By AMANDA MEUWISSEN

Coming Up for Air

DREAMSPUN DESIRES
#77 – A Model Escort

Published by DREAMSPINNER PRESS
www.dreamspinnerpress.com

COMING UP
for AIR

AMANDA
MEUWISSEN

Published by

DREAMSPINNER PRESS

5032 Capital Circle SW, Suite 2, PMB# 279, Tallahassee, FL 32305-7886 USA
www.dreamspinnerpress.com

Coming Up for Air
© 2019 Amanda Meuwissen.

Cover Art
© 2019 Tiferet Design.
http://www.tiferetdesign.com/
Cover content is for illustrative purposes only and any person depicted on the cover is a model.

Trade Paperback ISBN: 978-1-64405-176-4
Digital ISBN: 978-1-64405-175-7
Library of Congress Control Number: 2018963158
Trade Paperback published April 2019
v. 1.0

Printed in the United States of America

This paper meets the requirements of
ANSI/NISO Z39.48-1992 (Permanence of Paper).

To Regan Moore for always being an inspiration in both images and words that encourages more grand tales than I could ever write, but this one, which I hope you enjoy, is all because of you.

CHAPTER 1

IF HIS life had gone differently, maybe Leigh Hurley would have been an engineer working toward his master's in thermodynamics by now instead of sinking to the bottom of the river.

At least he couldn't tell how filthy the water was since it was midnight and he was plummeting fast into the dark depths, the glimmer of moonlight above him quickly disappearing. He was a good swimmer, not that it mattered with twenty-pound weights attached to his ankles. He had about two minutes before he passed out, and then it would be curtains.

Fighting against the panic clawing at his chest the same way his lungs begged for air, he forced his body to curl downward in a frantic attempt to reach the weights. They were cinder blocks attached with actual shackles. Under normal circumstances, he might have been able to remove them using one of his lockpicks, but he couldn't see. A bitter mantra of "if only" followed his path downward like the bubbles of air escaping as he tried to think of some other way, any way to get out of this.

If only he wasn't a criminal. If only he hadn't been so damn opportunistic. If only he hadn't gotten caught.

It had been a smart plan. The streets by the docks where Leigh lived were split in half between the Moretti brothers and Arthur Sweeney, who might have been Irish to their Italian, but that wasn't the root of their animosity. Everything revolved around power in Cove City. At the end of the night, what mattered was which family had the most territory, like some old-fashioned trade of land equaling wealth, which was always true, and Leigh owned nothing, not even the apartment he could barely pay the rent on.

Since his best friend was *Alvin* Sweeney, Arthur's son, Leigh played for their side, hoping to rise in the ranks on more than nepotism. Looking good to Sweeney Senior meant making a splash on the scene, so Leigh had been working overtime for months on small thefts that caused an increasing decline in how much the Morettis brought in from their protection racket.

Leigh gave most of what he stole to Sweeney, but some he returned to the neighboring mom-and-pop stores as a good Samaritan, and a little he kept for himself. This made the Morettis look weak, like they couldn't protect their own. It was all about the long game and how it would make things easier for Sweeney to claim those streets in the months and years to come.

It would have worked, too, if they hadn't been waiting for Leigh tonight.

"Nobody crosses the Morettis," Leo, younger brother to Vincent and in charge of their muscle, had said before his goons dropped Leigh over the side of the docks.

Now he was going to drown with no one to remember him other than Alvin and maybe the handful of people in his building who relied on his technical talents and didn't care if he was a runner for a mobster as long as their TVs and dishwashers worked.

It was such a waste, pushing him to struggle harder to swim upward after he gave up on the shackles, vainly trying to beat back fate, even though he knew he wasn't strong enough and barely made an inch of headway before he continued to sink.

Soon he'd disappear, another good riddance that he doubted even his parole officer would miss for how often she sighed and told him to make something of himself instead of falling back into bad habits. But what was there to make of a life without privilege? Leigh had no prospects, no family, no education, only honed skills of survival. He'd been a thief since he could fit his hand inside a passing pocket. With his record, even at only twenty-five, there was no hope for him in this city that didn't lean on Arthur Sweeney, and now he'd lost that opportunity too.

The water was cold even in spring since this part of the river was wider. The docks wouldn't see any activity until morning, and not much then either at this location, though with a few shortcuts, it wasn't far to Leigh's apartment. He'd die close to home, if that meant anything. He just wished he'd been smarter, faster, and had another chance to do things better.

Those two minutes had to be up, because it was getting harder to fight, his mind sluggish and unable to think of a solution to save him. He was even starting to hallucinate, maybe dreaming, maybe already dead and fading away. A light shone in the blackness as he hit bottom. More like a glimmer of bare skin, because he'd swear he saw a face approaching as his mind grew hazier and his vision dimmed.

Somehow the face became clearer, though, beautiful too, like something ethereal—flawless features, concerned eyes, dark hair swaying in the water. If he was real, he would have been the exact sort of man who would have made Leigh take notice. Maybe the man was an angel, and Leigh's passing wouldn't be as painful or as terrifying as he'd feared, despite his lungs burning with the struggle to breathe.

But he didn't deserve an angel. He wasn't good in any sense of the word or worthy of heaven. He didn't believe in love, not even in saying the words, because that was more damaging and hollower than being hated if it came from somewhere fake or turned into rubbish along the way. His father had taught him that early, and life only reaffirmed the dangers of love and trust over the years.

Scared as Leigh was, part of him believed he had this coming, but the angel in the water didn't snarl or fade away. He came close enough that Leigh could make out every detail of his face, including occasional freckles and a wide smile. Then the beautiful man floated closer, looking back at Leigh in wonder, and captured his lips in a cold kiss.

A song filled his mind like when one got stuck in his head, playing distantly and sweet like he imagined this man's voice might be—lovely but understated, just a tune without words.

Leigh was dying. He should have been filled with terror, but in his last moments, he felt calm to have had such a pleasant final dream.

The next moment, he was gasping for breath, somehow on shore, on the riverbank far enough from where he'd been dropped that Leo and his goons couldn't see him, but still close enough to walk home. It didn't make sense. The man in the water couldn't be real. Cove City didn't produce unknown saviors, yet when Leigh looked down at his ankles, the cinder blocks were gone.

Coughing into the sand and dirt, unsure how he'd been saved or if he'd been touched by some miracle, all Leigh knew was that he had to get home, and after he rested, he'd have precious little time to prevent this same fate from befalling him again tomorrow night.

With a mighty push, he thrust up onto his knees, staggered to his feet, and began the slow trek back to his apartment, trying to banish the vision of that lovely face from overriding what he knew could only have been a trick of the mind.

LEIGH DIDN'T mean to fall asleep when he reached home and shed his soaked clothing. He only planned to rest his eyes for a moment, but he'd underestimated how exhausted he was, and when he roused it was to a loud knock at his door, with the clock on his nightstand blinking 7:00 a.m.

He didn't have time to be tired. That could already be Moretti goons or Sweeney himself, furious at Leigh for failing. It didn't help that he didn't feel as though he'd slept. His dreams had been filled with the face he imagined in the water. He didn't think he'd ever seen a man like that before, but his mind had conjured such a perfect specimen for his final moments.

The kiss had been nice too.

Leigh couldn't get distracted by phantoms, though. While he had no idea how the weights had come loose from his ankles or how he'd ended up on shore, it couldn't have been some mystery man.

"I'm coming!" Leigh called when the knocking refused to cease. It wasn't the Morettis or Sweeney or they would have kicked down the door by now. It had to be Miss Maggie. Only she ever got this uppity before 9:00 a.m.

Yanking the door open, Leigh stood in his sweats and long-sleeved T-shirt, barefoot and still chilled from his time in the river, but clean after a shower when he'd arrived home. He rubbed the sleep from his eyes and scrubbed at the closely shorn length of his hair.

"What?"

Miss Maggie was indeed the person on the other side of his door, but she looked particularly surly this morning. "William," she said sharply, using his given name, which he despised. "About time. I might be an old woman, but that does not mean I want to see some young man walking buck naked through my halls at all hours just because you had a wild night."

"Excuse me?" Leigh took a moment to process what she was complaining about. He hadn't started to undress while still in the hall last night, had he? He was out of it when he returned home, but not that disoriented.

"You know I support your lifestyle, whatever it may be, just so long as you keep the volume down after 11:00 p.m. and act respectfully, but this was just vulgar. Are you playing some game with the boy?"

"Game? Miss Maggie, I have no idea what you're—"

But before he could finish, she yanked someone else into view, who was wearing what appeared to be one of her housecoats and nothing else, not even shoes, though that wasn't what stopped Leigh short.

It was the man from the river. Same hair, same eyes, same everything.

Leigh really had died last night.

"*William.*"

Which meant he was in hell if he was still dealing with Maggie's temper.

"Keep your evening activities confined to your apartment. Now, mind yourself, young man," she said to the flesh and blood figure who'd saved Leigh's life, "because I expect that nightgown returned at some point, preferably washed."

She shoved the man into Leigh's arms, and he had barely a second to register the full form of him, slim and tall, maybe half an inch taller than Leigh, and just as beautiful as he remembered, before Maggie hurried down the hall in a huff.

Leigh stumbled backward, causing the man to stumble with him, and pushed the door closed more on reflex than conscious choice. The man was real. Leigh hadn't imagined him. But if he'd saved Leigh's life, why was he only showing himself now?

And why the hell wasn't he wearing any clothes?

"I found you," he said in a breathless voice, as if in awe of Leigh, immediately evoking the memory of that same voice *singing*. "I knew I would, but still, I found you."

Carefully Leigh pushed at the man to hold him in front of him so they could get their bearings. He didn't seem very stable on his feet. Had he been drunk last night? Was that why he was swimming in the river at midnight naked and wandered all the way here in the same state? His eyes, large and almond-shaped, didn't look intoxicated. With olive skin, a reddish tint to his black hair, and freckles, he looked as likely to be of South Pacific descent as Greek or Jewish, maybe all three.

"You are even more handsome than when I saw you in the water," he said, with an intensity to how he stared that made Leigh shiver. The peek of long legs out of the housecoat was not helping his straying thoughts.

Leigh's generally fair looks with blond hair and blue eyes had gotten him out of sticky situations before. He knew what he had and how to use it, but he didn't think he compared with this lithe elfish beauty before him with a smile that lit up the whole apartment.

"It's you," he said, unable to articulate anything more than that. He pulled his hands from the man's shoulders, thinking it too intimate considering he was wearing nothing more than a nightgown.

"Yes." The man stepped into his space as if beckoned by a magnetic pull.

"You saved me. You found me."

"My apologies it took so long. I hesitated to follow, and once I decided to, I had trouble finding my feet, as they say. I knew the Breath of Life would lead me to you, though. Our souls are intertwined now, William. Ah, but you prefer Leigh, don't you?"

How…? "How do you know that?" And what was he talking about?

"You know my name as well."

"No, I…. Tolomeo. Tolly," he said before he could finish denying it. Had they met on the shore after all and Leigh simply didn't remember?

"Yes," Tolly said, smiling wider still.

This was too strange. Leigh's head was pounding, he was exhausted, and he still had to worry about Sweeney and the Morettis. He could not get caught up with some weird nudist—flower child—whatever this man was—when his life was in shambles.

"Look, I don't remember everything from last night, so if you explained this before, who you are, I'm sorry. I appreciate what you did. You saved my life, but it won't stay saved for long—"

"Those people who tried to drown you will continue to wish you harm," Tolly said.

"Yes. So if you came here expecting something more than my thanks, I hate to disappoint you, but I don't have much to offer."

"Oh, I am not like my brethren, I swear to you. I wish for no boon or life debt."

Okay. Was this guy a method actor or something? Maybe he was just crazy. "What do you want from me, then?"

"I wish to stay with you," Tolly said as matter-of-factly as asking for cab fare. "Forever."

Definitely crazy.

Holding up his hands to ward off whatever reaction might come next, Leigh chose his words very carefully. "Tolly, I will give you something to wear and then maybe there's someone we can call, okay? Or a hospital you came from?"

"I came from the sea," Tolly said, unfazed by Leigh's line of questioning. "Well, the river in this case, but all water is connected in my world. We can transport between depths through magic. I like bodies of water close to cities. The rest of my kin stay away, which I prefer, and I get to experience more of the human world."

"Human world? Your... kin?"

"Merfolk."

Leigh curtailed his reactions as best he could. "Tolly, is there anyone I can call to come get you?"

At last, a bit of that sunshine disposition flickered. "I have no one. No family or friends to speak of. That is why I chose to follow you. I was drawn to you, Leigh"—he stepped forward, making Leigh step back—"in the water, in your last moments, like I have never been drawn to anything. Others of my kin would have let you die, drowned you themselves, or forced a more self-serving pact, but I knew I had finally found the one who could give me legs."

If this guy snapped, Leigh was fairly certain he could take him, but he hoped it wouldn't come to that. "You are not a mermaid. You're a man. You're on legs right now. You did not have a tail last night."

"You only saw my face."

"You didn't have a tail because mermaids don't exist!"

"I shall prove it to you. I need only to submerge in water to call out my tail. Then will you believe me? Your bathroom should have what I need." Without waiting for an answer, he glanced around the apartment and pushed past Leigh, deeper inside.

Leigh needed to get this guy out of his home, even if he had saved him last night.

Merfolk? Seriously?

Tolly found the bathroom quick enough and proceeded to turn on the taps to the tub before Leigh could organize his thoughts for a proper protest.

He tried anyway. "Listen, I don't have time for this."

"I am used to cold water, but perhaps I shall try something warmer," Tolly said as he held his hand under the water and adjusted the taps accordingly. "Is warm water nice?"

"I… yeah, usually. Can we please just talk about this—"

Tolly disrobed without shame, right there in front of Leigh, just shed the housecoat and stood there nude. He was even more beautiful bare, entirely hairless below the neck, thin like a swimmer but well-muscled, without a single scar or imperfection other than the sunspots that Leigh thought only enhanced how beautiful he was.

Being gorgeous and naked in Leigh's bathroom did not change that he was clearly insane, however.

"Tolly, you can't just…. We need to talk about this." Leigh turned to stare at the wall. He was a hardened criminal. Sort of. *Sometimes*. It should not be this difficult to throw someone out of his home!

"Not until you believe me. Our conversation will go nowhere if you think me mad."

He was a smart crazy person at least, but that didn't help the situation. Leigh had to focus on the Morettis, on what to say when he saw Sweeney, on how to get himself out of this mess so he didn't end up dead some other way tonight, without having to flee the city. He'd break parole if he did that, and the money he'd saved so far wouldn't last him long on the run.

Maybe the Morettis didn't know where he lived. If they did, surely they would have sent someone to rummage through his things, looking for that extra cash. Maybe they did know and someone was on their way now. No point in rushing over when they thought him dead.

"Tolly, just put the housecoat back on or grab a towel. I'll get you some clothes—"

"Do you not find my form pleasing?"

Out of the corner of Leigh's eye, he could tell Tolly stood facing him, hands running down his hips and thighs like he really was unused to legs. "It is very pleasing, but it's not…. I hardly know you."

"Ah yes, human decorum. I might fail at that on occasion, but I will try my best. I know so much of your world, but I have not experienced it firsthand. Still, you know me better than you think through our connection. The Breath of Life is a powerful bond. I am yours now. You are welcome to look at me."

Leigh was certain some of the porn he'd watched over the years had lines like that. "Tolly...."

"I do not wish to make you uncomfortable. I will get into the tub to conceal myself until the water is high enough. Hopefully you will not find my tail displeasing."

Tolly lowered himself into the tub, and Leigh allowed a glance in his direction. Even mostly hidden, he was enchanting to look at. Despite having come from the water last night, his hair had perfect body and poof to it. Why did someone so gorgeous and who had saved Leigh's life have to be nuts?

"I have to figure out how to handle those men who tried to kill me. Do you understand?"

"Of course. I will help you."

"No offense, but you're a little skinny to be a bodyguard. This is going to take strategic planning."

"I am an excellent planner. I often have to dodge others of my kin. I am not popular, as I do not conform to the merfolk ways. Kill or be killed—it loses all the magic of life, even when magic surrounds me in the water. How can one live like that?"

Leigh almost took the words as an attack, though he knew Tolly didn't mean it that way. He'd never killed anyone before, but his plans to rise in the ranks with Sweeney meant one day he would. Kill or be killed was the only way he could survive in this city.

"You were right, warm water is nice, though the cold can be pleasant too." Tolly tilted his head back and sank lower into the tub.

Scrubbing a hand down his face, Leigh was thinking of how to get this naked delusional poet out of his apartment without drawing the attention of his neighbors when he heard a strange wet slap and a contented sigh.

"There, you see? I am merfolk, but you gave me legs, and now, I am yours."

The red glimmer in Leigh's periphery before he looked up had to be an illusion because of how tired he was. There was no way it could be anything else.

But when his gaze focused on Tolly in the tub once more, it wasn't a pair of feet propped on the edge but the unfurling of the most beautiful deep red tailfin he had ever laid eyes on, trimmed in gold-tipped scales.

"Holy shit."

CHAPTER 2

TOLLY HOPED it was not disgust he saw filling Leigh's face. He understood that it must be a shock. Humans did not believe in Tolly's kind anymore, or much of any magic, but surely Leigh felt their connection, that Tolly meant him no harm and only wanted to be....

Well.

Loved.

But he could not tell Leigh that. The magic of the Breath of Life prevented it. He could tell Leigh that he was his. He could ask to stay with him. He could try to court him the way he had never attempted with any of his kin—he stayed away from other merfolk and was lucky he was such a fast swimmer and had never been caught—but he could not tell Leigh plainly that the only way he could keep his legs for longer than the next full moon was if his pact-bearer, the one who had given him legs, offered him a vow of love.

He also could not tell Leigh that if that did not happen, he would be put to death when the spell broke and the others came for him.

Some of his fellows would jump at the chance to pursue him for that purpose.

"Holy shit," Leigh said, more stunned than horrified, Tolly hoped.

"You are welcome to touch it if you like," he said with a light flick of his tailfin, just enough to fan it out, not to splash any water. Maybe that was too forward, but Tolly could not remember a time when anyone caressed his tail in kindness, and Leigh had such exquisite hands.

Leigh's eyes widened, wonder overtaking him the way magic often affected humans, but he shifted a small step closer to look on Tolly fully.

His tail was not the most impressive, but Tolly had always been fond of his colors. Deep red and gold made him sparkle in the right light. Leigh said his human form was pleasing. He hoped his tail was, too, even if Leigh did find it strange at first.

This version of himself was much lovelier than his true form.

More than anything, more than his own life, Tolly did not want the pact to break and for Leigh to recoil when he saw what he truly looked like beneath the spell. He did not want Leigh to think of him as ugly or monstrous. The illusion was better.

Leigh reached out, but before his fingers could touch the edge of Tolly's tail, it gave another unconscious flick, and Leigh flinched like he had blinked awake from a gripping dream.

"I'm losing my mind," he said as he backed toward the door, then turned to escape the room entirely.

"Leigh…." Tolly tried not to let his heart sink as deeply as it wanted to. If Leigh shunned him now, all would be lost. But he knew Leigh had to be the one. His kin might call him a hapless dreamer for wanting anything more than cruel fun at a human's expense, but he thought the old legends beautiful.

The stories said that if one of his kin found the right human, the one destined for them, they would feel it, know it, and be drawn to save them from a watery grave. A single kiss was all it took to seal the pact, the Breath of Life connecting them as it gave the human the ability to breathe once more and sealed their fates together.

Afterward, if the merfolk chose to step out of the water, they would find themselves on legs, unsteady but surer with every step. They needed only to follow their human and woo them to love them, and together they could live happily on land or sea.

Tolly wanted that so badly, he could barely stand the thought of one more day alone in the depths.

He did not need to be dry to recall his legs, but it still took him a moment to change back and stagger onto his feet to find a towel as Leigh had suggested so he would not drip water all over Leigh's home. Humans preferred things dry usually.

"Leigh!" he called as he wrapped the towel around his waist and hurried into the main room.

He did not see Leigh at first and panic overtook him as he feared the man had fled, but then he saw him standing out on the—what was it called?—fire escape! He had climbed out the window and stood outside gripping the railing.

Not trusting himself to climb after him while encumbered by the towel, Tolly pleaded through the window. "Do you find me so terrible?

So startling? I do not need to call out my tail. I can be human for you. I only wished for you to believe me."

"I believe you. I don't think you're crazy. Or that I am. Or that I'm dead. Dammit, don't be dead...."

"You are very much alive, I promise you."

"Because you saved me." Leigh turned around. "A mermaid saved me. Mer*man*."

"Folk," Tolly corrected with a smile. "Though I do not mind anything you wish to call me."

With a sigh like finally catching his breath, Leigh came back in through the window, and Tolly backed up to give him room. "You aren't terrible. Startling maybe. Your tail is gorgeous. It's the fact that you have one that I'm having trouble with."

He was so handsome. Tolly loved the way humans looked. He loved the way Leigh looked especially—tan skin, shorn hair, intense and hypnotizing blue eyes like the iciest parts of the ocean. He also loved how Leigh looked at him, curious and unsure but not unkind.

"You may ask me anything you like," Tolly said. But oh! He should not have said that. He could not truly answer *anything*.

"What happened to your... I mean.... When your tail is out, you're smooth down there like a fish, like... there's nothing...." He gestured vaguely in front of himself below the waist.

Oh.

"Your sex is always in the open if not clothed. Ours is concealed unless we are using it. Would you like me to show you—"

"*No*," Leigh said before Tolly could undo his towel. "That's fine. I don't know if I could handle that right now." He took another deep breath and nodded. "You're a merman."

"Yes."

"And you want to stay with me because you saved my life, and doing that, for some reason, allows you to grow legs whenever you want?"

"Yes. I have nowhere else to go but back to the water. I do not wish to go back to the water. My kin are cruel to me. Vicious. I do not belong there. Please, do not cast me out—"

"Hey." Leigh stepped forward and reached for him, but like before when he had been about to touch Tolly's tail, he did not complete the act, as if it was not the sort of gesture he had ease finishing. "I'm not casting you out. You saved my life and this is somewhat… insanely… *cool* that you even exist. Just a lot to take in."

"Cool?" Tolly tried to recall the meaning of the word in this context.

"Amazing. Good."

"Oh." Tolly smiled widely. "*Cool.*"

"But I am not someone anyone should want to stay with right now. Those men—"

"I will help you defeat them," Tolly said surely. He knew cruelty was not only a trait of his people but existed broadly amongst humans as well. While he had no idea what it felt like to drown, it seemed a torturous thing to do to someone.

"It isn't a matter of defeating," Leigh said. "This isn't a battle. It's more complicated than that."

"Then explain it to me, and I will help however I can."

"No, I… I mean, it's a long story and—"

Rapid knocking startled them, rhythmic, like the beat of a song, very different from how Miss Maggie had knocked when she brought Tolly to Leigh's door.

She was a fine woman, Tolly had thought, just scolding at having encountered him undressed. He had not been able to find clothing between the river and Leigh's home, though he knew it would be needed. His only goal had been reaching Leigh. Though admittedly, the pull to Leigh's location had gotten confusing in a building where people stacked on top of one another, so he had been unsure of which floor was Leigh's.

Miss Maggie had been quick to correct him when he went to her apartment instead.

"Wait!" Leigh called at the continued knocking, familiar with its rhythm and who it belonged to, it seemed, but the person on the other side did not listen.

A young man entered, thin like Tolly though not as tall, smiling and friendly-looking with smatterings of bright color in his clothing, unlike Leigh's monochrome.

"Hey, what was Miss Maggie talking about down—" He stopped short when he saw Tolly and his smile shifted into something sly. "My, my. Who's the twink?"

"*Alvin,*" Leigh admonished, though Tolly was unacquainted with the word.

"Just calling it like I see it. Good for you. No wonder you didn't pick up the phone last night." Alvin sauntered closer with a slow scan down Tolly's body. He did not seem displeased with Tolly's form either.

"That isn't what happened." Leigh moved to intercept him. "Wait. You don't *know* what happened? You didn't hear?"

"Hear what?"

"Moretti gave me a dip in the river."

"*What?*" The smile dropped from Alvin's face as he focused on Leigh with a start.

"Leo Moretti himself had three goons weight my ankles and drop me in to swim with the fishes." Leigh paused with a glance at Tolly, and his eyes shone wide with sudden fear.

Tolly might be slow with some things about the human world, but he was not a fool. "I was walking by the shore. I saw what happened and jumped in to save Leigh once the men had gone. I helped him home, and he allowed me to stay with him to get dry."

Leigh's distress instantly receded and he mouthed a silent "thank you." Tolly would not reveal to anyone but Leigh what he truly was. He knew the dangers in that.

"Since last night?" Alvin said.

"We fell asleep."

"Sure ya did. A little victim and savior action?" His eyebrows bobbed, but his playfulness turned serious when he looked at Tolly. "You saved Leigh's life, Stretch. I owe you one."

"Stretch? My name is Tolly. Are you a friend of Leigh's?"

"His bestest. So I'm allowed to be both jealous and happy for him." He winked.

"*Nothing* happened," Leigh said.

"Plenty happened," Alvin countered. "What are you gonna do about the Morettis? Does Dad know yet?"

"I was hoping to ask *you* that."

Alvin chewed his lip in thought, eyes darting between Leigh and Tolly. "You two stay put. I'll do some recon and figure out where we stand. I'm sure Dad will know what to do, and this will all blow over in no time."

"I'm sure *Dad* will be next in line to fit me with cement shoes if I don't fix this myself."

"Relax. We'll figure it out. First, let me see who knows what. They must not know your address if no one's here yet. You sit tight, buddy. And you sit pretty, Tinker Bell." He winked at Tolly again.

"My name is Tolly, not—"

"Oh he is adorable. Definitely a keeper." Alvin scanned Tolly's body like before. Then, when he turned to Leigh, he tapped him in the center of his chest in a subtle gesture of affection.

Tolly was used to seeing hugs between humans to express such a thing, but Leigh did not seem comfortably physical in that way. Tolly had a feeling Alvin would have preferred to hug his friend, but he held back as a sign of respect and understanding. Tolly would have to remember that. After all, he would not like it if anyone was physical with him without permission either.

"I'll message you as soon as I know something. Be ready to move but take a breather, okay? Treat this fine specimen to breakfast," Alvin said, scanning one more time along the towel Tolly wore before he turned on his heels.

He was out the door as swiftly as he had entered, like a quickly moving storm, but Leigh seemed calmed after his appearance. Tolly decided that Alvin was welcome and would be his friend too.

"He seems nice, ready to rally to your defense. But why does he not refer to me by name?"

"Don't worry about it. Just means he likes you. Now… clothes." Leigh scanned Tolly's body with far less hunger than Alvin had, more with uncertainty despite the glow in his cheeks. "Let me find you some."

Tolly followed him into the bedroom. He was curious about beds and what it would be like to sleep on one. He had only ever floated or cushioned himself on sand. Usually he found dark, hidden places to rest. Leigh's bed wasn't overly large, but big enough for two, should Tolly be allowed to share it.

Leigh pulled out something blue for Tolly's legs, white for his feet, black to go on before the blue—*underwear*—and red, a *sweater* like the darkest parts of Tolly's tail, for his chest.

"There. You can, uhh…. Do you understand how to…?" Leigh trailed off when Tolly removed the towel and held it out to him. He thought it damp and perhaps rude to drop it on the floor.

"Yes? I know where everything goes. I can dress myself."

"Great. Good." Leigh accepted the towel but kept his eyes skyward.

"It really is all right to look at me."

A shaky chuckle fell from Leigh's lips and there was a brief, bashful flick of his eyes downward before he looked Tolly in the face. "Listen, that whole human decorum thing is important. You can't act like this with other people."

"I understand. I am yours alone. You need not worry."

"And what does that mean exactly?"

Tolly thought of all the stories he knew of love and romance. Coming on "too strong" was often a negative. He needed to be clear to Leigh but not overwhelming. "It means that I hope the kiss I gave you in the water will not be our last."

The glow in Leigh's cheeks darkened to a lovely shade. "I need to focus on one thing at a time. So you put those on, and I'll see what I have for us to eat."

Tolly nodded, but Leigh halted after only a step toward the door.

"What do merfolk… eat?"

"We are mostly carnivorous, but I am an omnivore like you. I can eat anything."

"Bacon and eggs?"

"I would love to try that if it is what you wish to eat."

"Okay." Leigh seemed to want to glance down again to look at Tolly but refrained and promptly left the room.

Tolly was not being shunned. He still had a chance to make this work. He would show Leigh how useful he could be, how well suited they were for each other, how happy he could make him. He started by putting on the clothing Leigh had given him. They were only slightly too large for him and seemed fine when he looked in the mirror on the closet door. He stood perhaps too long taking in his new form, but he liked it very much, even if the legs were an odd replacement for his tail.

When he ventured out of the bedroom, he found Leigh in the kitchen, from which wafted a wonderful smell as he cooked at the stovetop. "Cooked" was not something Tolly had experienced before either. Everything he ate was raw or still alive.

"Bacon and eggs must taste delicious. It smells amazing."

"Yeah?" Leigh peered at him with a look of relief. "Good, coz I don't have seafood in this place."

"I also eat birds on occasion."

Leigh froze. Perhaps that was a queer thing to say? Humans did not pursue prey the way merfolk did. "Well, uhh… you'll probably like chicken, then."

Tolly hovered in the doorway so he could watch Leigh. The movement of his hands and the fidget of his bare feet were mesmerizing. He had a vague vision through the connection of the Breath of Life of Leigh doing the same act as a boy—cooking in bare feet, alone.

Leigh had no one either. Alvin, it seemed, and Miss Maggie, a few others perhaps, but he had no family. Tolly could feel it as keenly as he knew his own loneliness.

"Here, why don't you fill some glasses with water to put on the table and I'll get this dished up?" Leigh said. "Glasses are in there, water from the tap."

Easy enough. Tolly was not used to drinking as humans did, but he was eager to learn everything Leigh could teach him. He followed the instructions, and when he returned, Leigh handed him two plates laden with food.

"I'll bring the forks. Do you know what a fork—"

"Yes. I am not the little mermaid."

"You know about the little mermaid?"

"Of course." Tolly preferred the colorful version with the singing. The ending was happier.

"Oh. That's good, I guess."

They sat at the table in the corner of Leigh's living room, and Tolly carefully picked up his fork. Knowing what something was and using it were two very different things. He watched Leigh for the right cues, how he used the fork to cut into the bacon, then speared a piece of egg with some of the yolk. Tolly copied the act and took his first bite.

Bliss.

"Oh my. This *is* wonderful."

Leigh laughed. "Wait 'til you try something more complicated like Miss Maggie's casserole."

"I look forward to it." Tolly dug into another bite.

All too soon, Leigh seemed troubled again and asked, "About this whole you being mine thing…."

"I do not mean as a slave without my own will. If you wish it, I can be your… companion. Your partner. What is the word? Your *boyfriend*."

Leigh nearly choked on his next bite of food but chuckled in the aftermath of his coughing.

Tolly might be imagining what he wanted to see, but he thought Leigh looked at least a little smitten with him. He could not afford to make even a single misstep.

"You said we're connected because of how you saved me," Leigh said. "That you know things about me, like my name and how to find me. Do you know… everything about me?"

"No. More a sense of you. But that is more than I need to know that I chose well."

The food was not yet gone from Leigh's plate, but still he set his fork down. "Tolly, I need you to hear this. I am not a nice person. I wasn't some innocent in need last night. Those men wanted me dead because I did bad things to them first."

"What things?" Tolly set his fork down too.

"Stole. I stole from them. I'm a criminal and a liar. Do you understand? I'm a bad man. I'm not some destiny for you to—"

Another knock at the door interrupted him, this time causing Tolly to jump.

"Who now?" Leigh grumbled. "Just hold on," he said with a gesture for Tolly to stay seated, then rose to answer the door.

Tolly could not believe Leigh meant what he had said. Even if it was true, there had to be good reason for him to steal. Tolly would feel it if Leigh was a bad man. There had to be good in him.

He watched Leigh peer through a tiny spyglass in the door before yanking it open.

"Ralph, what is it this time? I've had a long night. Shouldn't you be on your way to school? I'm not awake enough for this."

It was a boy, a teenager, nearly as tall as Leigh but whose face betrayed his age, and his voice cracked when he spoke.

"Come on, Hurley, it's not that early. Heh. See how that rhymed?"

"*Ralph.*"

"It's my laptop! If I lose this paper I gotta turn in today, I'm dead meat."

"How many times do I have to say it? Computers aren't my area."

"But you always figure it out anyway, whether it's a radio or a carburetor. Please? Just two seconds before I miss my bus."

Leigh sighed, holding firm for as long as he could before he gestured the boy inside. He had a backpack over one shoulder and what Tolly believed was a laptop in his free hand, though he did not understand what one was used for exactly. The boy was quite skinny with angular features and a pointy nose.

"Oh," he said when he saw Tolly, then turned to Leigh with a snort. "*Long night*, huh?"

"Don't even start. Now give me that." Leigh snatched the laptop. "Ralph, this is Tolly. Tolly, Ralph."

"Hello." Tolly smiled warmly.

"Hi." He tilted his head as if trying to read Tolly like a crooked signpost. "New runner?"

"You should not be asking questions like that," Leigh snapped as he returned to the table and pushed his plate aside to make room for the laptop.

"Sorry. Just figured anybody you brought home would have to know you're a… secret mobster," he whispered far too loudly for Tolly not to overhear.

"Not much of a secret with you around." Leigh shook his head, fingers clacking away on the keys. Tolly had never seen a computer in person. He wondered what Leigh was doing to it, but he focused instead on the word.

Mobster. It was true, then, but surely Leigh's profession was function more than form.

"Ralph, do you know Leigh well?" Tolly asked the boy.

"I guess so. He's lived in this building since I was a kid."

"Still are, *kid*," Leigh said without looking up from his work.

"Do you think he is a bad man?"

"Him? No way." Ralph made an exaggerated expression. "He acts tough but he's a big softie. Ain't ya, Hurley?"

Leigh sighed again but did not respond.

"I thought as much," Tolly said.

"Ralph…. First off, update your OS more than once every two years." Leigh turned the laptop around, which appeared to be showing a string of text that Tolly assumed was the "paper" Ralph had been concerned about. "And stop Googling porn sites. Stick to the safe ones I told you about if you have to be hormonal."

Ralph gave a jubilant cry as he collected his laptop. "You are the master, man. And yep, pretty sure as an exceptionally attractive teenage boy, it is basically law that I'm hormonal. So—" He looked at Tolly after snapping the laptop shut. "—if you're not a runner, who are you?"

Panicked eyes looked at Tolly across the table.

"I... am Leigh's bodyguard."

"Is that, like, a euphemism?"

"*No*," Leigh said. "Look, kid, I might be into some trouble, all right, so you need to steer clear for a while. No dropping by like this unannounced for a few days."

"Wait, he really is your bodyguard?" Ralph looked appropriately troubled. "Is it Sweeney? Or the Morettis?"

"Don't stick your nose where it doesn't belong," Leigh said sharply, but even such an authoritative tone did not seem to affect the boy.

"You're kinda scrawny, no offense," he told Tolly. "You sure you can protect him?"

"I will let no harm befall Leigh, I promise you."

"Cool. Weird, but... cool."

"Bus. *School*." Leigh stood from his chair.

"Going! Thanks, Hurley. Be safe, okay? You're the only one I can talk to about girls without worrying you'll steal the ones I like. Like Deanna. I am totally wearing her down. The other night—"

"*Go*." Leigh pushed him toward the door.

"I'm going! Keep it loose, Bodyguard Man!" he called, then gave a little salute before rushing out the door.

Tolly was all smiles when Leigh turned back to him. "You see. You are a good man."

"What, charity work for that brat?"

"You helped a child in need with no benefit to yourself. A true scoundrel would never do that."

Something chimed in the living room, and Leigh hurried to the coffee table to pick up his cell phone. That Tolly understood as something humans used to communicate long distance, which he thought very useful, but Leigh's lips pursed tightly when he looked at the screen. "Alvin. He wants me to meet him at one of his father's clubs."

"I will go with you." Tolly gathered his last bite of food to clear his plate.

"Hang on…." Leigh started to dissent but stopped, hand dragging down his face as he looked about his apartment, no doubt debating if he wanted to ask Tolly to stay.

"I will go with you," Tolly said again. "Merfolk are stronger than humans, even if I do appear… scrawny. I can protect you."

"Better than leaving you here to fend for yourself. Fine. I need to get changed first. Just put the dishes in the sink, okay?"

"You have not finished eating."

Leigh scratched back along his scalp, clearly antsy. Returning to the table but not sitting, he gathered his own last bite and shoved it into his mouth. He gestured at the plate in irritation before storming away to his bedroom.

Tolly was annoying him. He had to be careful. He had to prove his worth to Leigh.

Once again, he did as he had been instructed, even rinsing the plates first to make them cleaner. He itched to peek into the bedroom while Leigh changed. He wanted to know what Leigh looked like bare, but given how he had reacted to seeing Tolly, he doubted he would appreciate having an audience.

A minute later, Leigh returned in a more subdued combination of similar clothing to Tolly's, put on his shoes, a jacket, and thrust like items at Tolly. Shoes were especially odd to walk in, but he could adjust. He did not want to cause Leigh any trouble.

"You are upset with me."

"I'm sorry, I'm just…. My life is on the line, you got that?"

"Yes. I got that. I meant what I said to Ralph. I will not let any harm befall you."

"Fine, whatever. Let's go."

Tolly stuck close to Leigh as they locked up the apartment and headed down the hallway, then farther down the stairs toward the front entrance. Leigh seemed to be in a great hurry, either to reach their destination faster or to escape the apartment building before any additional interruptions arose.

Unfortunately, they were not quite fast enough to reach the exit before two young ones flew out of their apartment almost directly into Leigh's legs.

"Whoa, Gar, Gert, slow down! Where's your mother?" Leigh tried to collect them, but the youngest of the two, a girl about four or five, continued zipping about as what must be her seven- or eight-year-old brother chased her.

"Gert!" the boy called. "You don't always get to be the Jedi! It's not fair!"

"Is too! I'm the *girl*!" she shouted back, darting around Leigh's legs at great speed, making it impossible for him to move. Unlike with Ralph, however, who was older, Leigh did not jump to frustration with these two, but stood still, patient and waiting for them to settle down.

"That doesn't even mean anything! Girls aren't always the good guys!"

"*Hey*," Leigh said louder but without raising his voice too harshly. "How can you play Sith and Jedi without lightsabers, huh? Maybe worry about that first."

"We only have one and Gert broke it," Gar said, stopping finally as he crossed his arms in a huff, while his sister clung to Leigh's legs and stayed hidden behind him.

"Did not! The sword part wouldn't come out. I was just helping."

"Sith and Jedi?" Tolly asked. "Like the movies?"

The children seemed to notice Tolly for the first time, and while the boy looked at him warily, the little girl came out from behind Leigh's legs. "Do you like *Star Wars*, mister? Are you a friend of Mr. Hurley?"

"A new friend, yes." Tolly crouched down to be closer to her level. "And I like those movies very much. Would it not be more fun to play the Sith? You could be 'bad' but be turned to the light side. That story is more interesting than starting as the hero, do you not agree?"

Her big brown eyes blinked before she exclaimed, "I wanna be Sith! Gar can be the Jedi this time."

"Well…. Wait, I…." Her brother tried to backtrack as the Sith suddenly sounded more appealing, but Tolly laughed to discourage them from fighting further.

"What else do you like to pretend?" he asked Gert.

"Uhh… that I'm a Jedi or a princess or a dragon. Or a mermaid!" she added excitedly.

Tolly saw the way Leigh tensed, but he knew what humans thought of his kind. "The nice kind of merfolk, I hope?"

"Why would a mermaid be mean?"

Tolly wondered that too. There were no nice merfolk outside of fairy tales other than himself. Maybe somewhere, but none that he had met. "Then you are a very nice mermaid, Miss Gert. Quite lovely, in fact. Your hair would look beautiful in the water. May I ask what color your tail is?"

"Umm… purple!"

"Royalty indeed," he said. Not among his people, but it was a royal color, he had heard, and very pretty. It would look gorgeous on scales. "Perhaps you are a merfolk princess."

"I can be both?" Gert lit up at the thought.

"Of course. Was not Ariel both?"

The little girl seemed enchanted now, and because of her reaction, Leigh seemed enchanted, too, which made Tolly feel as though he had succeeded in something.

"Mermaids are boring," Gar said firmly.

"And what if one were like a shark?" Tolly snapped his teeth to prove his point.

"Mermaids aren't like that."

"Have you ever met one?"

"No, stupid." The boy kept his arms crossed. "Mermaids aren't real."

"Garfield Sean Richardson, do we call people 'stupid'?" A commanding voice came from the children's apartment, preceding the appearance of a woman who was clearly their mother, with the same dark skin, hair, and eyes. She multitasked with ease while waiting for an answer, locking the door and juggling several bags.

"No, Mama," Gar said dutifully.

"I didn't think so. Oh! Who are…?" She startled at the sight of Tolly, who stood from his crouch to better greet her, but she relaxed when she saw Leigh there too. "He with you?"

"Yeah, I'm keeping some extra muscle around for the next few days."

"*He's* muscle?" She eyed Tolly with scrutiny.

"Looks can be deceiving, apparently," Leigh said. "We were heading out too."

"Aww, but Mama"—Gert rushed to her mother's side—"I wanna play mermaid."

"Gertrude Ann, your brother needs to get to school, I need to get to work, and you need to get to Miss Maggie's."

"Miss Maggie looks after you?" Tolly asked the girl. "Well then, perhaps she will play make-believe."

"Nah. She's nice and all, but she can't play much, coz her back hurts her sometimes."

"Then perhaps later, when we have all returned, I can play with you instead."

"Really?" She clung to her mother as she had Leigh but looked at Tolly with a sparkle in her eyes.

"If Leigh and I have the time, I would be honored."

"Honored," she repeated, like she only half understood the word. "Did you hear that, Mama?"

"I did indeed," the woman said, still eyeing Tolly before speaking more quietly to Leigh. "Where'd you find this guy?"

"Long story, but you can trust him. This is Tolly. Tolly, this is Deanna, Gar, and Gert."

"A pleasure." Tolly bowed his head. "As are your children."

"Watch 'em for a few hours and see if you still say that."

"I would be delighted to."

The way her eyes widened made Tolly wonder if she had meant the comment as sarcasm. "I'm gonna hold you to that. See you later, Leigh. You let me know if I should be worried."

"I will," Leigh said. He let Gert hug his leg and gave a fist bump to Gar before the family hurried away.

"Bye, Tolly!" Gert called to him.

"Goodbye, Miss Gert!" He waved but realized after a moment what the mother's name had been. "That was Deanna, the one Ralph mentioned? But they are quite divergent in age."

"He's got a crush," Leigh said.

"A crush?"

"He *likes* her, even though he doesn't stand a chance."

"The father of her children is not with her?"

"No," Leigh said with sudden coldness in his eyes, "and everyone's better off that way."

"I see. Perhaps, though, Ralph should focus on someone closer to his own age."

"I've been trying to tell him that since he hit puberty. He's a stubborn one." Leigh began to move forward toward the exit, whereas the family had headed to Miss Maggie's.

"We all have difficulty giving up on the ones we want," Tolly said, catching Leigh's eye and making no attempt to veil what he meant.

Leigh averted his eyes, but Tolly could feel that it was not disinterest that plagued him. "Children are lovely, though. Even my kin can have pleasant ones before they are trained to be cruel."

"Why aren't you, then?" Leigh asked. "Cruel? If all the others are?"

"My parents thought differently."

"What happened to them?"

"They were not fast enough swimmers."

Leigh stopped just as he was about to push open the door, hand outstretched but hovering. He looked at Tolly in sympathy, but there was more that had him frozen. "I can't believe I'm letting a mermaid come with me to see Arthur Sweeney."

"I will not fail you, Leigh."

"I know you won't try to, but you need to follow my lead, got it?"

"I will go wherever you tell me to."

"No, I don't just mean follow me, I mean.... If I say a lie about you or the situation, you need to go along with it as though it's true. No one can know you're a mermaid. Man. *Folk*."

Tolly appreciated that he was trying to use the right word. He was a kind man, no matter his profession or past deeds. Tolly just needed to convince him that they could trust each other. "I am braver than you believe, stronger than I seem, and smarter than you think."

"Did you just paraphrase *Winnie the Pooh*?"

Clearly, they were a proper match if Leigh knew that. "There are many outdoor movie showings near bodies of water. It is quite wonderful the way people sit together on blankets and enjoy stories told that way."

"*Star Wars. The Little Mermaid. Winnie the Pooh.*" Finally Leigh's hand dropped from the door. "Tolly, does everything you know about humans come from movies?"

"Mostly."

Leigh's eyes shone with fear again. "Great. This is going to go… great." He pushed on the door at last, leaving Tolly to follow him.

Tolly liked to think Leigh was right—things would go "great"—but unless he was mistaken, he was fairly certain that had been sarcasm too.

CHAPTER 3

A MERMAID. Leigh was walking down the streets of Cove City with a flesh and blood mermaid.

If he hadn't been so dumbfounded when he first took in Tolly's tail, he would have spent longer cataloging the way it looked and touched it like Tolly had offered. Deep red-and-gold scales adorned by fins along the sides as well as the tailfin at the end. The fins were near transparent, while the scales glittered like precious metal.

Low at Tolly's hips, the red began to fade into his olive skin, leading into his human half. He still had sunspots. In fact, the ones that had been on his legs freckled his tail in darker red. Whether showing off his tail or sporting long limbs, he was positively breathtaking. Magical, even.

Leigh was in so much trouble.

Tolly was a literal walking disaster—his entire knowledge base of humans came from films he'd watched at outdoor drive-ins and movies in the park—but at least he was good, selfless, and endearing. Leigh couldn't let someone like that, a mythical creature no less, get messed up in his life of darkness and misdeeds.

If he had lived a different life, he would have welcomed having a beautiful man like Tolly enter it, so open and heartfelt, already professing a desire to know Leigh, to be with him—to *date* him. To stay with him forever.

Leigh wasn't worth that kind of blind devotion. Tolly didn't *know* him. Love was a burden in Leigh's eyes, something people used against each other more than positively, and Leigh would be no exception if handed a fragile heart like Tolly's. Once Tolly came to see the kind of person Leigh was, he would dive headfirst back into the water.

When Leigh glanced at the merfolk-maid-man beside him as they hurried down the street to Sweeney's club, he expected to see disappointment creeping into Tolly's expression. The neighborhood by the docks wasn't exactly a glowing example of city life. The streets were dirty, shops run-down, some closed, fewer and fewer families or children about other than Deanna's kids and Ralph. It wasn't a place anyone wanted to be other than aging folks like Miss Maggie with rent control and stubborn resolve to never move. Or criminals like Leigh.

To his surprise, though, with the morning light glinting off oil stains along the street and people smoking on corners and eyeing pockets to pick, Tolly looked captivated and smiled at everyone they passed. The sheer joy on his face to simply be here made it hard for Leigh to suppress his own smile.

"Are they moving in?" Tolly asked as they paused at a street corner for the walk sign to change. The shop there, a little electronics store that Leigh had thought would be there forever, had boxes all around and bustling activity of employees packing up. "Are they new?"

"No. Must be rearranging." Or *leaving*. Leigh wouldn't be surprised, but he didn't have time to stop and ask. The light changed, and they continued.

"I know this is urgent, but perhaps when we return home, we can take more time to explore. It is all so thrilling. I would like to see more."

Leigh tried not to be tripped up by Tolly already calling his apartment "home." He really was naïve if he thought the ghetto was thrilling, but his exuberance was hard to say no to. "Maybe," he said. "If we have time." *And if I'm not running for my life.*

"Do you think—" Tolly started to ask another question but broke off when Leigh's cell phone trilled from his pocket. He was lucky he'd only had a burner phone on him last night when he was dropped in the river. He always left his real phone at home if he was on a job.

Answering it now, he wondered if it would be Alvin telling him to hurry—or scram—but his parole officer's name blinked instead.

"We have an appointment in fifteen minutes," Leigh answered by way of greeting.

"Yes, we do," Tabitha Beckett said. She was a good woman but tough as reinforced leather. She tended to call in reminders of their check-ins since he'd missed a few, and she'd made it clear that many more would not end well for him.

"Gotta ask a favor today, Beckett. Can we make it tomorrow?"

"Give me one good reason, William."

Leigh glanced at Tolly beside him, who looked back at him curiously. "I have a new roommate I'm showing around the neighborhood."

"A roommate?" Tabitha deadpanned.

"Someone to keep me out of trouble. Figured you'd be pleased."

"In that case, bring him by tomorrow. I can't wait to meet him."

"Already planning on it." Honestly, Tolly meeting Tabitha was a lot less terrifying than where they were headed now. "8:00 a.m. sharp. I owe you one."

"Be on time tomorrow and stay away from Arthur Sweeney. That's all you owe me."

Leigh reached out to push open the door to the club as he said, "Don't even remember the last time I saw Sweeney. Later, Beckett. See." He turned to Tolly after hanging up the call. "*Liar*."

Tolly's lips pursed in concern or maybe deep thought, but he didn't reply. Better if Leigh started pushing him away now, before he got it into his head that there was anything redeeming about him. He was exactly what he'd told Tolly, and that wasn't going to change.

The club was quiet as they entered, not open to the public at this hour but still housing Sweeney's best and brightest loyal goons.

Bruiser Jake Theilen and honeypot Rosa Brookes were immediately visible, as well as hacker Cary Pettinger, the resident expert for getting around security or into bank records. Leigh ignored the gauging stares at Tolly and headed for Alvin sitting at the bar with a glass of milk. Even if it hadn't been morning, he wasn't one for liquor.

"You brought the boy toy. Hi again." Alvin spun on his stool. "Dad's waiting for you in the back. The Morettis think you're good and gone, and the word on the streets is minimal."

"Good. How mad is he?" Leigh nodded beyond the bar.

"You know Pops. He doesn't get mad."

Just homicidal.

"And you're my best friend. He'll fix this."

Right. Tolly wasn't the only naïve one in Leigh's company. "Watch him so he doesn't try making friends," Leigh said to Alvin, and Tolly immediately straightened.

"You are leaving me? I cannot protect you if I am not with you."

"I don't need protection from Sweeney." At least Leigh hoped not.

Not wanting to risk an argument, he pushed past Tolly. He'd be fine in Alvin's company.

The back room was Sweeney's private office, where ledgers were kept and dirty dealings done. As Leigh entered, Sweeney wasn't sitting at his desk but poised on top of it, expertly shuffling a deck of cards to the feigned delight of runner Selene Cook. Everyone knew to pretend to enjoy his magic tricks or risk his wrath.

He was an average-looking man, shorter than Alvin, though Alvin had his father's same pronounced nose and wide grin. "Pick a card, Miss Cook, pick a card." Sweeney held them out to her.

She obediently reached for one, but just before her fingers touched the edge, the cards burst upward in a shower of rectangles that ended in the appearance of a fake bouquet of flowers.

"Got me again, Boss." She chuckled.

"Mr. Hurley, care for the bouquet?" Sweeney dramatically thrust the flowers at him as he continued his approach, while Selene bent to attend to the fifty-two-card pickup.

Leigh knew better than to refuse the offer and pulled on a smile as he got in close to smell the plastic, expecting a spray of water or something equally childish. Instead, Sweeney reached into the center of the bouquet and gave a tug, reverting the illusion to a cloth bag that he then pulled from his hand to reveal—

A *gun*.

The flowers and bag fell to the floor and Sweeney was left grinning with the barrel pointed in Leigh's face. He really should have expected that.

"I can explain," he said, hands rising to delay the inevitable.

"Can you? Well that might change everything." Sweeney tilted the gun upward and stepped back, but a second later, his smile dropped and he pointed the gun at Leigh's head again. "Then again, it might not."

Click. Leigh's heart very nearly stopped as a flag with the actual word BANG on it shot out the end of the *fake* gun to go with the *fake* flowers. He hated this man. Alvin was a good sort, Leigh's best friend, no doubt, but that didn't excuse his father, and it certainly didn't protect Leigh from him.

"Your face!" Laughter erupted from Sweeney, which meant Selene had to laugh too, and Leigh forced a chuckle of his own. "You didn't actually think I'd shoot you for some little tiff with Leo Moretti, did you?"

"Well...."

"No, no, no. *William*, if I decide to shoot you, I'll let Mark do it."

Click—this time from behind Leigh, where his spatial awareness should have alerted him to the presence of someone else there, but he'd been too distracted. That click was a real gun that he soon felt pressed to the side of his temple.

Selene never went anywhere without Mark Gaines. This whole damn mob family traveled in pairs, aside from Leigh.

"Now," Sweeney said with deadly seriousness in his wild eyes, "explain to me why I shouldn't have Mark put a bullet in your brain."

"TA DA!" Alvin said as he pulled the bag from his glass of milk to reveal a bouquet of plastic flowers that he thrust at Tolly in offering.

Tolly clapped joyously. He loved human magic. Sleight of hand and illusion were much more fun than real spells.

"You're a gem, Slim," Alvin said, setting the bouquet on the bar top. "Leigh barely cracks a smile at my tricks anymore."

Perhaps Leigh needed an opportunity to relax to find the humor in life again. Having someone attempt to murder him was hardly helpful.

Tolly intended to ask Alvin about that, about what specifically Leigh had done to these Moretti men that had upset them so, but before he could, he noticed Alvin's eyes drift into the distance. Tolly followed his gaze to one of the other men in the club, near their same age but slight of stature, with glasses and a sharp edge about him like his tongue would cut quick if Tolly attempted to talk to him.

Regardless of the man's countenance, Alvin looked at him with longing that Tolly recognized too well.

"Is he yours?" Tolly asked, though he assumed the answer to be no.

"I wish. Cary's a bit of a cold fish. More the love 'em and leave 'em type," Alvin said with a shrug, "and me, well... I'm a romantic."

"Your flower trick is romantic."

"He'd laugh in my face if I tried that." Alvin turned on his stool to stare down at the bar.

Tolly mirrored his posture. "But you do desire him?"

"All the partners around here are just that... *partners*. Not warranted by my pops or anything, just sorta happened. We're the only ones who aren't."

"But Leigh...."

"He's always been a loner, that's different. Odd number and all. Though not anymore with you around." The playful smile Alvin afforded Tolly was encouraging, though he was concerned he might have already overstepped.

"I worry that Leigh, too, is a… cold fish."

"He doesn't mean to be," Alvin said, as though there was a story there.

"Did someone break his heart once?"

"Yeah. His parents. Mom died when he was little. Dad was an asshole until he died too. Leigh's been alone ever since. We've been friends for years and he still closes off sometimes. Cutie like you would be good for him." Leaning to the side, Alvin nudged Tolly's shoulder, but his friendly smiled turned mischievous. "I gotta ask, though. What aren't you telling me?"

"What do you mean?"

"You're hiding something about last night. Come on, you can tell me if you two shared the bed."

If only, but Tolly had been slow to believe the magic would work, slow to believe he would be wanted, so he had not found Leigh until morning. "We did not. I convinced Leigh to let me stay so I could watch over him. I am quite strong, I swear to you. I wish to help so that he does not take any more… swims with the fishes."

Alvin snorted. "Okay, but… why? You're divine, honey, but you don't even know Leigh."

Leigh had said the same. But Tolly did know him, deep in his soul. The rest, the little things, the details would only prove to make Tolly want him more once he learned them.

"Would you believe in love at first sight?"

"Seriously? No, I don't believe in that. I believe in lust at first sight and love over time. You want Leigh, that's fine by me. You saved his life. You want to love him, you gotta earn that, and it won't be easy. Maybe you'll change your tune after you get to know him." Alvin was testing Tolly because he cared for his friend. Tolly appreciated that, but he knew the truth.

"I will not. I feel it. We are a good match."

"Good luck, then," Alvin said. "You're gonna need it."

"It is not luck. It is faith and perseverance. Which is all you need as well."

"I think I need more than that." Alvin tilted his head to look at Cary again, sitting far from the other pair in the club, who kept eyeing Tolly in open contempt despite not knowing him yet.

"May I help?" Tolly asked.

"Help how?"

"You are afraid to make a wrong move but wish to know more of your partner to woo him. I do not think a ruse like in *Roxanne* would serve you here."

"You mean that Steve Martin flick where he does all the thinking and coming up with poetry but the dumb guy does all the talking?"

"Precisely!" Tolly had seen many movies over the years, but his favorites were modern romances, which he also took as the closest to normal human life, since he recognized early that films like *Star Wars* were not applicable to reality. "You are hardly dumb, however. How about I befriend your quarry to find out what would work best and let you know what I discover?"

"Not like hitting on him, though?"

"Oh no. I would make sure my intentions are clear, that I only wish to have Leigh."

"You'd do that for me?"

"I would like for us to be friends. Friends help each other, do they not?"

Alvin snorted and patted Tolly's back. "You got a weird way of talking, String Bean, but I like you."

"I am glad. But please, I would prefer that 'String Bean' not be a lasting nickname."

Alvin laughed harder.

It was then that Leigh reappeared from the back. Everything about him from his face to his walk was visibly tenser. Tolly immediately hopped down from his stool.

"Is everything all right?"

"Fine," Leigh answered curtly.

Alvin hopped down as well, not appearing to notice Leigh's distress. "See. Told ya Dad would fix everything."

"Yeah. Good ol' *Dad*."

"You can work it off, right? He's got a plan?"

"He does. We'll talk about it later. For now, I'm off the radar and playing dead as best I can. So if anyone asks…."

"I never saw you," Alvin said. "Really broken up about your disappearance too."

"Thanks, Al," Leigh said gratefully.

"Anytime. Be safe. And you be good, Tol-man."

Tolly understood that as their cue to leave, to "lie low" as the saying went, so he wished Alvin well as he followed Leigh to the door. Hopefully he would get the chance to speak with Cary soon and fulfill his promise. For now, he cast the man a quick glance, but Cary sat alone at a table in the corner with an open laptop, completely engrossed in his work. Tolly saw him reach up to rub at his ear, but he otherwise gave no indication that he cared to meet Tolly's stare or had even noticed it.

The pair at another table, however, stood as if to stop them.

"Hey, Hurley!" the man called. "Aren't you gonna introduce us to your friend?"

"Nope," Leigh said without looking at them and grabbed Tolly's arm to usher him out the door.

"You were not being truthful with Alvin," Tolly said once they were outside.

"No, I was not."

"What does Arthur Sweeney wish for you to do? Will he not help you?"

"He'll help. But I have to prove myself first."

Oh. That was never a good thing, not in the movies or in Tolly's world. "How?"

"Well ain't that just the least surprisin' thing," a gruff voice said before Leigh could respond, coming from behind them, farther down the street. "Runner Hurley coming out of Boss Sweeney's nightclub."

Tolly whirled about to see two men getting out of a car. At first he worried they were Moretti men, but they wore neat suits, one with a tie, the one who had spoken without, and had detective badges hanging from their necks.

Police and mobsters rarely got along.

Leigh turned around much slower than Tolly had. "Detective Perez. What, a guy can't go to a club anymore without being harassed?"

"Like we don't know what goes on in that place," Perez said, burly and large and mean-looking as he approached, in contrast to the man with him, who while taller and also large, had a calm and gentler expression.

"Now, Nick, wait a second...," he tried.

"Don't see a warrant on either of you," Leigh said. "Fairly certain that means you can't prove anything you just said."

"Yeah, well," Perez huffed, coming to a stop in front of them beside his companion, "I heard the Morettis finally caught wise to all that thieving you been doing, turning over the extra cash to Sweeney."

Tolly weighed his options for protecting Leigh from this situation. Other mobsters he could fight. Police made things complicated.

"Don't know what you're talking about, Detective," Leigh said. "I was just paying a friend a visit."

"Sweeney's brat, right? Yeah, you're just swimming in upstanding friends." Perez's eyes darted to Tolly. "Who's he now? Another runner?"

"I am here to protect Leigh from people who wish him harm," Tolly said.

Perez huffed once more and gave an unimpressed scan down Tolly's body. "Some bodyguard you must be. Can you even throw a punch?"

Leigh's eyes betrayed his concern that Tolly would make the situation worse. He did not wish to worry Leigh, but he also could not let this behavior stand.

"I would show you, Detective," he said, "but then you might arrest me."

"*Tolly*," Leigh snapped, just as Perez reared up, ready to seize him.

"Hey! We're just trying to keep the neighborhood safe," the other man intervened, the "good cop" to Perez's "bad," in truth more than any game, because Tolly could read in his eyes that he did not share the same aggression.

"You work together?" Tolly asked.

"I'm Detective Horowitz," the man said. "We're partners."

"I see. I hope to be the same with Leigh someday."

"Not those kind of partners," Leigh hissed at him.

"What's he tryin' to say?" Perez glanced between them.

"Are you not boyfriends as well?" Tolly smiled.

Perez lunged at him, grabbing Tolly by the lapels of his borrowed jacket and lifting him off his feet. "Ya think yer bein' funny, Slick?"

"Hey, hey, hey." Horowitz stepped in to intervene again, pulling his partner back and forcing him to release Tolly. "No need to get riled up. Hurley, you think about how you want all this to end someday.

Sounds like things are heating up for you. I hope we don't run into each other again."

"I couldn't agree more," Leigh said as Horowitz pulled Perez back to their car.

"Next time we won't be so friendly!" he warned, and moments later, they were back inside the vehicle, headed down the street.

"Prick," Leigh growled.

"He means to keep the law," Tolly said, understanding what detectives did. "He is merely angry that you are not on the same side. Perhaps in another life, you would have been friends."

"Doubtful," Leigh said, then seemed to recognize the hint of smugness Tolly wore. "You goaded him on purpose, didn't you?"

"I am a fast learner," Tolly said. "I am good at watching people. They have nothing to… pin you on."

"Pin on *me*. And you're right—they got squat, but they keep trying anyway. If I end up in the clink again, I'm gonna be there awhile. Never did more than a few months so far." Leigh turned back around to head down the street.

Tolly followed. "Months locked away? For what?"

"I told you, I'm a thief."

"No. For what benefit? Why? Is this truly the life you want?"

Tension rippled up into Leigh's shoulders, and he clenched his fists. "We gotta get off the streets. Come on."

They made quick work of the intersections they needed to cross, but eventually they ended up at that same shop packing up boxes. This time, Leigh paused and caught the attention of one of the men.

"Don't suppose you're moving new inventory," he said.

"Hey there, Hurley. Nah. We're moving to Bay Park, I'm afraid," the young man said, stretching after loading another box into a truck. "Can't make anything work in this part of town, worrying about hustles from Sweeney or the Morettis. Even with a little help." He winked. "My ma can't take it anymore, so we're out. Bet this place'll stay empty awhile. No one wants to buy a shop that'll cost them three times as much in protection fees. Too bad too." He glanced up at the place that obviously had great meaning to him, just like it seemed to have great meaning for Leigh. "No other electronics stores or repair shops around this neighborhood."

"Yeah," Leigh said, "the docks are for the birds these days. Sorry to see you go."

There was a unique sort of ache in Leigh as he looked up at the shop, but he did not say anything more before continuing down the street. He was quiet the whole rest of the way until they reached the inside of his small apartment.

"Leigh, please," Tolly said after shoes and jackets had been shed and still Leigh had not said anything. "What does Arthur Sweeney wish for you to do?"

Leigh remained facing away from him, looking toward his window and the fire escape as if longing for an exit. "To kill Vincent Moretti."

CHAPTER 4

TOLLY FELT a cold chill race through him as though he were narrowly escaping the grasping claws of his brethren.

"Kill Vincent Moretti? The older brother of the one who tried to kill you? But you are not a killer, Leigh."

"You don't know what I am," Leigh said with bite, remaining facing the window.

"I know your heart." Tolly moved slowly around him so as not to spook him. "That is what I feel through our connection. And what I feel is good and kind and resilient. You know my heart as well, so you know I speak the truth. If you do not believe me, tell me otherwise." He took Leigh's wrist, and while he felt him tense, he was able to lift his hand and place it over his heart.

Tolly did not mean for Leigh to feel the rhythm as anyone could, but the truth deeper than flesh and blood, everything he was and longed to be, just as he could feel the same in Leigh.

Leigh shook his head as if to dissent but stopped, eyes growing distant as he allowed himself to experience the connecting thread between them. To Tolly, there was much conflict and loneliness, Leigh's exhaustion and desire for peace. Tolly assumed Leigh could feel something similar in turn, because Tolly, too, was tired and lonely.

"There is much more goodness in you than in me," Leigh said with a drop of his eyes.

"That is not true. It does not have to be true. What did you do to these men? Stole, you said, but what and why? Are they so terrible that they deserve death?"

"Cash," Leigh said, snatching his hand away. "I stole cash, okay, which might as well be life and death to these people. I intercepted deposits after they made rounds of the local businesses to collect protection money. Then I gave some back to the shops and the rest to Sweeney. Only kept a little for myself.

"For a good long while, I was a ghost. They never saw me, never knew who was behind it, never knew which drops I'd hit and which I'd ignore. But last night they were waiting for me." Leigh's eyes darted up as he said the words. "Last night they were waiting for me...."

"Leigh?"

"Alvin said word on the street was minimal, but the detectives knew, which means somebody talked. It wasn't common knowledge, but someone knew something, and it's too convenient for the answer to be Moretti men being smarter than usual."

Tolly tried to remember similar situations from stories he knew. "You have a... snitch?"

Leigh snorted, which at least meant his standoffishness had loosened. "Couldn't be any of the lower-tier runners. They'd be too scared of Sweeney. Has to be one of the inner circle. Not Alvin. Maybe he'd betray me for the right reasons, but never his father."

Tolly doubted that. Alvin was loyal and cared for Leigh deeply.

"So that leaves Cary, Selene, Mark, Jake, or Rosa. Maybe more than one."

"Not Cary, I hope. Alvin is smitten."

"I know." Leigh rolled his eyes. "Which means we can't trust his opinion. We don't tell him about this, understand? He has trouble keeping his mouth shut, and it could be any one of those people."

Concern made Tolly press his lips together. "Killing Vincent Moretti will not be any easier if you have a traitor in your midst."

"I'm aware. But I still have to kill him if I want to stay alive myself. And yes"—Leigh stepped closer to Tolly as if to challenge him—"he is a bad enough man that he deserves it, just like his brother."

"Perhaps he does," Tolly said solemnly, "but you still do not wish to be the type of man who kills."

"Tolly...."

"I will help you, however, if that is what you want."

"You're not helping me kill a man," Leigh said.

"Then I will help however you tell me to." Tolly accepted Leigh for who and what he was. He hoped for Leigh to believe better of himself, but he would not try to change him if Leigh was set on this course.

With distress bleeding into the cracks in his expression, Leigh looked ready to say something more, but a knock at the door interrupted, as was so common here. Leigh gestured for Tolly to be quiet and walked back to the door to peer through the spyglass.

"Mrs. Johnston," he said as he opened the door to reveal a woman a few years younger than Miss Maggie, holding an appliance in one hand and a pan of some sort of baked goods in the other. "Toaster acting up again?"

Tolly wondered how Leigh had time to be a mobster when his neighbors came by so frequently. Mrs. Johnston was very sweet, however, and asked politely for Leigh's assistance with her appliance. The pan was filled with brownies as payment, and after Leigh introduced Tolly as his roommate, he tried one of the treats while Leigh worked on the toaster.

Brownies were even more delicious than bacon and eggs, sweet and melty like an explosion of decadence. Tolly must have betrayed his love for them, because after Mrs. Johnston left, fixed toaster in hand, Leigh said he could have another if he wanted.

Tolly accepted the offer gratefully, but he was only halfway through eating it when he heard Leigh hiss at the kitchen sink.

"Damn. Must have cut myself on something," he said, turning on the faucet to rinse away the blood.

Setting his unfinished brownie aside, Tolly rushed to grasp the wrist of Leigh's injured hand.

"Hey, what are you—"

"I know it is only a small cut, but there are benefits to being merfolk when water is near." Holding Leigh's hand under the spray, Tolly kept his wrist in one hand and placed the other over the cut.

There was the barest hint of illumination through Leigh's veins, and then Tolly lifted his hand to show that the cut was gone.

"How…?" Leigh marveled at Tolly's magic. It must be so strange to live without any. There was a faint tug as though Leigh might pull away, but he looked at Tolly and seemed to decide against it. "There are so many strange things about you. Even how you talk. Why so formal all the time if you learned English watching movies?"

"I did not. Merfolk learn languages differently from humans. Our magic allows us to comprehend whatever we wish. How I speak is a reflection of how my people communicate, simply translated into your words. Would you prefer I spoke more colloquially?"

"No. It's nice. I like the way you talk."

This close, Tolly could see Leigh's eyes glitter, navy and bright blue combined, lips slightly parted and so inviting. Tolly wondered if Leigh had any idea that their kiss in the water had been his first. He meant it that he hoped more than anything that it would not be their last. It appeared another was imminent as they stared, Tolly's thumb circling Leigh's pulse point and the distance between their lips shrinking.

The trill from Leigh's pocket—his cell phone again—was a rude reminder that magic was not prominent in this world but technology was.

Leigh pulled out of Tolly's hold to answer it, and Alvin's name blinked on the screen. "He must have plied his dad for details." Slamming his hand down on the handle of the faucet to turn it off, Leigh answered with impatience. "If it's not intel or good news, I don't—" A sigh. "Yes. I'll do what I have to. We all know this neighborhood would be better off without Vinny, even if his brother would just step up to take his place."

Tolly forgot his brownie as Leigh looked at him in apology and finally escaped the kitchen. He moved to the doorway to listen in.

"Right now, I need you to be my eyes and ears. Talk is minimal on me being alive, right? Well make sure it stays that way. Who all knew the Morettis were after me and when did they figure out I was the one hitting their drops? That's what we need to know so I can make a plan of attack."

Leigh was serious about pursuing this, and while Alvin did not seem pleased with the idea either, he was having no more luck than Tolly at convincing Leigh to give it up. When they finished talking, Leigh thanked Alvin and promised they would see each other soon.

"I need a disguise," he said after he hung up, "and I need to make a few rounds with the people in the neighborhood. I wish I knew whether someone was watching from the alley without sticking my head out there." He nodded toward the fire escape.

"Oh. That is a very good idea," Tolly said, moving to the wall beside the window and placing his palms against it.

The sound that erupted from him was not so much a cry like a whale might make but more a mystical pulse to see beyond the depths, which worked on dry land just as well. The ripple effect projected back to Tolly a general sense of the surroundings in the direction he faced, and he had an instant image in his mind of the building beyond, the alleyway, and in this case, the lack of people in it, though there were a few birds on the ground pecking at crumbs.

"The alley is clear for now if you wish to exit this way," he said, glancing back at Leigh, who stood in seeming awe once more. "I can check again when you are ready to leave so you can find a suitable disguise."

Leigh's mouth opened, though no sound escaped, not until he closed it again and started over. "Sonar?"

"In a manner of speaking."

"How clear of a picture can you see when you do that?"

"If there *were* people? Their number, and general height and weight."

A smile crept into Leigh's expression. "That will be useful. Let me get ready so we can go."

We. Leigh would not try to leave Tolly behind. He was making progress.

Tolly took it upon himself to finish his second brownie while Leigh changed. Leigh kept on his darker wardrobe but added a pair of glasses, a ball cap, and a hooded sweatshirt.

"How Captain America of you," Tolly said. He had managed to see all the recent Marvel movies and had especially enjoyed the one where Captain America hid by dressing that way. Stories of heroes and tales of great love always kept Tolly captivated.

He hoped that was the sort of story he was in now.

CAPTAIN AMERICA? Leigh didn't mind Tolly's taste in films, but he couldn't live up to references to comic book characters.

Not unless he was the villain.

He was skulking about his own streets like a tourist, using Tolly to case shops before they went inside. He was protecting himself, sure, but also laying the groundwork for murder. There was no way he could feel good about this.

The route Leigh took Tolly on was the same one the Morettis would make when collecting fees. Leigh lived right at the border of territories, and technically he was on the Moretti side until he crossed that last street to Sweeney's club. The shop owners all knew him and who he worked for, so if one of them had given him up, it would be easy to suss out.

Tolly was the decoy and it gave him his wish to explore the neighborhood, not that Leigh felt any less low about it. He would send Tolly in first to put the shopkeeps at ease with a new and friendly face. Then he would enter after and wait for the right moment to reveal himself. If any of these people had talked, they would be startled to see him, but everyone seemed relieved. A few even laughed.

"William," said the surly old man who ran the corner store, "what are you playing dress up for? We got a problem brewing?"

The shopkeeps knew the money Leigh slipped them from time to time was from the Morettis. Sweeney liked the Robin Hood act because it made the people love Leigh, and in turn love *him*, but people tended to talk, so he had to wonder if any of them had.

"You're with him?" the man said to Tolly. "You go ahead and take that soda on the house, son. William is good people."

The pit in Leigh's stomach deepened to hear that, made worse by Tolly's smile.

The other businesses turned out much the same, from the mechanic shop to the little antique store barely holding on. Tolly was especially enamored there, hands skimming edges of old tables, pictures, and a collection of ancient VHS tapes. Leigh had to break it to him that he didn't have a VCR to watch them on, but Tolly still enjoyed looking at them.

The last stop was the record store, the closest to being in good shape since it skirted the line toward nicer streets and got good spillover traffic on occasion. A lone and very bored young woman covered in piercings and tattoos manned it today. Leigh had dealt with her before, not that she ever seemed fazed by having mobsters around.

"I love this song," Tolly said. Iggy Pop's "Lust for Life" played, probably because *Trainspotting* was on the TV behind the shopgirl's head. "I love most music. Is this one from that film? I do not think I know it."

"I'm guessing you prefer happier tales, so stay away from *Trainspotting* and definitely stay away from *Requiem for a Dream*."

Tolly was only half listening, sifting through records and CDs as he hummed along to the song, his voice far sweeter than Iggy's. It reminded Leigh of hearing Tolly sing under the water, though he wondered if he'd really *heard* him because he didn't remember seeing Tolly's lips move.

When the song changed to David Bowie's "Golden Years," Tolly's eyes closed, and his humming seemed to shift more than simply switching melodies. Leigh felt drawn in, as if only Tolly's voice were singing, as if only Tolly existed in all the world, calling to him like a siren.

Leigh gasped as he broke free from… whatever that was, feeling like he'd been dreaming, only to see the shopgirl out of the corner of his eye, staring at Tolly with a blank expression, eyes unblinking and glazed over.

Like a siren.

"Tolly." Leigh grabbed his arm.

Tolly's eyes flashed open, his humming ceasing, and in that same moment, the shopgirl blinked and shook her head.

"I am sorry," Tolly whispered. "Usually I have more control over it."

"Are there any other mermaid abilities you need to warn me about?" Leigh said.

"I do not believe so."

Great. They'd finished their errands and needed to get back before any other surprises arose.

Leigh thanked the shopgirl and left, tugging Tolly behind him. He could see the disappointment in Tolly's face at leaving, but there were more pressing things to be done than browsing records. Leigh could introduce Tolly to YouTube later, and he could listen to any song he wanted.

The outing had at least proved that local businesses were loyal. Leigh should have been happy, especially with Tolly's powers proving beneficial. Sonar, hypnotism through song, a healing touch under water. It would be so easy to exploit those gifts.

Then Leigh really would be like his father.

"This is good, yes?" Tolly said when they returned home, climbing in through the fire escape the same way they'd left. "Your neighborhood shop owners are all fine people. I could sense their honesty and goodwill."

"Sense?" Leigh tossed the ball cap onto the sofa. "Like with me?"

"My sense of you is much stronger, but yes, a bit like that."

Next, Leigh removed his glasses. He'd worn them once for a Halloween costume. Alvin thought it would be hilarious, given his closely shorn head, if he went as Walter White. "Sure, it's good, but it means I'm right that one of the inner circle has to be the one who betrayed me, and all of them saw me alive this morning."

"With me," Tolly said, standing straighter in alarm. "I wish only to keep you safe. Please, continue to use me however you need."

Didn't Tolly understand how easily he could be taken advantage of if Leigh were a different man? "Using people isn't usually seen as an endearment."

"But I am offering," Tolly said, his smile sweet as he moved closer and reached to take Leigh's hand, but then hesitated. Usually it wouldn't have been something Leigh allowed—the touch when Tolly healed Leigh's cut aside—but he must have shown some sign that it was okay this time because Tolly grasped him firmly. "Regardless of the end goal, this was nice, seeing where you are from, your home."

"Born and raised on these very streets," Leigh said. "Other places are a lot nicer than here, though. If you're a movie buff, you have to know that."

"This feels more real," Tolly said with a shrug, both hands holding one of Leigh's now and caressing his fingers almost as if he didn't realize what he was doing. "Everything is new. The people are kind. And there is you. Are you a… movie buff?"

"When I can be. Usually watch 'em at home or at Alvin's. Don't get to the theater much. Except for this one…." It came to Leigh as he said it, a reminder of an old theater he and Alvin used to sneak off to. "Maybe I can take you sometime."

"I would love to see a movie with you. Do you have a favorite?" Tolly's eyes, dark and shimmering, could capture Leigh just like his singing, and the touch of his hands sent shivers racing beneath Leigh's skin.

"I always like mysteries. Hidden villains, hidden heroes, secrets to be unraveled. Ever see *Princess Bride*?"

"I have not, but I have heard of it. Does it have a happy ending?"

"Definitely. We'll watch it sometime. Assuming we're still alive in a few days." Reality kept creeping in no matter how remarkable Tolly was.

A fresh knock was so well timed that Leigh wondered how many knocks he'd missed while they were out. He pulled his hand from Tolly, who seemed to recognize what he'd been doing finally and looked sheepish.

It was the kids from the apartment below Leigh, teens who might have been runaways, high on something and needing their air conditioner fixed even though it was spring and still crisp outside. Leigh also noticed a few Post-it notes on his door, one from the super, who needed assistance with the fuse box. Leigh couldn't blame him. The guy was ancient and shouldn't be superintendent for any building anymore.

Before agreeing to help the kids, he checked his phone to be sure Alvin hadn't sent any warnings. Nothing so far.

Tolly accompanied him—his roommate, he introduced him again, rather than tell anyone new that Tolly was his bodyguard. He would have been annoyed to have so many errands to run, being the "real super" as Deanna often called him, but it took his mind off what he'd have to face soon.

Killing a man. Killing a bad man. A really bad man. A murderer himself who'd sent his brother to kill Leigh. There should be no conflict of conscience. But then Tolly would smile, sweet and adoring, and Leigh felt like throwing up.

"Must be bad karma in the building today," he said when they were finally finished with everyone else's needs, gathering laundry he'd thrown in so they could return Miss Maggie her housecoat. "It isn't usually this steady."

"Perhaps if people from other buildings knew of your skills, you could do this instead of stealing," Tolly said so easily, like anything could be easy if you simply believed enough.

"I can't pay the rent in brownies."

"Oh. Yes. You need money. You should ask for money."

"Not from my neighbors."

"From others, then. Surely others would appreciate your knowledge."

"It's not that simple. I'd need money first to buy a shop. People can't just come to my apartment if they're not my friends."

"Like the shop we passed that will be empty soon?"

Tolly was observant, Leigh had to give him that. "There are too many pieces to running a business," Leigh said, leading Tolly out of the laundry room.

"You have considered it, then?"

"It's a catch-22."

Tolly stared at him dumbly.

"To get enough money to start a business," Leigh said once they were inside the apartment, "I need to do bad things. But if I do bad things, maybe none of my neighbors will want me to fix things for them anymore. So the only way to get what I want ruins what I want. Story of my life."

"But... you have me," Tolly said softly, "assuming you wish for me to stay. And I am not ruined. Am I?"

"Of course you're not—" Leigh started to say, but another knock prevented him from finishing.

He longed for a moment's peace, but Tolly seemed to know what he'd been about to say and smiled gratefully before Leigh went to see who was calling.

It was Miss Maggie.

"Apologies for last night," he said as he allowed her inside, followed by Gert coming in at a run. "For the record, it wasn't what it looked like."

"No?" Maggie said, hands on her hips. "And why not? I actually like this one."

Tolly's head darted up, but the next moment Gert was hugging his legs and exclaiming, "Can we play mermaid now?"

"Don't get ahead of yourself, young lady," Miss Maggie said. "We came to cook dinner for these boys."

"What? No, Maggie, now isn't a great time—"

"Is it dinner already?" Tolly asked.

They'd grabbed sandwiches from the corner store for lunch, nothing special, though Tolly had acted as though turkey and swiss on a croissant was as amazing as everything else he'd tried.

"Miss Maggie heard you walk by from the laundry room," Gert said. "She said you wore her nightgown last night. Did you really?"

"I did." Tolly crouched down like before to get on Gert's level. "She was very kind. I lost my clothing and had nothing else to wear."

"That's silly." Gert giggled. "I bet you looked funny."

"Speaking of," Maggie said, "I assume that was part of the laundry you did."

Tolly pulled the nightgown from the bag and handed it to her bashfully.

"Great, you have that back." Leigh hoped to usher them out after realizing how late it was. "Now you need to go."

"William." Miss Maggie was an immovable wall. "It's casserole night."

"I appreciate that, but I've had enough visitors today. Anyone staying for too long... it could be dangerous."

"You in trouble again?"

"I'm fixing it."

"Fine, then you can come with us," Maggie declared. "We'll cook at my place. Gertrude, Tolly, come along. Deanna and Garfield should be home soon."

Leigh imagined this was what having an overbearing mother must be like—not that he remembered much of his own. He knew he was no match for Maggie, though, or Gert and Tolly's excitement.

He checked his phone again. Alvin had done a good job of grabbing intel during the day, but without telling his friend to look into the higher-ups of their crew, he couldn't be sure where he stood. He'd need to tease out more info himself, and he had to be careful. He couldn't just walk over to Moretti-run territory and pop Vincent on a street corner.

Maybe he did need a dinner break.

Gert held Tolly's hand and talked his ear off about what she had done all day while they headed to Miss Maggie's, brownies along to share. Tolly explained with equal excitement how Leigh had shown him around the neighborhood. His earnest nature made him right at home entertaining a child.

Deanna didn't seem surprised to find Tolly with them when she and Gar showed up for dinner. Neither of the women brought up Leigh being in trouble or pried for details. It was dinnertime, and the children didn't need to hear about that. Leigh didn't always get roped into casserole night, but if Maggie happened to catch him, he usually gave in. It was nice to have more than himself at the table sometimes.

"You like sharks?" Gar asked Tolly when he finally got a word in around his sister.

"I do," Tolly said. "Sharks are very intelligent and affectionate creatures. Their bite is only for eating as long as you are nice to them."

"You've seen one in real life?"

"Many times. They like to be petted on the nose like a... puppy! Ah, but you should not try that yourself if ever you meet one. They should only be approached in such a manner by a friend they trust."

"How do you become friends with a shark?" Gar asked.

"Very carefully," Leigh said so Tolly wouldn't dig any deeper holes.

"How did you two meet again?" Deanna asked.

"I needed a roommate who could watch my back," Leigh said, "and we sort of... found each other."

"Roommate, huh?" Maggie said.

"It's not what you think."

"Tell that to my nightgown."

Deanna snickered from behind her next bite of food, while Tolly kept the children distracted with chatter and cast smiling glances at Leigh, not minding at all what these women thought of them. Leigh didn't mind either; he just couldn't believe someone like Tolly could actually be happy with someone like him, who wasn't capable of loving openly.

"Can we play mermaid *now*?" Gert asked once everyone had finished eating.

"Of course." Tolly smiled at her. "We will have to imagine the water."

"We could go to the pool, right, Mama?"

"You have a pool?" Tolly's eyes brightened at the suggestion.

Crap. Leigh hadn't thought of that.

"I suppose we could," Deanna said, "for a little while."

"Tolly doesn't have a suit," Leigh spoke up quickly, "and I don't have one he can borrow."

"Aww...," Gert whined.

"I'm sure Ralph has one," Maggie said. "He should fit Tolly well enough."

When they knocked on Ralph's door, he offered up his suit easily as an excuse to do homework with company while his parents worked the late shift. Somehow, Leigh ended up poolside in minutes with Ralph on his laptop, Maggie knitting, and Deanna and Tolly swimming with the kids. If it hadn't been an indoor pool, the weather would have been too cool for this.

He'd pulled Tolly aside before they got there. "Your tail won't just come out?"

"No, I can control it. You need not worry."

"What about the chlorine?"

"What is chlorine?"

"It's a chemical they put in pools to keep it sterile." Though Leigh doubted theirs was the cleanest pool around.

"Chemicals do not affect my kin. If they did, I could hardly go into any water near human cities. We adapt well. I will be fine."

He was. He was also an amazing swimmer, not that that was a surprise.

Trying to use the time to clear his mind and consider his next steps, Leigh lay back on his chosen pool chair and closed his eyes. The Morettis didn't know where he lived, or at least didn't know he was alive—yet. No one had talked, but one of the inner circle might be behind it. They would likely play it safe for a while—Leigh would have—but then what? He had maybe one more night of peace before things got dicey. He needed to lay a trap. He needed to save his own skin. He needed to...

Get in the water.

Leigh had the sudden desire to be submerged, and somehow it didn't scare him despite having nearly drowned last night. The water felt calm and peaceful and welcoming around him, like he'd never known in his entire life. He wanted so badly to let his *tail* out.

Startling awake from his half-dozing state, Leigh realized he'd been thinking like *Tolly*, feeling what Tolly felt. They really were connected.

Tolly was enjoying his time in the water, pretending to play mermaid with his ankles crossed, but there was longing in his eyes to let the real thing free.

Sitting up fully, Leigh instinctively reached to check his wallet, mostly because he always did that, paranoid as he had to be in this neighborhood, but also because he'd sworn as he lay there he'd felt something....

Ralph.

"Wipe that smug grin off your face and give it back."

Ralph's sticky fingers were impressive on occasion, but he had no poker face. He held the wallet up from where he'd hidden it behind his laptop. "Actually got it away from you this time."

"I fell asleep."

"You said being opportunistic didn't count as cheating."

"Trust me, you don't want to be like me." Leigh snatched the wallet back from him. He didn't mean to sound so angry, but he'd started out just like Ralph once. Ralph's parents cared at least; they just weren't around much. "You need to get out of here someday. Stick to your studies."

"Like you did?" Ralph shot back. "My parents work so hard, I barely see 'em. My only chance to have something better is with skills, and these are the skills I got. What am I supposed to do, become a cop, fight the good fight?"

"Why not?"

"Because if I did that, someday I'd end up arresting a familiar face." Ralph petulantly returned to his laptop, and all Leigh could do was frown.

"All right, you two, time to get ready for bed," Deanna said as she climbed out of the pool, gesturing for Gert in her floaties to reach up to her. Both kids groaned and begged for more time, but Deanna was firm, and soon the party was ending, leaving only Tolly in the water.

"Leigh, do you mind if we stay a bit longer?"

"Sure," Leigh said, not ready to get up himself yet. "We can stay."

Deanna and Maggie were cordial in their farewells, the kids, too, but Ralph didn't say much more than a "Later" thrown at Tolly.

Seeing the expectant look on Tolly's face after the others left, Leigh went to the doors to lock them.

"Go ahead. But we can't risk it for long."

Tolly pushed off the side of the pool in a backward dive, disappearing swiftly. Before Leigh returned to the edge, the borrowed swim trunks came flying up to land with a splat on the side. He ventured closer and saw the transformation already complete, a vision of red cutting through the water in twists and turns, sparkling like Tolly was covered in sequins.

He really was glorious, every bit the fantasy conjured in paintings and fairy tales. The pool wasn't deep enough for him to shoot up like a fish and dive back down, but he still kicked with his tail a few times, allowing Leigh to take it in and see how large the tailfin was when it fanned out behind him with a flourish.

Sitting at the edge of the pool, Leigh didn't care that his jeans got a bit wet, though he still took off his shoes and socks and rolled his jeans up to the knee before dropping his feet over the edge.

"Leigh." Tolly came up with a splash, swimming to him like he was floating on air. "Why is it you feel you have no family? Clearly you do, much as you are not related by blood. They love you."

Love never gets anyone anything but pain, Leigh's father used to say, and he'd taken that to heart, but some people kept wheedling their way in.

"Join me," Tolly said when he didn't answer.

"I don't have a suit, remember? And I'm not putting on the wet one or getting my clothes soaked."

"Then… what is the phrase? Skinny-dip!"

"Not happening," Leigh said, sharper than he meant to, but stripping by moonlight for a near stranger, no matter how magical or adorable, was not something he was up for tonight.

"You do not wish for me to see you," Tolly said glumly.

"It's not…. I'm just not feeling it right now, okay?"

Tolly swam awhile in silence, sometimes with his head above the water, tail splashing playfully, other times like a blur in the depths, but eventually he came up, his dark floof of hair slicked back, and drifted closer to Leigh.

"Will you really kill this man?" he asked, and Leigh gave a deep sigh.

"I have time to figure out how. Sweeney's not expecting it overnight."

"But you have not killed before."

"No."

"Why do you wish to start?"

"Because I have to." Leigh kicked at the water angrily, and Tolly floated around him to approach from the side.

Not that Leigh would have…. He hadn't meant to….

"Do you? Have to?" Tolly pressed. "I can protect you."

"Tolly…."

"I come from a race of killers, but I choose to be different."

Killers? Looking like that? Leigh hardly believed it, but he didn't think Tolly was the type to lie. "Because you *have* a choice."

"You think it has been easy for me?"

This was getting too heavy too fast, and Leigh still wasn't sure about his plan. "Are you done?" He gestured at the water as he pulled his feet free and stood. "I need to get some sleep and don't want to leave you down here alone."

"We can go up. All I ask is that you allow me to help you."

"Let me sleep on it."

Tolly lifted out of the water without any effort, and right then he had legs, *naked* again, since his suit was on the floor. "May I sleep with you?" he asked as he picked up the trunks to slide on for the walk upstairs. "I mean, may I *share* the bed with you?"

"Of course. It's fine." It wouldn't help Leigh sleep, but he couldn't ask Tolly to take the couch, and he didn't want to sleep there himself.

Leigh got ready for bed, while Tolly, somehow, without showering or brushing his teeth or doing more than patting gently at his head a moment with a towel to get rid of the denser drops of water, was clean and fresh as a daisy. Even smelled it, like rain after a storm.

It might not be a power Tolly understood, but it was definitely magical.

He said he would prefer to sleep naked but agreed to wear underwear. It didn't help, however, to watch that long, lithe body, clad only in too-tight boxer briefs, climb into bed with him. He needed to get Tolly some clothes of his own tomorrow.

Amazingly enough, Leigh drifted off easily. He'd nearly fallen asleep earlier, after all, bone-weary from almost dying and having his world turned upside down.

Only his dreams weren't the pleasant ones of sun-kissed skin and boyish grins he'd hoped for, but of drowning again, very different from his shared half dream with Tolly at the pool. The water wasn't welcoming anymore, but dark and hiding terrors.

Something deadly was in the water with him, something with skin the color of blood and razor-sharp teeth. Something with claws like knives and eyes that same deep red, almost black as a void.

And it was hungry, wanting nothing more than to possess Leigh entirely.

He awoke with a gasp like choking on water again. He'd almost died. He'd learned mermaids were real. In a few days, he'd either be a murderer or dead himself. Of course he was dreaming about monsters.

After catching his breath, he reached toward Tolly to make sure he was okay, but his hand came down on nothing. Leigh sat up quickly. He couldn't hear anything, so Tolly couldn't be awake. Had something happened? Had Tolly left? Had Leigh dreamed it all?

Then his tired eyes took in the lump in the covers below the empty space, and he lifted the comforter to peek beneath, discovering Tolly curled up in a very small ball in the center of the bed. No wonder, really; he was used to sleeping beneath several tons of water.

A knock at the door brought Leigh right back to yesterday, only at least this time he knew it wouldn't be Miss Maggie holding Tolly by the arm in her housecoat. Padding across the apartment barefoot and in sleep clothes like the unfairest of déjà vu, he was still only half awake when he wrenched his door open.

"What—" But his greeting died on his tongue when he saw the three Moretti goons who'd weighted his ankles.

Leigh desperately tried to shut the door, berating himself for being so careless when he'd known this could happen, but they were too strong for him, armed and ready to take him out.

The largest burst in first as Leigh stumbled back from the force of their push. "Hey there, Hurley. Fancy seeing you here—*alive*. Guess we're gonna have to remedy that."

CHAPTER 5

LEIGH THOUGHT of anything nearby he could use as a weapon, anywhere he could run, but there were three of them and one of him, and two of the goons already had their guns out. He couldn't fight his way out of this, and he wouldn't be fast enough to find an exit before they fired. Then, once they took him out, they'd ransack his place for that extra cash and find *Tolly*.

He had to bargain.

"We have an opportunity here, gentlemen, if only you'd see that." Leigh dropped his fighting stance and stood tall. "Sweeney has a soft spot for me, being close friends with his son and all. Might have a soft spot for you, too, with cold hard cash or anything else you want if you forget you found me."

The lead goon, the largest, who'd burst in first and hadn't yet drawn a weapon, gave a sinister laugh as he stalked up to Leigh, while the others circled behind him to box him in. "Always heard you had a silver tongue, even though usually you fly under the radar. Not under the radar anymore," he said close in Leigh's face. "I don't know how you escaped that drop in the river, but you're gonna tell us, and then this time we're gonna be more thorough making sure you stay dead."

Before Leigh could say anything, the butt of a gun slammed against the back of his head and he stumbled to his knees, gasping to get his bearings. The blow hadn't been brutal enough to knock him out. They didn't want him *out*. Just less likely to fight while they got what they wanted.

"I'm not saying we'll go easy on you if you talk sooner." A large hand grabbed Leigh by the neck and slammed him into the floor, laying him out prone. "But we're definitely gonna go harder until you do. Now *spill*." A gun barrel pressed against his skull. "How did you get out of the river?"

"*Me*," Tolly answered, his voice harder than Leigh had yet heard and far too close.

No, he thought, because Tolly against three men wasn't any better than just Leigh, not when he couldn't help.

He wasn't prepared for how little help Tolly needed.

The gun and the hand on Leigh's neck left in a blink. He was still too dazed to push onto his feet, no matter how loudly he internally screamed at himself to move. Tolly needed him, he had to—

A howl left one of the goons before a body thudded beside Leigh, the forearm he saw in his periphery looking bent at a ninety-degree angle in the *wrong* direction. Several oomphs and hard smacks followed, like someone punching a slab of meat, and then the second goon landed on Leigh's other side.

"The *hell*—" The leader spoke in a huff as if swiftly backpedaling, but Tolly's bare feet darted past Leigh, moving like lightning, like the blur he could be when swimming underwater, as Leigh finally pushed onto his knees. "What *are* you?"

The stabbing pain after a blow to the head made it difficult for Leigh to focus, but what he could make out was the goon pushed up against his door, staring in terror at Tolly, who slammed him back with frightening force. Then Tolly pulled the goon toward him to slam him back even harder.

"Wait!" Leigh called. "We need answers. Don't knock him out."

Lurching to his feet, he pushed past the instant surge of bile. The goons with guns were both splayed out, the one on Leigh's left bleeding from his temple, unconscious, the one with a broken arm whimpering into the floor, while the leader kept staring at Tolly.

Tolly didn't turn, and Leigh wondered if he was as enraged as his brutality suggested and didn't want Leigh to see his expression.

"How did you know where to find me?" Leigh focused on the task at hand. "Who told you I was alive?"

The man trembled in Tolly's grasp, staring forward like he didn't dare glance away.

"*Tell me*," Leigh demanded, "or I'll tell him to keep showing you what a mistake you made coming here."

"It was…." That got the man's eyes to dart to Leigh. "*Theilen*!"

Jake. Figured. "Who else knows? Leo? Vinny? Is Jake working with anyone else?"

"I don't know! I only ever dealt with Theilen. The bosses don't know you're alive. We were gonna tell 'em when we brought in your body."

Tolly slammed the man's head back. "You will not touch Leigh again, do you understand?"

"Tolly…." Leigh didn't know how to finish the reprimand, because he couldn't let these men go—they'd rat him out for sure and be back with more—but he didn't want to put Tolly in this position.

"Do you not wish for them to die?" Tolly asked, turning only partially so Leigh still couldn't see his eyes.

"I don't want *you* to kill anyone."

"But it is too dangerous to let them live."

"I know, but—"

"P-please," the man stuttered. "I won't turn you in. I'll make something up. Anything! I won't tell anyone I saw you."

What must Tolly's expression look like for the man to be so terrified, even if he was a surprise powerhouse?

"Leigh," Tolly said, strange-sounding, stiff and cold, "cover your ears."

"What? Why?"

"Because I am going to sing."

Leigh obeyed with a jerk, but in the moment before he did, he heard the goon gasp as Tolly's song began. Leigh could still hear him, mutedly, but it wasn't enough to draw him in or affect him like before. It was hauntingly beautiful, the simple tune without words, and caused the goon's eyes to glaze over like the shopgirl's.

Then Leigh heard Tolly murmur commands, telling the men to forget what they had seen, where Leigh was and that he was alive, and to go back where they'd come from as if they'd failed in what they had set out to do.

Leigh looked down to see the man with the broken arm staring at Tolly in a similar daze, and the unconscious man was awake now, lying with his eyes open, frozen by the spell. It wouldn't last forever, not if Jake was a traitor, but it would buy Leigh time.

When Tolly stepped away from the leader, the man moved mechanically to open the door. The men on either side of Leigh got up to follow. The one with a broken arm cradled it, the other holding a hand to his head, but what caught Leigh's attention were the deep scratches through both their shirts, drawing trickles of blood.

"Some sharp nails you have," Leigh said once they had filed out of the apartment.

"Yes," Tolly said, though he sounded sad now, off.

Finally, after shutting the door and taking a breath, he turned to look at Leigh, and Leigh honestly couldn't say what the goon had been so afraid of.

"Are you all right?" Tolly rushed to Leigh's side, traces of blood smudged on his skin as he grasped Leigh's hands.

"You know what they say, it's not the years, it's the mileage," Leigh said, letting Tolly fret and fawn, because it was nice to have someone worry over him so much.

"*Raiders of the Lost Ark?*" Tolly tilted his head like an inquisitive puppy. He really was a movie buff to catch that.

"I think Indie and Karen Allen's character had it easy compared to us. I'll live, though, maybe a concussion. You weren't kidding about the bodyguard bit. You're officially hired."

A crack of Tolly's more familiar smile emerged. "I will keep you safe, however I can, I promise." He stroked one hand down Leigh's cheek before blushing in embarrassment and retracting the touch. Leigh hadn't minded, but they had larger concerns.

"If Jake's a snitch, then so is Rosa. Maybe more, but the two of them for sure."

"The unfriendly pair in the corner of the club? You must tell Arthur Sweeney."

"Can't. My word against theirs and I'm already on the shit list. I need to prove it or it won't matter."

Tolly pursed his lips in thought. "Careful planning?"

"Exactly." Retrieving his cell phone from the coffee table, Leigh checked his messages. Nothing new from Alvin, but it was 7:30, and he had an appointment at 8:00 a.m. he couldn't miss. "We'll get to that. First, we have a date to keep."

TOLLY FELT shaken from his morning wake-up call. He had felt the loss of Leigh's warmth and reached out beneath the covers to find the line of his body only to discover emptiness. He had not meant to curl so small and deep within the blankets, though it had been soft and warm, much nicer than he expected. If he could have had such safety and comfort under the water, nothing would have been more perfect.

Before he could worry that Leigh was gone, he heard voices in the other room, a scuffle—*trouble*. He was up in seconds to go to Leigh's aid, but he nearly lost himself in the attack, swift and brutal like his instincts fell to so easily, even though he hated the part of himself that could snuff out human life without thought.

He was grateful Leigh had held him back, but he worried that some of his true form had come out. He could not risk that happening when Leigh could see him.

"I am not certain I understand what a parole officer is," Tolly said as they neared the woman's office at the Department of Corrections.

"You've never seen a movie with parole mentioned?" Leigh asked.

"Mentioned, yes, but only in passing, never fully explained."

"I served time for theft but got out early for good behavior. Beckett makes sure they didn't make a mistake. Keeps an eye on me, has me check in from time to time, that sort of thing. If I step out of line too much, a word from her could send me right back to jail."

"Ah, which is why you lie to her."

"Say that a little less loudly inside," Leigh hissed before opening the door to the building. "And let me do the talking. Follow my lead again, got it?"

"I understand."

Tolly was not a fan of this corrections facility, as it was very drab and lifeless, and no one seemed particularly happy to be there. The building was mostly small, however, and they reached the office of Tabitha Beckett quickly, even a few minutes early.

"Who says I don't deliver?" Leigh said with a wide, *false* smile. He was shaken from the morning too, his head in great pain. Tolly could feel it through their connection, despite the medication Leigh had taken before they left, but he hid it well, pushing on as any survivor must.

"The roommate's real, huh?" Tabitha stood from her desk to reach out to Tolly and shake his hand. "Tabitha Beckett. Pleasure to meet you."

"You as well, Miss Beckett. I am Tolly."

"Tolly what?"

Oh. Right. Leigh had two names. Most people did, some three or even more than that, but Tolly was simply Tolomeo.

"Allen," he said quickly, thinking of the actress from *Indiana Jones*. Certainly, Leigh was the Indie between them. "Tolly Allen."

"Planning a background check already?" Leigh said. "You won't find any records on him. Totally on the up and up. You looking for ID?"

"I'd be within my rights to ask," Tabitha said.

"Excessive, considering I haven't done anything."

She sighed.

"You're here to grill *me*, not Tolly." Leigh took a seat in one of the two chairs in front of her desk, so Tolly took the other.

"I must say, Miss Beckett," Tolly said, "I appreciate that you wish to keep Leigh out of trouble. I only wish the same."

"Oh?"

Tolly could feel Leigh's flare of concern that he was going off script, but he could sense that this woman had no hidden agenda. They need not be at odds. "Oh yes. He is a good man, and I enjoy staying with him. I would not want for him to go back to jail."

She was clearly used to reading people and must have been appeased by what she read in Tolly, because after a moment of sizing him up, she nodded. "All right. I can play ball. You got a roommate to keep you honest. Couldn't be happier. Now let's hear how that happened and what you've been up to."

As requested, Tolly let Leigh take the lead, amazed at how seamlessly he weaved a tapestry of mixed truths and lies about them meeting by the docks, Tolly needing a place to stay, and helping Leigh with chores around the apartment building.

"No pay stubs yet, they can't afford to offer me much as backup super, but I'm looking into other options now that I got some help with the rent."

"I'll expect a little more than that come next month before I sign off and you're free of me."

"I know. I'll blow your socks off, I'll be so straight and narrow." Leigh smirked, and she shook her head in amusement.

"Tolly, can you give us a minute?"

Tolly straightened. His instincts were to not let Leigh out of his sight, but he knew they were on safe ground, and he trusted Tabitha to want only what was best for Leigh. "Of course. I will return to the lobby so as not to disrupt anyone," he said to reassure Leigh, whose eyes flashed briefly in concern.

After excusing himself, Tolly moved down the hallway to find the chairs near the entrance. Just as he was coming around the last corner, however, he nearly ran headlong into a large man.

"Whoa! Sorry about that." The man grabbed Tolly's arms to keep them from knocking heads, the suddenness of being touched without permission nearly causing Tolly to flip him over his shoulder before he realized he knew him. "Hey. You were with Hurley yesterday."

It was the nicer of the detectives they had encountered. Tolly read only genuineness from him, but still he steeled himself for confrontation as he pulled from the man's grasp. "He is seeing his parole officer, Detective Horowitz."

"Good. That's good," Horowitz said. "Look, I know Nick—I mean, Detective Perez—is a bit of a hothead, but he just cares really strongly. I swear! He's from the same neighborhood as Hurley, and he hates seeing how it's devolved over the years to all this crime. He used to try to steer Hurley in a better direction, but the next thing he knew, we were hauling him off to jail. Really broke Nick up."

"I see," Tolly said, better understanding now why Perez had been so sharp. "It is like Leigh and Ralph."

"Ralph Abbott? That teenager who's only barely escaped juvie a few times?"

Much like the term "parole," while Tolly had heard of "juvie" in films before, he did not fully understand what it was, so he simply said, "I do not know any other Ralph. He is young and unsure of himself, and Leigh hopes to lead him down a better path."

"That's great!" Horowitz said with enthusiasm. "Having a hard time, though, huh? Yeah, what goes around comes around. We're just trying to keep what's *around* to better things for the people here, you know? So, if you ever see anything…."

"I am sorry, Detective. I appreciate your concerns and goals, but I will not *snitch*. I will, however, continue to help Leigh do better. He is a good man. Ralph is a good boy. I do not want to see either of them in jail."

"I guess that's good enough," Horowitz said. "And hey, I know it's tough out there. I won't say anything to Beckett about seeing Hurley at Sweeney's. He was just exiting a building, after all. But you keep a good eye on him, okay? These are dangerous men, Sweeney and the Morettis."

"I understand, and I will endeavor to keep Leigh safe and away from all of them."

"That's all I wanted to hear."

Tolly was not sure how he was going to keep Leigh away from any of those villainous characters, but if the only way to keep him safe was their demise....

He hoped it never came to that.

"HE'S CUTE," Tabitha said once Tolly had slipped out the door.

"It's not like that."

She stared him down with a well-groomed eyebrow raise.

"Fine. It *could* be like that, but right now we're just friends. Roommates."

"You don't have a second bedroom, William." She called his bluff. Not that it really *was* a bluff, things were just complicated. "Relationships are good. I'm glad you made a friend without a record for once, but there's chatter on the streets about Sweeney and the Morettis heating up. I don't want you caught in the middle."

"I won't be. I can't help it if I happen to live in their territories. Moving is expensive. Maybe if the cops could catch either of them on something, we wouldn't be having this conversation."

"You got some leads you want to throw my way?" she asked. She had to try.

"Sorry, fresh out."

"Same old tune? Do you really want to turn out like your father?"

Leigh looked away from her. She always brought that up, because his deadbeat dad had been in and out of jail most of his life before he drank himself to death. The last thing Leigh ever wanted was to be even a shadow of him, but some things were inescapable. It was one of the reasons he never drank.

"We done here? I showed up on time, didn't I?"

She had no legal reasons to report badly about him—yet—but that didn't make her any less upset with his evasion. "I need pay stubs or a real plan of action for a job next time or I'm done with you. You hear me?"

The last thing Leigh needed right now was her breathing down his neck for the next few weeks. "I guess there is something I wasn't sure how to ask about."

"I'm listening."

"How's an ex-con supposed to get a business loan?"

"Business loan?"

"I'm not exactly appealing to the banks, but there's a place in my neighborhood about to be empty. Could be an opportunity. Always wanted my own shop, maybe get some of my neighbors to stop hitting me up in my home and start becoming paying customers. Tolly's been pushing me toward it." Leigh shrugged, taking to the lie easily because it wasn't a full lie. "See, good influence, just like you'd want."

"Want me to put in a good word, see what's possible?"

"Worth a shot, right?"

"I'm proud of you, William," she said. "These are tough decisions, but isn't it better to try something different than to get sucked into all that drama with Sweeney again? Petty theft is one thing, but I'd hate for you to end up doing something you'd regret."

Heaviness settled in Leigh's stomach like it was filled with the same cement that had once weighted his ankles. "Me too, Beckett. Me too."

It was only meant to get her off his back while he planned a man's murder. He shouldn't be so curious about how things might turn out if she returned with good news.

Leigh worried he wouldn't find Tolly in the lobby right up until he turned the corner and found him waiting patiently. It still threw him for a loop that Tolly even existed. Though as far as the system was concerned, he *didn't*, and Leigh needed to fix that before Tabitha did any real digging on "Tolly Allen."

"Where to now?" Tolly asked.

"Now, we get you a backstory and an ID."

They left the building, and Leigh couldn't help but notice how Tolly seemed more determined in his step, though about what, Leigh wasn't sure yet. He just hoped he never had to see him come to his defense with such brutality again. It didn't suit him at all.

Not like the monster following at Leigh's heels.

He froze, nearly tripping over his feet as he passed a long row of glass windows, because for a split second, he could have sworn that beside him was the monster from his nightmare. He hadn't gotten a good look in the dream, not really, but he remembered bloodred skin, black eyes, the fangs and claws and deadly intent....

"Leigh?" Tolly came up beside him, looking into the reflections as well, but there was no monster. It was just him and Tolly.

"I'm fine," he said, because he was good at lying, after all. Forcing a grin for Tolly's sake, he pushed aside his fears and focused on what he could control. "Let's go make you a real boy, Mr. Allen."

CHAPTER 6

TOLLY COULD hardly believe that by tomorrow he would be able to pass as a normal human, with identification and a history, however falsified. Apparently it was much easier for a criminal to accomplish such things than other people, so for once he did not mind that Leigh was a gangster. It made the possibility of starting a new life seem that much more attainable.

Leigh wanted him to stay. Now Tolly needed him to want him to stay forever.

"All right, Smiley, you and me need to have a chat," Alvin said the moment Tolly and Leigh joined him at the café, passing Tolly a cell phone Leigh had requested. "Next time Leigh pulls a stunt like that and leaves before telling me the whole story, you give me a call. My number and his are already in there for ya."

Tolly accepted the phone gratefully, though he had no idea how to use it.

"Play with it later," Leigh said, meaning he would show Tolly how to use it later, so Tolly put it in his pocket. "Thanks, Al. And I didn't want to tell you what your old man requested until I'd had time to process it myself. Right now, we need to talk strategy, unless you want to fish me out of the river sometime this week."

"Cary is here," Tolly said, seeing the other man at the café counter with his laptop again. He must never go anywhere without it. "Why is he not sitting with you, Alvin?"

A sigh left Leigh at the interruption, causing Tolly to smile in apology—though perhaps Leigh was more concerned with Cary's presence, since he worried about other snitches. Tolly did not think Cary was one, however, not if Alvin loved him so.

"He wanted to keep working," Alvin said. "Dad likes his partners to stick together so someone's always watching the other's back. I told Cary we were getting Leigh's new partner papers, why lie, and that Dad has you both working on something big. You're his bodyguard, right? But why do you need all this anyway? You running from something?"

"Not your business," Leigh said with a growl.

"I don't want anyone getting you into more trouble, even if he is this cute."

"I will not bring Leigh trouble," Tolly said. "I wish to help him out of it."

"Tolly's getting out of a bad living situation, okay?" Leigh offered a not-quite lie. "He's not running from the law or anyone who's going to make our lives more complicated."

Alvin seemed satisfied with that. "Just checking. I like you, Mystery Man," he said to Tolly. "I'm just protective of my boy. We go back a long way. Used to skip rope in juvie even."

Leigh snorted. Tolly would have to ask about juvie later, since it kept coming up.

"Also, gotta ask—are you wearing Leigh's clothes?" Alvin scanned the dark gray sweater Tolly wore with a playful twist to his smirk. "Were you wearing his clothes yesterday?"

"Shopping is next on our agenda," Leigh said. "That dicey situation Tolly left, he left *quickly*, got it? Now can we stop with the twenty questions?"

"Fine, fine. You two shouldn't be out and about much, though. Hit the strip mall on Eighth to avoid prying eyes. And don't worry about Long John's creds. I'll bring them by tomorrow after they're done. Now, you gonna get me up to speed on all this Moretti business or what?"

"Please, keep me informed on what you decide and what you need of me," Tolly said, "but perhaps now would be a good time for me to make good on my promise. I shall go introduce myself to Cary."

"Wait, what?" Leigh reached across the seat to stop him.

"I will be all right. If you love him so," Tolly said to Alvin, "I am sure he is a fine man to know."

He thought Leigh and Alvin looked fearful as he headed for the counter to meet Cary. Surely, being afraid of one's heart's desire was no way to live. If Alvin could not "take the plunge" as people said, then Tolly was happy to do so in his stead.

Cary seemed preoccupied with his computer and did not notice Tolly's approach. Holding back to better read him, what Tolly noticed was the way he tugged at his ear like he had the other day.

Then Tolly saw why. Cary had a tiny, high-end hearing aid in his ear. He was deaf, or partially so. One of the first films Tolly ever saw explained hearing loss and the technologies created to help, and he had his first experience with sign language, instantly choosing to learn it since he knew the difficulties someone without hearing or a voice had to face. He had always been drawn to tales that focused on communication barriers, since his kin communicated quite differently than humans normally.

Tolly wondered if Alvin knew about Cary, but regardless, this knowledge gave him confidence in fulfilling his task.

"Hello," Tolly said, speaking aloud but also signing with his hands in fluid motion. "I am Tolly. We did not officially meet yesterday, but you are Alvin's partner as I am Leigh's."

Cary was at first disinterested at the sound of Tolly's voice, but when he glanced up, he froze as he saw the signing that accompanied the words. "You were with Hurley. You sign?"

"I know many languages." Tolly continued to use his hands as he sat on the stool beside Cary. "But I have always thought this was a particularly beautiful way to speak."

"Most people wouldn't call a handicap beautiful," Cary spat.

Defensive. Tolly understood Alvin's trouble now.

"It is merely a difference," Tolly said, ceasing his signing for fear of offending the man. "Differences do not make us ugly, even if we have a hard time telling ourselves that." He certainly did some days, but when Leigh looked at him, he thought perhaps now he was beautiful like he had always wanted to be.

"Did you want something?" Cary asked without looking at him. "Alvin and I are only partners coz his dad doesn't like loners earning targets on their backs. He'll love you for ending that trend with Hurley, but I don't care who you are."

He had his cell phone beside the laptop with headphones plugged into it and took one of the earbuds to place in his empty ear.

"I merely wished to say hello while Leigh and Alvin talk," Tolly said. "I do not want anything from you. You like music? I love music. May I ask what you are listening to?"

Cary made an effort to ignore Tolly for a span before his expression scrunched. "Look, it's tinnitus, okay? Hearing loss as a kid so there's this ringing all the time I need to drown out. Sometimes that makes it hard to hear people, but I'm not…. I don't need to sign."

He was embarrassed. Someone must have made him feel like his condition was something to be embarrassed *about*. "You know how, though, I can tell, and it is easier to hear and understand people if they sign for you while they speak."

"Why do you care?"

"Because Leigh and Alvin are my friends, and I wish to be your friend too. For that to happen, we need to understand each other."

"Are you for real?" Cary slid his eyes to Tolly without turning his body fully.

"I am hardly a figment of your imagination."

For a brief but important moment as Cary coughed a surprised laugh, the reticence slipped from his face.

"What was the first song you ever heard?" Tolly asked.

"You mean really heard and paid attention? 'You've Lost That Lovin' Feelin'' by The Righteous Brothers."

"Good choice." Tolly loved the deep, resonant vocals in that song. "Does Alvin not know about your… handicap?"

"I don't broadcast it. If people notice, I just play my music louder so they think I have wireless headphones."

"Why? Alvin would not adore you any less if he knew."

"Alvin adores me?" Cary said with a scoff.

"It is obvious by the way he looks at you. Do you not notice?"

Cary glanced at Alvin and Leigh's table, and in that moment, Alvin darted his attention away as if he had been taking another longing glance. "Guess I didn't. Who are you exactly? Hurley's partner, fine, but you don't work for Sweeney."

"I am Leigh's bodyguard."

"*You're* a bodyguard?"

"I am stronger than I look," Tolly said. "Would you like to know the first song I ever heard?"

There was a pause, and Tolly knew Cary might easily dismiss him now and end their conversation. When instead he pulled his hands from his keyboard and turned to face him, Tolly knew he had accomplished something profound.

"WHAT IS he doing? Is he crazy? Cary could eat him alive!"

Leigh was more concerned about Cary being in cahoots with Jake and Rosa, but Tolly's certainty that he wasn't eased him somewhat.

Tolly had a sixth sense about people. He should be able to tell if Cary was a conniving bastard. And Alvin was so damn lost on the guy, he needed a win.

"Can we focus on the Morettis trying to have me killed and how now I need to kill Vincent?" Leigh couldn't afford to be distracted by Tolly's obsession with romance, endearing as it may be.

He explained the attack that morning and how Tolly had scared the guys off.

"Pretty Boy scared off Moretti goons? I would have paid to see that."

Then Leigh explained the harder part—that Jake was a traitor.

"That asshole. Rosa's gotta be in on it too."

"My thoughts exactly," Leigh said. "And maybe others."

"You didn't send your playmate over there to grill Cary on purpose, did you?"

"Do I look like I had anything to do with that? If Tolly said he was going to help be your *wingman*, then that's what he's doing." Leigh should have seen it coming, honestly, since Tolly knew about Alvin's crush.

"But you think we could be compromised by more than just Bonnie and Clyde?"

"Maybe. Probably."

"Shit."

"Don't start poking your nose in too deep." Leigh leaned across the table to make sure Alvin remained calm. "You'll tip them off, and whoever else might be a traitor. All I need from you is to know where Jake and Rosa are headed today. I'll handle the rest. You keep an ear open for any chatter and get me Tolly's papers when they're ready like you said."

They discussed logistics, a few ideas about who other snitches might be, and possible larger plans the Morettis had in the works, before Tolly returned, leaving Cary with his laptop and looking oddly content instead of surly for once.

Tolly was also humming what sounded like "Killing Me Softly."

"What did you talk about?" Alvin asked the second he slid into the booth.

"Music mostly. Would you like to learn sign language, Alvin?"

"What?" So that's what Tolly had been doing with his hands. "He told you about his hearing aid?"

"You knew?" Tolly said in surprise.

Everyone knew, they just didn't care. It wasn't as if it affected how Cary hacked a security system.

"I'm not an idiot," Alvin said. "Wait. You can teach me how to sign?"

Tolly was full of wonders Leigh couldn't have predicted. Who knew merfolk would know sign language? Or maybe it was just Tolly, in love with the human condition in all forms.

His hands moved beautifully in sync with his response. "I would be happy to. As well as the importance of the right song."

SHOPPING FOR Tolly's new wardrobe would have to wait. As would teaching Alvin anything more than a handful of ASL phrases. Jake and Rosa were scheduled to be smuggling in the latest drug shipment soon.

Arthur Sweeney dabbled in a little of every kind of organized crime. Diversity of resources made it harder to pin much on him when he had his hands everywhere and could drop anything in an instant without hurting his business overall.

Thievery was Leigh's specialty. It required thought and skill and could even be a little fun—when he wasn't getting caught and dropped into the river afterward. Drugs and guns and the like he preferred to stay away from.

He'd brought his hat and glasses along to be incognito, not that it made it any easier to head to the docks, considering Leigh's last memories of being there. His steps slowed as he tried to think of the best route to sneak up on Jake and Rosa. This was a daylight transaction. Not everything happened at night. Police expected that, so the right location or conducting business at the right off-time could be even more effective than the cover of nightfall.

"Ah, I see. You believe them to be meeting there." Tolly pointed through the many shipping containers at the meet-up spot.

"Yeah, but if we make any noise or get seen, we're screwed."

"I shall go alone, then," Tolly said, and suddenly he was stripping, right there at the water's edge.

"What are you *doing*?"

"I can listen more easily from the water." He already had his jacket and sweater off, then kicked away his shoes and slipped his pants and underwear down his legs. "They will not see me. Trust me."

Leigh was at a loss for words, scrambling to think of something, anything to prevent Tolly from diving headfirst into the water, *naked*, in the middle of the day—but then it was over and Tolly was gone.

What if he never came back? What if they saw him, saw what he *was* and....

It would be crazy for Leigh to follow, so he ended up pacing back and forth between the crates for ten solid minutes before he started seriously considering jumping in after Tolly. When he heard a splash, he turned to see Tolly climbing up from where he'd gone in, looking satisfied and no worse for wear.

"We are in luck," Tolly said, casually returning to his clothes to put them on over wet skin. "They were talking about more than drug smuggling, as you had hoped. There was a Moretti informant present. He was concerned about the men who returned to their base injured with no memory of what happened to them."

The goons Tolly roughed up. Leigh should have expected that a concussion and a broken arm wouldn't go unnoticed, but hopefully it just made things more confusing on the Moretti side.

"They think it careless and dangerous to send anyone else after you for the time being, but Jake and Rosa are expected to meet with Vincent Moretti soon, within the week, once the umm... heat dies down, they said. They also mentioned another snitch, but I believe there is only one other."

"Who?" Leigh asked eagerly.

"They did not say a name, merely mentioned a... runner. Not like you, someone inconsequential. This other person told the Morettis that you were alive and at your apartment. That is why those men came."

It wasn't Selene or Mark, then. Had to be one of the nobodies hoping to rise in rank. That didn't narrow it down, but it was a start. Leigh was going to have to get cozy with some of the lackeys.

"Jake and Rosa were told to lie low and to wait for a message about when and where to meet Vincent Moretti. We must be vigilant, Leigh, but that would likely be your best chance to strike at him."

It would be. If Leigh learned about the meet-up in time, he could set the perfect trap. No one suspected they knew about the snitches. The only people who had any idea were Leigh, Tolly, and Alvin.

"Did I do well?" Tolly asked once he was dressed, though he looked like a drowned rat and definitely in need of fresh clothes.

"You did very well," Leigh said. "But next time, no diving into the water without warning me."

LEIGH FELT comfortable returning home without fear of another ambush after Tolly's eavesdropping, but he still listened to Alvin's advice about the strip mall outside Sweeney or Moretti territory. Tolly was somewhat drier by the time they got there, though a few store clerks still shot them dirty looks.

They didn't spend an excessive amount of time, just enough to get Tolly the essentials. He looked like a kid at Christmas anyway, when Leigh told him he could choose whatever he wanted.

Tolly had simple tastes but gravitated toward more color than Leigh, especially red. It was his color for sure, complimenting his dark hair and eyes. One signature piece Tolly fell in love with was a red bomber jacket with a black collar and cuffs.

"Thank you," Tolly said when they left, changed into one of his new outfits and the jacket while his wet clothes were in a separate bag. Somehow, like before, he didn't seem in need of a shower after his dip in the river. He was fresh and clean, hair dried already into the perfect coif.

"Don't mention it."

"Why not? It bears mentioning since I am truly grateful."

"It's an expression. It means it was my pleasure, so don't get mushy about it."

Tolly tittered a giggle, which was almost as captivating as his singing. "Language is fascinating. There are always new turns of phrase to learn."

Leigh wished he had that sort of zest for life, but then, being around Tolly made it easier to appreciate the little things.

When they returned home, there were a few Post-its on Leigh's door, like usual, which he'd deal with later. He needed to clear his head first.

"Leigh, can you elaborate more on what 'juvie' refers to?" Tolly asked after they had arranged his clothes into spaces in Leigh's dresser and closet, which felt oddly intimate, but where else were they going to put it? "I know it is short for 'juvenile hall,' but I am not sure I understand."

"It's jail for minors. Kids under eighteen who get in trouble end up there sometimes. Not a nice place really, since it's meant to be a punishment."

"I see. The laws in your world are quite complicated."

"What, no baby jail for merfolk?"

"No. If a child goes against their parents or merfolk ways, they are hunted and killed just like an adult."

Leigh froze with a fresh shiver clawing up his spine. He kept forgetting that Tolly's people were dangerous and cruel, however beautiful they must be if they looked like him. He'd seen how strong Tolly was, but it was still difficult to picture his people as killers.

When a knock sounded at the door, Leigh's instincts were to tense before he reminded himself that they should be safe for now.

It was Ralph he saw through the peephole. The kid didn't look like he wanted to continue their fight from last night. Quite the opposite; he seemed cowed and nervous.

"What's your problem?" Leigh opened the door. "You get into trouble again?"

"You're home." Ralph sagged in relief. "You weren't here earlier."

"I have a life outside this place, you know. What were you coming around earlier for? Weren't you at school?"

"Most of the time."

"*Ralph.*"

"I'm sorry I got bitchy last night," Ralph said, pushing past Leigh into the apartment. "I was pissed and not thinking. But sometimes you rag on me even worse than my dad."

Leigh resisted the urge to fall into that compulsion now since this wasn't the best apology. "It's fine. But you get why I don't want you turning out like me."

"I know. Just doesn't seem like I got many options."

Leigh let the door shut behind him and looked Ralph up and down. He was a mess of tension in his gangly limbs. Must have had a rough day. "You like solving mysteries, good at sneaking around and sleight of hand. Doesn't mean you have to be a thief. Might make a good detective someday."

Ralph finally looked Leigh in the eyes only to ooze cynicism. "My kindergarten transcripts said the same thing my teachers tell me now. 'Does not respect authority. Does not play well with others.'"

Sounded about right. Leigh's would have said the same. "Who says you gotta work for anyone but yourself?"

It might have been a romantic suggestion, being a private eye, but romantic was what Ralph needed right now, a bit of a dream to cling to, something to strive for that would ignite a fire in him to get out of this place. It seemed to work, too, because his eyes glittered at the possibility.

"Hello, Ralph." Tolly came out of the bedroom. "How are you today?"

The way Ralph relaxed further at Tolly's appearance said he approved of his continued presence. "Wired. But good. Nice jacket."

"Thank you. Leigh bought it for me."

"He did, huh?" Ralph said, returning to the mischievous shit Leigh was used to.

"Mind your own love life," Leigh snapped, then flushed when he realized what he'd said. He didn't know how to handle the hope that filled Tolly's eyes when that was the only way he'd ever let a phrase with "love" in it pass his lips.

"Hey, Hurley," Ralph said more quietly. "Are you still in deep with Sweeney?"

"I don't want you involved—"

"I know, I know, just wanna be sure I don't have to worry about you. Even if you do have a *bodyguard* around," he said like he still didn't believe that was Tolly's function.

"I got some reprieve, all right? No one's gonna come looking for me for a while."

"Good."

There was another knock before Alvin called, "You guys having a party in there without me?" and barged in without waiting, carrying pizza boxes with a bag over his arm.

"You got Tolly's stuff already?" Leigh asked.

"Nah, not till tomorrow, but I figured you could use a night to relax. Hey, Ralphy-boy. You eat? Got plenty. Plus *RoboCop* 1 and 2 from the bargain bin. You know you want to be educated tonight."

"Hell yes." Ralph flocked to Alvin like the bad example he was. "All over the yes. I haven't seen those yet."

"That's because you're still in diapers," Leigh said, but he wasn't against the idea. In fact, he almost wanted to hug Alvin for it.

"The first one is quite violent for someone so young." Tolly came forward to protest.

"He'll be fine. You've seen *RoboCop?*"

"I prefer the second one."

Tamer and more tongue-in-cheek made sense coming from Tolly. "Pizza and mini movie marathon it is," Leigh said.

He was interrupted a few times to make good on those Post-it notes that had been on his door, but for the most part, Leigh got to relax, eat pizza, and watch flicks with his friends like someone almost normal.

When he came back from his last house call about a third of the way into *RoboCop 2*, Tolly was on the sofa with Alvin, teaching him more signs, while Ralph remained glued to the screen, sitting probably too close to the TV.

"How do you do 'beautiful' again?" Alvin asked, and Tolly fanned his fingers across his face.

"Beautiful. See?"

Alvin copied him. "Beautiful."

"I will teach you more. No need to rush. Simply be open with Cary. Talk to him. And when the time is right, you will woo him."

Leigh cracked open a soda he'd grabbed from the fridge, and Alvin turned to look at him.

"You're keeping this guy around, right?"

Tolly's proud expression made it impossible for Leigh to hold back his own smile.

"Haven't come up with a reason to get rid of him yet."

TOLLY WAS succeeding and it had only been a couple of days. He had until the next full moon to complete the pact, but the night he saved Leigh had been some days after the last full moon. Tolly could feel the time he had left almost like a ticking clock in his head.

Twenty-four days and counting. It had to be enough.

Trust and companionship had come easily between them, but Tolly needed more—he needed a true vow of love to stay with Leigh forever. It was no secret that Leigh desired him. Tolly could feel his gaze on him when Leigh thought he was not paying attention. He could feel Leigh's desire in their connection, too, a spike of heat, of affection, but despite the lingering gazes at Tolly standing in his underwear at the edge of the bed that night, Leigh simply crawled under the covers and made no move to touch him or draw him close.

Should Tolly make a move instead? He wanted to but feared scaring Leigh away if he pushed too much too fast. He had to be calculating and patient.

That was difficult, however, when he could hear the steady beat of Leigh's heart pounding so close to him, and when a mere glance afforded him the most gorgeous sight. Leigh's expression while asleep was young and smooth and unencumbered. Tolly wanted to keep that sort of peace on his face always.

Peace was difficult as well, it seemed, because Tolly woke the next morning to muffled whimpers and rustling of the sheets. He had burrowed down in his sleep again, curled up beneath the covers, but when he crawled up into the light, he found Leigh still asleep, gripping the sheets in clenched fists like he was having a nightmare.

Merfolk did not dream. Perhaps that was why Tolly sought movies and other storytelling so often, because he had so few outlets to escape reality. He did not want Leigh to have nightmares. Dreams should be sweet.

"Shhh," he hushed him, crawling closer, bold enough to allow the lines of their bodies to become flush as he stroked a hand down Leigh's cheek. "You are safe. Nothing can harm you while I am here. Be calm." He hummed a quiet tune meant to soothe, and his magic entered Leigh with a relaxed sigh.

Tolly smiled. He should have rolled away then, given Leigh space, but it felt good to be in contact with him, to touch his cheek and watch his face as his eyes blinked open to reveal that deep yet icy blue like an arctic ocean.

For a moment, Tolly worried Leigh would pull away, but he understood that it had been Tolly who chased off his nightmares. Leigh had been so scared, like a shock of dread in Tolly's chest through their connection. Now he was content and grateful for Tolly's song.

He lifted a hand to place over Tolly's on his cheek, and Tolly felt that spike of heat again, of affection, of *arousal*. He could not deny how affected he was by it, drawn to Leigh because of their proximity and the surge of adrenaline still strong from the terrors in his dreams.

Tolly wondered what the dreams were about, but he was far more interested in the bow of Leigh's lips.

He kissed him, a simple press like they had shared in the water, and Leigh's hand moved to his wrist to squeeze in encouragement as he deepened the kiss with a subtle opening of his mouth.

Leigh's tongue felt wonderful against Tolly's. He wanted to get closer and rolled on top of Leigh to straddle his hips, kissing back deeper still. Tolly wanted more and wanted it *now* with a hunger he did not think anything else could satisfy.

CHAPTER 7

LEIGH WAS only half awake, but even in his sleepy state, he knew he wanted this—*Tolly* and the comforting weight atop his hips while they kissed much more deeply than they had when Tolly saved him from drowning.

Tolly had saved Leigh again only moments ago, his song chasing away the monster that plagued Leigh's nightmares, because while at first the creature had been vicious and terrifying as it circled him in an endless ocean, Tolly's song transformed it into something beautiful, elegant and ethereal, like Tolly himself with his glittering tail.

Leigh had soon realized he was dreaming, eyes opening in the wake of that song to find Tolly against him, lean body pressed to his with a hand at his face. As he kissed Tolly now, slow and heated in the morning light, his mind and surroundings fuzzy, Leigh felt almost like he was still asleep, but this was much sweeter than any dream or monster that wasn't real.

He moved his hands to Tolly's waist to hold him closer, and Tolly responded by grabbing both sides of his face. Scooting lower, he straddled Leigh and rocked his hips forward, brushing his underwear against Leigh's sleep pants.

While Tolly ground into him, he slid his hands from Leigh's face down his chest to the hem of his shirt and pushed up underneath. Leigh's instinctive urge was to flinch, but Tolly's touch wasn't harsh like the world around them; it was kind and giving, like a beacon home.

They were both starved for contact, but even though Leigh usually shied from what was offered, Tolly dove in headfirst the same way he'd jumped into the river. Their connection—Leigh could feel it, the calm Tolly projected like his soothing song, contrasting the ravenous desire in him to get Leigh's shirt off. He pushed it up Leigh's chest as they kissed, but he didn't want to break away so he drew one hand downward again and slipped beneath his waistband with tentative but curious fingers.

"Tolly...," Leigh panted.

"I want to be inside you."

Whoa. "Uhh... Tolly...."

"Or you inside me. I have no preference," Tolly said, palming Leigh with only enthusiasm pouring through their connection. It would be so easy to give in, but one of them had to think sensibly.

"Hey." Leigh grabbed Tolly's wrist to stop him, and *wow*, did he look even more beautiful kiss-bitten. "There's a lot of prep and thought and... and supplies we'd need. Plus, I don't.... It's, uhh... it's been a while for me."

Tolly blinked as if not fully understanding. "That is all right. It has been forever for me," he said and leaned in for a kiss.

Leigh gripped his wrist harder to keep out of reach. "You mean you've never...."

Of course he hadn't. He hadn't had legs until now, and he never would have been with one of his own. Leigh wasn't even sure what Tolly's anatomy was like when he had his tail out.

"Does that bother you?" Tolly asked innocently.

Innocently.

"No, I've just never been with someone who's... never been with someone. Even my first time, the other person was experienced."

"Oh," Tolly said as though he must have disappointed Leigh. "I will do my best to please you. You can tell me everything you want me to do."

There he went sounding like a porno again. "I need to process this." Leigh pulled Tolly's hand out of his pants. "We shouldn't rush, not when you've never.... Someone's first time isn't always special, but it should be."

Tolly sat back on Leigh's hips with a pout. He had no idea how much that made Leigh want to throw him to the bed. "It would be special if it was with you. But we can wait for the right time if that is what you wish." He chewed his lip like he needed something to bite to stave off his hunger, and slowly dragged his fingers to the edge of Leigh's sleep pants again. "May I still touch you?"

Clearly, Tolly had been sent here by the powers that be to torture him.

Leigh should've said no, even if he desperately wanted to say yes. He didn't want to take advantage of Tolly's inexperience, but when Leigh didn't respond, Tolly teased his fingers beneath the elastic like he very much knew what he was doing.

A knock at the door made Leigh's breath catch. Could he get *one* morning…?

"Must you answer it?" Tolly whispered.

"I have to."

"Then can we revisit this later?"

Later would be good. Leigh needed five minutes to think this through and untwist his insides. He and Tolly were both adults who knew what they wanted. That should be enough. But most crises of conscience didn't involve mythical creatures.

"Yeah," Leigh said since he was only human, even if Tolly wasn't. "Later."

At least the sight of Deanna and Gert through the peephole was the final bucket of ice water he needed to cool down before answering the door.

"Hey. What's going on?"

"Can you watch Gert today?" Deanna asked, looking frazzled while she held her little girl's hand. "Gar's waiting downstairs and we're already late. Maggie isn't feeling well, and you know that woman would power through a nuclear explosion if she had to, but she doesn't want Gert to catch anything."

Crap. This neighborhood wasn't exactly teeming with viable options for a babysitter, and Deanna couldn't afford normal day care. The desk job she'd finally wrangled after being a waitress for years paid well, but she hadn't been there long enough to save much.

"If there was anyone else, I wouldn't ask. I know things can be… complicated for you." She glanced into the apartment, no doubt looking for signs of trouble, but instead she saw Tolly wearing one of Leigh's sweatshirts and an extra pair of sleep pants. She relaxed at the sight of him just like Ralph had.

"It's okay," Leigh said. "Honestly, here might be one of the safest places right now. It's better for me to stay home anyway and wait on some info. We'll be fine. Tolly can help, right?" he said loud enough for both Gert and Tolly's benefit.

Gert peered around Leigh's legs with an excited smile, and Leigh looked back to see Tolly wave at her.

"It would be our honor to watch over Miss Gert," Tolly said. "I did promise my assistance. Shall we play merfolk again?" He winked at her.

"You two are amazing." Deanna sighed as she let Gert scramble inside and handed Leigh a bag he assumed was filled with toys she might want for the day. "I'll be back with Gar in time for dinner. You're sure it won't be any trouble?"

Leigh glanced back once more as Tolly dropped down to a crouch while Gert regaled him with tales of some cartoon she'd been watching that he *had* to see, and Tolly nodded along happily. It wasn't the morning they'd had planned, but maybe for the better.

"I'm sure. Tolly's a double threat, you know, as bodyguard and babysitter."

Deanna laughed. "At this point, I'll take anything."

Leigh set the bag down next to the sofa after she left. "You eat breakfast yet, little miss?"

"Nope!" Gert jumped on the balls of her feet, hair bouncing in two puffball pigtails. "Maggie was gonna make muffins."

"Don't think I got the right stuff for muffins. How about we have cold pizza and you don't tell your mama? We'll eat something healthy come lunchtime, deal?" He held up his hand, and she gave him a swift high five.

"Deal!"

"Pizza can be eaten cold?" Tolly followed them into the kitchen.

"Pizza can be eaten any way you want. Sometimes cold really hits the spot."

Taking the day off would have been nice, but having to play babysitter didn't mean Leigh could be lax. He still checked in with Alvin and kept the cogs in motion. He also discreetly asked Tolly to scan for any strange figures outside the apartment every couple hours. If Gert needed to use the bathroom or was distracted enough, Tolly would step up to one of the walls and project his sonar. Nothing ever came back suspicious, but it gave Leigh peace of mind.

He didn't like that most of his next move relied on sitting pretty at home while Alvin did the legwork, but he'd been out and about too much already. Everyone knew he was alive by now, but that didn't mean he should make it easier for them to take him out.

Naturally, as soon as he thought that, he realized he didn't have much of anything other than leftover pizza in the fridge or cabinets. He hadn't gotten groceries in a while, but he couldn't send Tolly out alone, and he didn't want to take them both along.

"I'm gonna run out for like twenty minutes to get groceries. We'll make sandwiches for lunch, how's that, Gertie, and I'll pick you up some chocolate milk?"

"Will you be okay alone?" Tolly asked. "Perhaps we could all—"

"Twenty minutes," Leigh reiterated, grabbing his ball cap and glasses. "If I'm gone longer than half an hour, then worry."

There was a general store not far away where he could get what he needed, though it did take him past the shop from the other day that was locked up now, empty. He hadn't heard anything from Tabitha about a loan. It was a shot in the dark anyway. He didn't think anything would come of it, but he wondered....

Picking up food went by uneventfully, until he passed the aisle with the supplies he'd been thinking about that morning. Did he even need condoms with a mermaid? Did Tolly know what condoms were?

Leigh probably stared for a solid minute in indecision before he swept a box into his basket—and a bottle of lube. He'd never been embarrassed purchasing such things before, but today he felt like everyone's eyes were on him.

He scanned his periphery. No eyes were actually on him, but when he stepped out of the store and turned an immediate right, he nearly ran into detectives Perez and Horowitz.

Making a smooth about-face, Leigh headed the other direction, circling back around to the alley where he could get a look without being seen. He wasn't close enough to hear what they were saying, but things were getting serious if they were hanging around this much. They were worried, which meant there was something to be worried about.

This wasn't only cat-and-mouse undermining from the Morettis. With multiple snitches in Sweeney's organization, they had to be planning something bigger. A takeover. Why hadn't Leigh seen it? And it had all started with getting rid of him.

Heading a longer but more hidden path back to his apartment, he contemplated how easily he could secure anything he wanted from Sweeney if he ended a war before it began. He wouldn't just be back in Sweeney's good graces, he'd be set.

Set for life and part of this world forever.

Seeing Perez—Nick—always spiked resentment through his chest. The detective had been understanding once, always giving Leigh a break when he was a kid, because he understood you couldn't change who your father was or how limited the options were coming from these streets. But as soon as Leigh started running for Sweeney in earnest, those slaps on the wrist escalated.

Sure, Leigh had let Nick down, but what else could he have done?

He was fully aware how much he sounded like Ralph.

After waving with a forced smile at Tolly and Gert, who were playing with a combination of dolls and action figures on the living room floor, Leigh retreated to the kitchen to put away the groceries. Their voices filtered to him clearly.

"Then what happened, Tolly?"

"Then Effie bopped it right on the nose so Keelan could steal the fruit. The pelican was not happy, but I splashed it with a wave and the three of us swam away before it could recover. We ate the fruit in the shade of a large cliff by the beach, laughing at our cleverness. After all, he stole the fruit first. I was not much older than you then."

"Are you still friends with 'em?"

Tolly's voice took on a sad edge. "No."

"Why not?"

"They had to go away," he said, careful not to tell any part of his story that would scare her or admit what he was. "I miss them, but it is nice to think of them sometimes."

It was only when Tolly came into the kitchen to help with the groceries that Leigh realized he'd been staring at the counter.

"I got it," he said, still embarrassed about the supplies tucked into one of the bags. But before Tolly could leave, he asked, "What really happened to your friends?"

"They were not fast enough swimmers either."

"*Tolly*," Leigh called to keep him just a moment more. "How long have you been alone?"

At first Tolly didn't turn, but when he did, there was a sparkle of wetness in his eyes. He didn't say anything but smiled as if to say it was okay, even though it obviously wasn't.

Leigh couldn't do this. He couldn't let Tolly be part of killing Vincent Moretti, but there was no way he'd agree to stay back. What was Leigh supposed to do without turning into the type of monster Tolly had escaped?

To distract himself, he focused on making lunch—sandwiches and chocolate milk as promised. Tolly devoured his pastrami. He had yet to try anything he didn't like. He also ate a lot for someone with such a small frame.

The usual interruptions came as the afternoon ticked on, and helped alleviate some of Leigh's unease. There was always something broken in this building. If it was brought to him instead of taking him out of the apartment, Gert and Tolly would watch over his shoulder. Leigh could see the same hunger in Tolly's eyes to learn and experience something new. Before long, he was offering Leigh suggestions on how to fix things, and he was usually right.

"I am a fast learner."

"So you've said, but you weren't kidding." Leigh smiled, and Tolly beamed back at him like all the loneliness he'd known could be erased if only Leigh willed it.

Maybe if Leigh could buy that shop, he could get out from under Sweeney's thumb. That wouldn't solve his Moretti problem, though. He'd be another business expected to hand over cash on the regular, and if he didn't, they'd do far more painful things to him than a drop in the river or a gun to the back of his head. He needed to solve that problem first; he just didn't know how without bloodshed.

Later, Leigh and Tolly did the dishes while Gert napped. Their hips would brush every now and again, and Tolly would glance at him with a hopeful smile. It was strange but also reassuring to feel Leigh's own anticipation and nervousness echoed back at him, just enough through their connection to be sure they both wanted the same thing.

"Out of curiosity," Leigh tried with an awkward clearing of his throat, "how would we have sex if we did?" He was twelve. He was twelve years old and making a fool of himself.

But Tolly didn't laugh. "You can show me the first time. As humans," he said as if it was a simple thing to be discussing over dishes. "Though I would like to know you with my tail someday as well."

Know you. It was just so… *Tolly.*

"And like that… we'd…?"

"Oh. I am quite different in that form. More like a… shark? Perhaps that is the wrong analogy. I do not know of other creatures exactly like merfolk. Do you fear you will find my sex hideous?"

Leigh looked at him, but Tolly kept his eyes on the dish he was rinsing. "I don't think it's possible to find any part of you hideous."

Tolly smiled so brilliantly then, dark eyes twinkling as they met Leigh's so that Leigh almost convinced himself he could be fine no matter what Tolly looked like as a merman *aroused*.

Then he made the mistake of Googling shark penises after they finished the dishes. He should not have done that. Tolly looked perfectly normal, extremely attractive and frankly well-endowed as a human. As a merman, did he have… *claspers?*

Leigh erased his search history and tried not to think about it.

TOLLY HAD seen the flush in Leigh's cheeks steadily growing ever since the afternoon. There was trepidation in him but also an eagerness to be alone with Tolly again. Tolly would be so good to him if only he gave him a chance. He would follow Leigh's every whim to please him. Then, surely, Leigh would speak a vow of love long before their time was up.

It was a joy to watch over Gert in the interim. Human children were precious and allowed to be precious. Gert behaved well, but even when she pouted tiredly after her nap to have another unhealthy snack, calmly getting down on her level and speaking firm but plainly brought back the reasonable girl Tolly knew her to be.

Children did not need to be treated harshly to get them to listen. They were still learning. One needed to be patient with them. It was careless and cruel to kill them simply for disobeying—for going off alone from a hunting party to play instead.

Effie and Keelan's parents had done their duty by merfolk law, but Tolly's had refused and escaped with him. It was for his sake they became renegades, and he would always be grateful for that.

Dinner was at Deanna's after she returned home. Leigh could not refuse the offer, not when she mentioned empanadas, which Leigh was certain Tolly would love. He did.

Ralph joined them as well. "Your cooking is always the best, Deanna," he said with a look that Leigh had called "moon eyes" to Tolly in a whisper.

"Thank you, Ralph."

"You know what else could be on the menu?"

Leigh kicked Ralph under the table. It seemed such an obvious action to Tolly, but everyone pretended it had not happened, and Ralph grew quiet.

Gert pleaded for another playdate at the pool, and since Tolly was happy to be in the water, he convinced Leigh to go along. Tolly had his own swim trunks now, red with yellow stripes down the sides.

"Why did you kick Ralph?" he asked when they were headed downstairs to join the others.

"You know what's on the menu? Me-N-U," Leigh said with a sneer. "Kid's a walking disaster of pickup lines. He's got no idea how to talk to a woman."

"Me-N-U," Tolly repeated, then laughed. "I get it. Perhaps he merely needs direction in how to be thoughtful and attentive toward a potential partner."

"I've tried. Kid always panics and defaults to cringy bullshit instead."

Ralph was in the pool with Deanna and the children when they arrived, since he had his own trunks back. He was talking to Deanna animatedly, while also playing with Gar and Gert. The subtle smile on Deanna's face said she knew exactly what his intentions were, but she did not have the heart to tell him to stop.

"Don't go trying to matchmake them like Alvin and Cary," Leigh said.

"Oh no. Perhaps if Ralph was twice his current age. He needs to find someone with the same qualities he admires in Deanna but who is more attainable. He should also not rush. Sometimes one must be patient for the right match." Tolly looked at Leigh with wholehearted affection, adoring the way Leigh glanced away, wide smile stretching his face like he too was young and bashful.

"You watch a lot of rom-coms, don't you?"

Tolly stared in confusion.

"Romantic comedies."

Ah. "Are they not wonderful stories? Love and humor are the best parts of life."

"You're a *walking* rom-com," Leigh said. "I've never met anyone like you."

"I take that as a compliment."

"It was meant as one."

If there were not others present, Tolly would have braved another kiss, but perhaps now was a moment to—what was the phrase? Play hard to get.

He dropped his towel on one of the chairs and backed toward the pool, eyeing Leigh with open hunger that made Leigh shiver. Tolly would make up for his lack of experience. He would show Leigh all the ways he could please him.

For now, he reached the pool's edge and dove in at the deep end before swimming around to join the others. The water rejuvenated him, even though in his new form, he no longer needed as much regular submersion.

It felt strange but still enjoyable to feel the flow of water around his legs. Being in the water made him want to let his tail out immediately, but it was merely a matter of will to resist. The occasional tug to let out his claws or any other part of his true form would increase as the full moon drew near, but he had time. Losing his temper and letting a few aspects out had been dangerous enough when fighting those men. Tolly preferred to be something Leigh looked at with desire.

Deanna and the others did not stay long, but she expressed much gratitude for their help that day. Gert gave both Tolly and Leigh high fives before they left, and Ralph trailed behind Deanna with those same moon eyes.

Leigh locked the door once they had gone, prompting Tolly to waste no time shifting forms. It was like a great stretch. Not that his legs were constricting, just different. Perhaps now he could convince Leigh to join him in the water.

"We can't stay long. Alvin's on his way with your ID."

"We can stay a bit longer, yes?" Tolly arched up to float atop the water on his back, arms and tail extended. He felt Leigh's eyes scan the length of him, tempted whether Tolly had legs or not.

Like before, Leigh shed his shoes, rolled up his jeans, and sat at the edge, dangling his feet in the water. Tolly dove down deep, zipping from shallow end to deep end and back again to show off for him, delighted at Leigh's chuckle when he surfaced. Then he floated toward Leigh, close enough to slide his hands onto the concrete, framing Leigh's thighs between his arms.

When Leigh's legs spread apart to allow him closer, Tolly moved his hands to Leigh's thighs and lifted up to angle for a kiss. Leigh tilted his head down to meet him, the chlorine on Tolly's skin making the taste between them salty but not unpleasant.

Tolly floated just out of Leigh's reach with a grin. "Come into the water with me."

Leigh's eyes strayed down the front of Tolly's tail.

"Do you want to see what I look like in this form?" Tolly asked, already having trouble keeping his sex from appearing since he felt the heat building between them. Flicking his tail up, he floated away farther to give Leigh a good view should the answer be yes.

A thud alerted Tolly to something behind Leigh, but the entrance had been so seamless, like someone used to picking locks, that he only saw Alvin over Leigh's shoulder after it was too late and his eyes were already taking in Tolly's tail.

"Holy shit."

CHAPTER 8

TOLLY'S LIPS were a constant temptation now that Leigh had given in, especially when he swam to the edge of the pool, hands moving to Leigh's thighs as he lifted up to claim a kiss. Tolly tasted far sweeter than he should.

"Come into the water with me," he said. Then, more seductively as he swam away, "Do you want to see what I look like in this form?"

Leigh did—he really did. His conflict stemmed only from fearing he was bad for Tolly, a bad element, bad example, bad everything. Here was this miraculous, beautiful being, offering himself up, and Leigh was caught in a net of violence and lies that could easily drag Tolly down with him.

Of course Leigh kept seeing something terrible in his dreams. Tolly might be from a race of killers, but Leigh was the one who would soon have murder on his hands.

"Holy shit."

The voice brought Leigh to attention, recognizing the alarm on Tolly's face only after he heard Alvin exclaim from behind him.

Alvin!

Whirling around, Leigh saw a bag on the ground that Alvin must have dropped—Tolly's papers—and the unmistakable shock on his friend's face as he saw Tolly's tail, that he had a tail, his *tail*. Shit!

"Alvin—"

"A mermaid? He's a freaking *mermaid*? No wonder he talks so weird. This is huge! Like talking dog huge! Like… are fairies real too?" Alvin rushed toward Tolly in the pool. "Unicorns? Wizards? Do you grant wishes?"

"*Al*." Leigh scrambled to his feet to ward him off. "He's not a fucking genie."

"I thought you were fooling around in here, not communing with Flipper!"

"Stop," Leigh warned him, since Tolly had already ducked down in defense. "You're freaking him out."

"What? Why? This is the coolest thing ever!"

"Leigh," Tolly called tentatively from the water, "I need to sing."

"No." Leigh spun to face him again. "You can't—"

"Sing? Like put a spell on me?" Alvin spoke over Leigh's shoulder. "I'm not gonna say anything!"

"Do you promise?" Tolly swam to the edge, his tail glittering beneath him but mostly concealed. "I would only wipe your memory of the past few minutes. I would never harm you, but should anyone untrustworthy discover what I am—"

"I'm trustworthy!" Alvin raised his hands in surrender. "You're helping me with Cary. You're my hero right now, Tolly."

Before Leigh could recognize what was happening, Alvin dropped into a cross-legged position right at his feet and scooted to the edge of the pool.

"We talked today. Like words exchanged. It was *the best* thing ever. No signing yet, I want to be better at that first, but it's progress and it's all because of you. Plus, you saved Leigh's life! I'll owe you forever, Nemo. Or should I call you Creature from the Blue Lagoon?"

"It's Black Lagoon," Leigh droned, calming now that he saw the warm smile blossoming on Tolly's face.

"Not looking like that he's not." Alvin winked. "Your tail, by the way, is gorgeous. Can I touch it?"

"*No.*" Leigh hadn't even touched it yet.

"You do not mind that I lied to you?" Tolly asked.

"You're a *mermaid.* Of course you lied. You tell the truth, people will think you're nuts. Or throw you in a government lab somewhere. But you can trust me, we're buds! So—" Alvin scooted closer, leaning forward enough that the proper momentum could have tipped him right into the water—and oh how Leigh was tempted.... "—if you sang, what would it do to me? Like hypnotize me?"

"In a way." Tolly glowed under the positive attention, surprised but pleased by Alvin's response. Leigh couldn't deny he felt the same, and really, he should have known better coming from his friend.

Suddenly, all the questions he'd been too afraid to ask could be asked by Alvin, who had no filter whatsoever, and Tolly didn't seem to mind answering a single one.

"Are there mermaid cities? What do you eat down there? How do you see underwater when it's so dark? Do you ever get attacked by scary ocean creatures?"

Tolly answered every question calmly and thoughtfully.

No, they did not have cities the way it showed in *The Little Mermaid* or stories about Atlantis. They lived near coral or in underwater caves in communities so they could hunt together and protect one another from predators. Some creatures might try to attack them, but most kept away from his kin. He ate fish and birds and anything he could get his hands on, but he loved fruit and vegetables when he managed to get some from a tree or garden near water.

"My eyes cut through the darkness and it looks as clear to me as daylight."

"Do they glow like a cat's?"

"No, it is different than that," Tolly said with hesitancy, and Leigh wondered if his eyes changed underwater. He didn't remember them looking any different.

"You wouldn't *eat* a cat, would you?"

"Why would I eat a cat?" Tolly said, offended. "They are quite intelligent from what I hear, and affectionate creatures. I would much prefer to pet one someday."

"You've never pet a cat?"

"Alvin," Leigh spoke up before long, "leave the poor guy alone so he can catch his breath. It's late. We should go up."

Alvin looked thoroughly betrayed at the idea of calling it a night, but Tolly nodded, and Leigh grabbed Alvin's arm to hoist him up.

"How do you change back?" Alvin jumped right in again. "Does it take a while? Does it hurt? Do you have to be dry?"

"Not at all," Tolly answered all his questions in one as he started to lift up.

"*Tolly*." Leigh stopped him. "Naked."

"Oh. My apologies." Tolly sank back down, hidden by the ledge of the pool. "Would you hand me my trunks, please, Alvin?"

"Spoilsport," Alvin grumbled after tossing Tolly his shorts. "I was hoping for some *Free Willy*."

Leigh groaned, though he had a feeling he'd tracked down the source of Ralph's pickup lines.

"That is so cool," Alvin said when Tolly finally lifted out of the water with legs and wearing his trunks.

They went upstairs so Alvin could give them the ID and papers. It was official—Tolly could get a job now, buy alcohol, drive a car even. Well maybe not *that* unless he really wanted to learn.

While Tolly went into the bedroom to change, Leigh told Alvin his suspicions about the Morettis planning a takeover and the detectives hanging around more lately.

"What do we do? Warn Pops?"

"With the way he reacts? It'll only make things worse. We need to wait for the meet-up between Vincent, Sam, and Rosa."

"So we can take 'em all out?"

"So we can… figure out another plan."

Alvin stared at him with none of the usual mischief. "You don't want to do it, do you? Off Moretti."

"Would you?"

"I don't know." Alvin shrugged, looking young and unsure despite the collection of crimes between them. "Dad's gonna expect it of me someday. What, you thinking of going straight for Shark Week? Figuratively speaking."

Leigh cracked as much of a smile as he could manage while ignoring the bile churning in his stomach. "Not only for him, but I don't know. I don't know what I want."

He must have betrayed his concern over leaving Alvin to this life alone, because Alvin said, "Hey, I'll be fine. You do you. And definitely do him." He winked toward the bedroom.

"Al…."

"Please tell me I interrupted something super kinky—"

"*No.*"

"Aw, haven't sampled the sushi yet?"

"Seriously?" Leigh sputtered a laugh.

"You have got to tell me once you do. Like every weird merperson detail."

"You can go now." Leigh pushed him toward the door, since he'd already said his goodnights.

"He is seriously the coolest thing," Alvin said, "like wow."

"I'm glad you think so. Really. Thanks for being so good about all this."

"Anytime, man. You're my brother, you know." He tapped Leigh lightly on the chest with the back of his hand, as close as they usually came to hugging. "Even if you are dating a fish person."

"*Out.*" Leigh pushed him out the door, and Alvin chuckled before waving goodbye.

Only he could have taken learning mermaids were real that well, but Leigh was grateful. Whatever the future held, he couldn't stomach the thought of his best friend not accepting his... whatever Tolly was.

Speaking of Tolly, Leigh was surprised he was taking so long in the bedroom. It shouldn't take that much time to pick out something to wear to....

Leigh's thought process stalled as soon as he turned to see Tolly standing in the bedroom doorway wearing a fresh pair of underwear that hugged him snug and a T-shirt Leigh had been meaning to throw away because it shrunk in the wash and was currently giving a peek of toned abs. Tolly had no idea how much hotter he looked like that instead of standing in front of Leigh nude. Or maybe he did and that was the point.

"Are you angry with me?"

"WHAT? WHY would I be angry with you?" Leigh said, eyes snapping to Tolly's face after raking down his form the way Tolly had hoped.

Not that his question was fabricated; he really was concerned he might have upset Leigh and wanted to help him forget his worries so they could return to more pleasant endeavors.

"I am making your life more complicated," Tolly said, moving toward him, "when I promised I would not."

"I make my own life complicated. *You* are not the problem. And Alvin will survive. He thinks you're amazing."

"I sensed only curiosity in him, not fear or opportunism. He loves you greatly."

"Yeah...." Leigh cringed and glanced down as they met in the center of the room. "He always wants to please 'Daddy,' but most of the time, for a long time, we've been all each other has."

"May I ask, since Alvin is interested in men, and you are as well, did you two ever...?"

"Once," Leigh said. "Just a kiss or two, don't get excited. Felt weird. We're too much like family."

Tolly had gathered as much but it still soothed any foolish notions of jealousy to hear that. He pressed his hands to Leigh's chest and slid them up his shoulders. "I hope it does not feel weird when you kiss me."

"N-no." Leigh shivered, almost like he might pull away, but he relaxed under Tolly's touch. "Not… weird."

Stepping closer into Leigh's body, Tolly wound his hands around his neck. He knew to go slow, to telegraph each motion as he would have wanted in return, but he did so want another kiss. He wanted more than that.

"May we continue now?" he asked.

Doubt splayed across Leigh's features.

"Please. You put something in the bedroom after you collected food for us. You picked up the supplies we need, I think."

Leigh chuckled bashfully. "Caught me."

"Then let us use them." Tolly pulled him closer with a gentle tug at his neck and kissed him boldly. When he felt the hesitant weight of hands at his waist, it urged him to press farther forward.

He knew the underwear he had chosen were tight. He knew the shirt was too small. He wanted to entice Leigh in a new way—in all ways.

Bringing his hands down from Leigh's neck, he reached for the hands at his waist and guided Leigh into the waistband of his underwear.

"*Tolly*," Leigh laughed, ceasing the motion of their hands with the smallest resistance. "You are trying really hard to seduce me."

"Yes." Tolly saw no point in denying that. "Is it working?"

Leigh laughed again, voice quivering as he closed his hands around Tolly's, not to push him away, just to touch. "Are you sure you want this? That you want it to be me?"

"I would ask for no replacement if I had all the choices in the world. And I have waited so long for you. I do not wish to wait anymore."

Perhaps it was his honesty, but finally Leigh stopped resisting, and Tolly was able to lead him by the hand into the bedroom. Tolly was in very little clothing. He wanted Leigh to catch up so he could finally see what he looked like.

"May I undress you?" he asked.

"Y-yeah," Leigh said, but there was still uncertainty in his eyes that Tolly hoped was not a prelude to disappointment. He would not allow it to be.

With gentle hands, Tolly felt the contours of muscle and contrasting softness beneath Leigh's shirt like he had that morning. This time, however, he lifted the shirt over Leigh's head, undid the closure of his jeans, and because they were closely fit, hooked his thumbs beneath the waistband of denim and underwear alike to slide both down in tandem.

Slowly, he went, and as he did, he dropped to his knees. Finally, here was Leigh, naked and perfect for all his scars and bruises and dustings of hair. Tolly liked most the hair on his chest that thinned as it traveled down until it was but a line that disappeared into the hair framing his sex.

Leigh was hard, yet as he stepped out of his clothing and Tolly's hands returned to the outside of his thighs in worship, he shuddered.

"Why do you tremble?" Tolly asked. "You are not afraid of me, I hope."

"No." Again Leigh laughed to hide the truth he was unsure how to speak. "I... I think you're too good for me."

"Nonsense," Tolly said as he slid his hands down, then up and inward, caressing between Leigh's legs. "What shall I do for you? This?" He grinned, already leaning forward, lips parting, eager to take Leigh in.

A gasp left him when Tolly descended, then a whimper, then a moan as Tolly's tongue set to work. He had never done this before but he knew to keep his teeth back. It was easy to get lost in the sensation, especially when Leigh's fingers twisted in his hair.

Familiar hunger stirred in Tolly, but now was not the time to let his true self slip. He had to retain control.

"Wait." Leigh stopped him, pulling his head back with tender insistence.

"Am I doing it poorly?"

"No. Definitely not." His eyes were heavy-lidded as he gazed down. "But I should be the one doing this for you."

"Would you?" Tolly asked in amazement.

He would have been perfectly content catering to Leigh, but Leigh lifted him from the floor, moved him to the bed, and laid him down. As carefully as Tolly had undressed him, now Leigh did the same in turn. Leigh had seen him many times, but he looked at Tolly with newfound wonder tonight. The excitement when he parted Tolly's knees and knelt between them could not be quantified; Tolly whimpered long before his lips landed.

Once they did, it was hot and wet and tight all at once. Tolly was unused to legs in many cases, but he knew he wanted to wrap them around something, any part of Leigh he could to pull him closer. For now, he settled on letting his legs fall open as Leigh gave languid twirls of his tongue. The grip of Leigh's hand at his base, the other sliding along his thigh, enhanced the sensation tenfold.

Tolly wanted to touch Leigh in return and ended up pulling him up for a taste of his lips again. They connected with equal appetite, their sexes sliding past each other hotter and wetter from each other's mouths.

Rutting up into the friction he found, Tolly kissed Leigh deeper, and their tongues trailed down each other's jaws and necks before long. Soon Tolly's hands were moving across Leigh's chest and stomach and thighs—and oh, how good it felt to have him everywhere.

"It's all so wonderful," Tolly gasped, feeling as though his skin was on fire yet somehow happy for it. "Please… may I have you inside me now?"

Leigh growled an enthusiastic affirmative but still asked, "You're sure that's how you want this to go?"

Inside *Tolly*, he meant, instead of Tolly inside him, since he had expressed he would be happy with either.

"You can better show me what to do that way," Tolly said, eager to learn and to please, but happier still that Leigh wanted to please him as any true partner would.

"Okay," Leigh said, all doubt washed from his face. "Relax. I'll take care of you."

Tolly believed that with all his heart. Still, he did not realize it could feel better than it had been until Leigh's fingers were stretching him with help from the silky liquid he had acquired. Tolly had a good enough understanding of what a condom was and was not bothered by Leigh wanting to use one, customary for new lovers. It also did not diminish the intensity of the sweet burn of Leigh pushing inside him finally, filling him as he had wanted to be filled.

Now, at last, Tolly had something to wrap his legs around as Leigh sank in deep between his thighs.

Leigh spoke little in the minutes that followed, but when he did, it was always asking for assurances that Tolly felt pleasure or offering praises for how good he felt in turn. The build to an end was warm, urgent, and magnificent. Tolly wanted Leigh to go faster, and he read the desire easily, always in synch with him without use of words, changing angles and rhythm to match Tolly's wishes until the crescendo was upon him.

He shuddered from the barest brush of Leigh's fingers and released with a whimper. The pleasure did not dwindle either, because the echo was in Leigh still deep inside him until he too finished with a tensing of his muscles and a tremble of relief.

What a beautiful thing to share with someone, Tolly thought, overjoyed that he had shared it with Leigh, chasing pleasure together until they claimed it.

"Good?" Leigh asked after wiping them clean.

"Better than I ever imagined," Tolly said, smiling adoringly back at him.

"You are not good for my ego." Leigh chuckled like he hardly knew how to react to Tolly sometimes, but he was charmed and that was what mattered.

"I think perhaps your ego could use more *strokes* on occasion," Tolly said, and giggled when Leigh laughed at the pun he had very much made intentionally. Then he gripped Leigh's face, mesmerized by his features more than his body, though he loved that too, and kissed him, getting close enough to tangle their legs together.

Leigh tensed at initiations of touch, but he did not shy from Tolly or push him away. He sagged against him, and Tolly took advantage to touch everywhere he was allowed.

"Tolly," he asked once they were lying side by side, "when you say you want to stay with me forever…."

"I mean just that. Nothing about our time together or what I have learned of you has changed my mind. You gave me legs. You are everything the stories said you would be."

"What did the stories say?"

"That when a merfolk finds their pact-bearer, that person will be their complement in all things. A friend and lover and partner in one, as you have proven to be."

Leigh was quiet for a time. "You know, if this was a movie, you'd be the Disney prince more than the little mermaid."

Tolly smiled, for he would happily be Leigh's prince. Leigh deserved one, just as Tolly deserved a home. Surely they could find all they lacked and needed in each other.

The hazy meeting of their gazes ended in a yawn as Leigh's exhaustion caught up to him.

"You are tired," Tolly said, lifting the covers so they could crawl beneath, though he curled close to Leigh again as soon as they settled. "You should sleep."

"It's okay. Not a big fan of sleep lately. Can't seem to shake those dreams."

"Ah yes. May I ask what your nightmares are about?"

"Always the same thing lately," Leigh admitted with a soft sigh. "A monster. It's silly, I know. It's like I'm drowning again, but it's darker, colder, and there's something circling me. Gotta be the scariest thing I've ever seen, only something a dream could make up, or a horror movie."

A sense of dread began to fill Tolly's stomach. "What does the monster look like?"

"Like something that would try to eat you. I never get a good look at it, but it has claws and too many teeth and bloodred skin like a demon. And its eyes... they're the worst part. No feeling, just empty. *Awful*. It keeps trying to reach for me, and the last thing I want is for that thing to touch me."

There were other parts to the stories, to the old tales of love found and love lost among Tolly's kin. If a pact-bearer were to ever catch a glimpse of the merfolk's true form, they would never love them. Who could, after all, when just as Leigh described, Tolly was nothing but a monster?

"Hey... you okay?" Leigh asked, gentle fingers brushing a tear from Tolly's cheek.

"Yes." Tolly smiled but felt further anguished, knowing that for the first time he was lying. "I simply feel your pain and do not wish for you to feel it anymore."

Starting at a low hum, he began to sing, not to erase Leigh's memories or to control him, he would never do that, but to ease his mind and wipe the dreams away.

"Tolly…."

"Sleep and be at peace. You will not dream of the monster again. You will never see it again. I promise."

Leigh's eyes were heavier already and slowly began to close. "Thank you," he said, and fell into a soothing sleep.

CHAPTER 9

LEIGH HAD no idea what time it was when he started to rouse, but it wasn't near dawn like he had been waking lately—or rather, been forced to wake from a knock. He'd slept, not only because he hadn't been disturbed, but because his sleep had finally been peaceful. Tolly had sung him to sleep after....

A smile and swirl of warmth brought Leigh to full alertness. Tolly wasn't buried under the covers for once, but slept with his arms clinging to Leigh's waist, creating a heat all down his side, their legs interlocked. There was not a single regret in Leigh that he had given in and stolen this remarkable creature's virginity. It hadn't really been stolen, after all, but freely given.

Though there was something nagging at the back of Leigh's mind, something sour that had almost pushed through their connection before Tolly began to sing, like maybe Tolly had been lying about something, but Leigh had no idea what it might be.

He chalked it up to paranoia and chose to enjoy the continued afterglow of waking up with someone in his arms.

Eventually, he decided to let Tolly sleep and carefully extracted himself from the bed without waking him. He watched with a fond smile as Tolly stirred only enough to roll farther onto Leigh's side of the bed and bury his nose in the pillow.

After taking a quick shower, Leigh returned to find Tolly still asleep and decided to wake him with breakfast. He still didn't have what was needed for muffins but he could manage french toast. He brought his phone with him into the kitchen to check for messages. Nothing of importance yet, but he knew that the powwow with Moretti could come any day, and the further along in the week it got, the more anxious he would feel until it happened.

For now, he tried not to think about it, until just as he was dishing up the French toast, his phone rang, and instead of Alvin, he saw Tabitha's name on the caller ID.

"Beckett. Good news for me, I hope?" he answered, excitement replacing his anxiety, which was not what he usually felt when speaking to his parole officer.

"Hello, William. I wish it was good news."

Leigh's stomach dropped as she continued, telling him plainly but sympathetically that an ex-con getting a business loan was not so easy an ask, something he *knew* and should have expected, but still he'd hoped.

He could get one, eventually, but not so soon after he'd been locked away. It would take a long time before anything would be possible, maybe years, to build back credibility, prove he was a worthwhile investment, and a handful of other phrases that meant society didn't trust him to become something other than what he'd always been.

He'd never get out from under Sweeney without a better plan, but as good as he usually was at forming new ones on the fly, he couldn't think of any way to escape his fate. How was he supposed to tell Tolly that he might have traded one prison for another by choosing to be with Leigh?

"Thanks for the heads-up, Beckett. I'm sure I'll figure something out."

"Call me if you need advice, anything more I can do—"

"I will," Leigh said and hung up promptly, because there wasn't more to say. He would figure something out, he had to, but it likely wouldn't be legal.

"That smells divine." Tolly startled him from his thoughts. He'd grabbed fresh underwear but had chosen to put on that too small T-shirt again, hanging in the doorway looking coy and delicious, even more so than the French toast.

Leigh had to smile despite fearing that someday he'd let Tolly down.

SOMEHOW, WITH seemingly so little to do, the rest of the week passed quickly, waiting on news from Alvin of Jake and Rosa's movements. Some days Leigh went out. Some days Tolly joined him. Every day there were people stopping by for Leigh's skill set, but never anyone unsavory trying to take him out.

Most nights they ended up at the pool—and eventually in bed to revisit their first experience. Leigh wasn't used to having a regular partner, but by getting to know each other's bodies, each successive time together felt better than the last.

They hadn't tried with Tolly topping yet or anything with his merfolk self, but after the first few days, Leigh couldn't stop thinking about both and almost asked several times before he chickened out.

He really was some nervous preteen when it came to Tolly, blushing and fumbling for words. He'd never been good at flirting, expressing feelings, seducing someone, but Tolly made him comfortable in so many other ways, made him happy—and that just made his inability to ask for what he wanted worse for fear of saying the wrong thing and screwing this up.

It wasn't easy to be someone else's fairy tale.

Maybe he could find some other way to get the money he needed to buy that shop and make an honest man of himself. It was hard to change one's stripes, but not impossible. After all, Tolly usually had a tail and now he had legs. Surely Leigh could manage something simpler.

He might have believed more in that too if his hope in the universe hadn't been dashed one afternoon late in the week when he and Tolly slipped out to grab lunch somewhere that wasn't his living room, and he saw a familiar figure pickpocketing someone.

"Is that Ralph?" Tolly asked.

Leigh quickened his pace, the victim already heading away, unaware that his wallet was gone.

Unfortunately, Leigh wasn't the only one who'd seen. Perez and Horowitz really did get around lately, and they crossed the street to intercept Ralph before Leigh and Tolly could reach him.

"Well I'll be, they sure are startin' 'em young, eh, Horowitz?"

"Mr. Abbott, shouldn't you be in school?" Horowitz said. "And returning that man's wallet?"

Leigh rushed forward as Ralph turned with wide eyes that proved he had no idea how to talk his way out of this. "I'm sure he was planning on informing the guy he dropped it, *detectives*."

All three spun at Leigh and Tolly's approach, Ralph looking cookie-jar caught before he mouthed an earnest "thank you" at Leigh.

"Hurley," Perez scoffed. "Showin' him the ropes to make sure his form's up to snuff?"

"Don't know what you're talking about. All I see is a kid trying to be a Good Samaritan."

Perez eyed Leigh with barely a glance spared for Tolly. "What are you pullin' a Captain America for?"

Again with the Marvel reference, but any time Leigh went out, he wore the glasses and ball cap to play it safe. "Trying something new. What, not a fan?"

"I'll, uhhh… catch up to that gentleman and let him know he dropped this," Horowitz said, taking the wallet from Ralph and dashing away.

Ralph inched closer to Leigh and Tolly's side of the standoff, causing Perez to shoot him a glare before he snarled back at Leigh.

"I was too easy on ya for too long. Maybe if Abbott lands his ass in juvie sooner, he'll learn better."

"No, you can't." Ralph shrunk behind Leigh. "The Moretti guys made me—"

"*Ralph*," Leigh snapped before he could incriminate himself further. Moretti guys? Shit. "Don't say anything else."

Horowitz came back over at a jog, having hurried to make sure his partner didn't lose his temper.

"Look," Leigh tried before this escalated, surprised at the plan forming in his mind that before today hadn't dared rear its head, but if all this was what it looked like with Ralph, it might be the only way. "Maybe you let this one slide for the kid, huh, because he's gonna *promise me*"— he looked at Ralph pointedly—"that this is the last time he ever pulls something like this."

"I swear!"

"And why would we let him off?" Perez growled.

Leigh was either a genius or out of his mind. "Coz maybe I know why you've been hanging around, and I might have a lead on bringing Vincent Moretti and a few rats on Sweeney's side down."

"Leigh?" Tolly questioned his seeming betrayal, but Leigh added:

"*Only* if you stop there and leave Sweeney and the rest of his people out of it."

"You mean leave Sweeney's kid out of it." Perez sneered.

"Whoever isn't at the location once I learn it, yeah."

"You don't even have a place? Or a time?"

"I'll have it," Leigh said, leaning into Perez's space.

"And you'll inform us?" Horowitz asked.

"As soon as I'm sure it's not a false alarm, I'll send a message and record everything I hear until you get there. I'll even testify if it comes to that," Leigh said, aware of how dangerous having this conversation in the open might be, but fairly certain there wasn't anyone around with traitorous ears—other than *Ralph*. "But you let the kid go and leave Sweeney and his people alone. That's the deal."

Horowitz looked all for it, the eager puppy type like an eternal rookie who never lost faith in people, even if he was pushing forty, but Perez was a realist.

"You must want something big from Sweeney to make this kinda play."

"Yeah," Leigh said—the biggest thing he'd ever wanted. "*Out.*"

"Ch. Heard that before."

"I mean it, Nick." Leigh used the man's first name like he hadn't in years. "I don't want to do this anymore. And I don't want anyone *else* taking my place." He shot another pointed look at Ralph.

Eventually, the gruffness seemed to soften from Perez's demeanor, if only a little. "This is the last time I trust you."

"I know. Blame *him* for being a good influence." He thrust a thumb at Tolly. The last thing he needed was for Perez and Horowitz to expect otherwise since Tolly wasn't a familiar face.

Tolly, of course, beamed at the compliment.

"Think I hear a call comin' in," Perez said to his partner. "Better get back to the car so we can check it out." He looked Tolly up and down like he didn't quite get it, but he nodded and turned on his heel.

"You got it, Nick!" Horowitz hurried to follow. "Thanks, Hurley. You got our numbers?"

"How else am I supposed to avoid 'em? I'll call, any day now."

As soon as the detectives were gone, Leigh seized Ralph by the shoulders and ushered him off the sidewalk into the nearest alley.

"Hurley, I owe you big-time—"

"You better believe you do." Leigh pushed him just shy of harsh as Tolly crowded in with them. "You're joining us for lunch and you are going to tell me everything you've been keeping to yourself. Then you are heading right back to school. Understood?"

Ralph's head nearly popped off as he nodded like a bobblehead.

They made sure to head the long way to a diner well out of any territories, and Ralph spilled his secrets. He'd been running for the

Morettis for months, but he'd also been running on the down-low the past couple of weeks for *Sweeney*.

"You *are* the last snitch," Leigh said, though he'd figured as much. He would have been more pissed if he wasn't impressed he hadn't caught on sooner.

"They said it was the only way they'd stop giving me grunt work and take me seriously." Ralph sat alone on his side of the booth, facing their scrutiny, shoving fries in his mouth every few sentences. "I figured a few tidbits of info wouldn't hurt anybody, and I'd be set."

"It never works that way, Ralph."

"I know. I didn't think mentioning your name would mean they'd send someone after you." He slowed his chewing and stared at his plate with a thick swallow. "Then someone said these thugs were in the building and you weren't answering your door when I went to check and I… I was so freaked I'd gotten you killed."

He almost had, but Leigh didn't want to make things worse by telling him that. "Jake and Rosa would have fed the Morettis the info I was alive within a day anyway. What matters is that you're in deep with both sides and your only way out is by letting me take care of this through those detectives. Hopefully after that, Sweeney will be so pleased to have the competition out of the way, he'll listen when I ask him to forget you ever did errands for him. But you stay low and you stay safe, you hear me? You go to school, you come home, that's it."

"Totally." Ralph nodded rapidly again as he glanced up. "I was thinking about what you said, really, about other options, but they wouldn't let me stop."

"It's a lot harder to get out than in, kid. But I'll take care of it."

"You are the best, Hurley." Ralph smiled brightly. "I'll make this up to you. I promise."

"The only way I need you making this up to me is by getting out of here someday any way other than by heading to lockup."

"Of course!" Ralph laughed, the way only a teenager could in a deadly situation he didn't fully understand, then he turned to Tolly as he shoved more fries in his face. "You *are* a good influence, Tol, but he's always been like this."

Tolly had been annoyingly quiet through it all, watching Leigh with a knowing smile. "He has trouble believing that, and I think you have very much in common in that regard."

"Yeah? Well, save the doe-eyed glances for *him*. I'm spoken for."

"You are not," Leigh said.

"Ralph, perhaps you should pursue someone closer to your own age," Tolly tried, since they all knew he was talking about Deanna.

"Hurley said that once I'm eighteen, the age difference won't matter."

"That is not what I said, I said…." Leigh sighed. "Aren't there any girls at school you like?"

"Sure, but they all laugh at me."

"Laugh?" Tolly repeated.

"The crappy pickup lines might have something to do with it," Leigh said.

"I don't sound like that around them!" Ralph defended. "I just… kinda fumble and don't know what to say." While Deanna, being her wonderful, motherly self, had never made Ralph feel like he was a gangly, geeky goofball, so of course he'd fallen for her.

"Would you like to practice?" Tolly said. "You could pretend we are one of the girls you fancy, and if you say the wrong thing, we can lead you in a better direction."

"Really?" Ralph brightened before instantly deflating again. "I don't know, Hurley's tried that before."

"Ah, but I think your problem is trying too hard to woo when first you need to befriend." Tolly took on an air of authority, maybe because he'd succeeded in wooing Leigh. "A friend will not laugh at you. A friend will make you feel comfortable enough to be yourself and express how you feel. Do you have any girl *friends*? Or boys, I suppose."

"Girls," Ralph affirmed, though without the reflexive disgust someone might have responded with when Leigh was that age. "And not really, I guess."

"Then we shall start there."

Tolly *was* a good influence, on everyone and everything in Leigh's life.

They let Ralph play hooky for another hour to help him forget his mess with the families and focus on romantic troubles instead. Then Leigh pushed him in the direction of the high school and threatened to call to make sure he showed up, but Ralph swore he'd be good. He would be, Leigh hoped. Better than *he'd* ever been.

"Are you sure about this?" Tolly turned to him on the way home.

He knew Tolly meant what he'd promised the detectives. "Don't tell Alvin. Not 'til it's over. If it doesn't work out, I don't want him to get hurt. If it does, then we'll come clean."

"Okay. I trust you."

Leigh just hoped that trust wasn't misplaced.

MAYBE TOLLY had banished more monsters than his own reflection in Leigh's subconscious when he sang that night, because the tides had been changing ever since, and he saw only hope on the horizon.

Leigh was getting restless again, however, as the days passed and no word came from Alvin of the meeting between the other snitches and Vincent Moretti. When they did see Alvin, it was for social reasons, which Tolly preferred. Alvin had not known Ralph was working for his father. Few people had, or Leigh would have caught wind of it sooner.

Thankfully, Alvin finding out Tolly's nature had only strengthened their bond, and the lessons in sign language continued. Alvin was very dedicated to learning and was making notable progress.

"You and Cary are growing closer, then?" he asked during one of their lessons as they sat on Leigh's sofa.

"Actual conversations are definitely the right direction," Alvin said. "And they're *friendly* too. Like he asks questions sometimes instead of only grunting and nodding, wanting to know my opinion and interests. Just a little longer and I'll be ready to ask him out. It's gonna be amazing, too, coz I'm gonna use everything you've taught me. Hopefully, he'll be so stunned, he won't remember to tell me to get lost."

"Oh, I am sure he will not respond that way. He will say...." Tolly signed the rest, and Alvin giggled as he understood: *You are my heart's desire too.*

"Done," Leigh called from where he had been sitting at the table fixing a microwave. "Hey, Al, think you can drop this at Roy's place downstairs so Tolly and I can head out? We're gonna be late."

"Late? Where you guys going?"

"Leigh will not tell me," Tolly said. "He says it is a surprise."

"I bet I know, then." Alvin grinned. "Galaxy?"

"Yep."

"Galaxy?" Tolly parroted.

"You'll see when we get there."

Tolly loved surprises. Or at least he believed he did, since he had never had one before. Leigh clearly wanted distraction as the week ended, claustrophobic from staying in so often, so he donned his hat and glasses as they headed onto the streets after dark on a path he seemed to know well.

"Most people would use a car, but Alvin and I always cheated a little since we never had one or much cash. If you don't mind a little criminal activity?"

Tolly was far too excited to say he did, unsure where Leigh was leading them until they reached a back alley and a fire escape that Leigh began to climb. Tolly followed. Only when they reached the top and Leigh walked to the edge of the roof did Tolly realize that beyond the building was a cleverly hidden outdoor movie screen.

A drive-in with a vintage sign proclaiming Galaxy Theater, and they had the best seats.

"When I heard they were playing *Princess Bride*, I figured we had to."

Tolly rushed to Leigh's side, bringing his hand down to lace their fingers together. "You said it was a happy story, yes? A romance?"

"One of the best." Leigh smiled in his half-crooked but adoring way, accepting Tolly's contact more readily every time. "You'll love it."

Little did Tolly know that Leigh had stashed sodas in his jacket, and a box of Milk Duds he had procured from the store. They sat on the ledge of the roof, feet dangling, with the perfect view of the screen and all the people in their cars below. The audio was loud enough echoing up to them that they had no trouble hearing, but there were subtitles as well to be sure everyone could clearly understand even if they were far away.

This was much better than watching from the water, especially with Leigh beside him. Tolly was riveted by the film, the humor, the cleverness of it all, and the romance—oh, what a romance, even with every obstacle in their way. The eels were not Tolly's favorite, but the rest was perfect, every moment of sharing it with Leigh and leaning into his body whenever something startling happened.

"All this love of film and there's still so much about humans you don't know," Leigh said with a fond smile.

"It is not the same as firsthand experience or being formally taught." Tolly blushed at the tease. "I suppose sometimes I do not pay as much attention to the details as I should, more the relationships and emotions. The way a film makes me feel. But I do so want to learn more."

"Happy to help with your continuing education, then." Leigh held him to his side.

It was fun watching everything close after the film ended as well, and the people started to drive away. A few noticed them up on the roof and waved, to which Tolly happily waved back, even if they had cheated and not had to pay for a ticket.

Their hands were clasped between them as they enjoyed the evening together, the stars above and Leigh warm against Tolly, with an air of wonder about them after watching a fairy tale with a perfect ending kiss.

"Are you sure you want this?" Leigh asked softly, not looking at him but keeping close. "Me, I mean?"

"Why do you continue to ask that? My answer is not going to change."

"So much could go wrong, I just... I want you to be sure." Leigh sighed as though he had never believed in happy endings for himself, but Tolly was determined to have one now that he had banished the plague of his true form from Leigh's nightmares.

It must have slipped in through their connection somehow, from Tolly's subconscious, but it was gone now, and Tolly meant it that he would never allow Leigh to see it again.

"Did you ever hear the line: a bird may love a fish but where would they live?" Leigh asked.

"I have, and it has an easy answer: the fish must grow wings and the bird fins so they can live wherever they wish."

"It's not always that easy, Tolly."

"For us it could be, if I am able to keep my legs."

"Able to?" Leigh repeated, pulling away to look at him.

What a fool he was for letting that slip when he could not tell Leigh more. "Forgive me, I... I cannot explain. The spell prevents me from giving you details about the pact." Even that much was difficult for Tolly to say, but if he tried to explain more, the words would vanish on his tongue, unable to flow past it.

"You could lose them?" Leigh asked with the dawning fear Tolly had been holding at bay.

"I hope not."

"I can't grow a fin, you know."

Tolly smiled because Leigh did not know how wrong he was. "Magic makes many things possible." While his left hand remained tangled with Leigh's, Tolly reached with his right to draw him into a kiss.

A honk from below startled them, one of the last cars leaving with smiling faces inside. Tolly and Leigh both laughed as they broke apart, that rare, lovely flush in Leigh's cheeks again.

"Hey, umm, I think I'm ready to try—"

Leigh's phone cut him off, sounding with Alvin's ringtone—the only reason Leigh had not put it on silent.

"Yeah?" Leigh answered, and Tolly was close enough that he could hear Alvin on the other end.

"I got a time and location."

"Where?"

"East docks, that old warehouse that's been out of commission."

"When?" Leigh asked with hardening resolve.

"Tomorrow night."

THE EVENING of their movie date ended with restless sleep that had nothing to do with nightmares. Getting through the day proved even more difficult, time passing like a glacier, but when evening rolled around again, it grew worse.

Tolly did not think he could feel the sort of fear he used to experience when being chased by his brethren simply by waiting to watch a group of humans meet in a warehouse. Perhaps it was Leigh's fear feeding into his own, but he worried as Leigh worried that this would not go as simply as they hoped.

If it went well, the detectives could do what Leigh did not wish to—take care of Vincent Moretti. But it was not the same as killing him, and Arthur Sweeney might not like that when they spoke with him later.

"It'll be fine," Leigh said as he had many times already. "Stay quiet and follow my lead like always. I know this warehouse and how to get there without being seen. We just have to hope it stays that way."

Tolly had never seen Leigh like this. He was not the type to outwardly show if he was frightened, but he kept wringing his hands, his gestures more pronounced. He was scared. For himself and for Tolly.

The docks were familiar to Tolly now, but the route Leigh took them on was winding and well before the scheduled time for Jake, Rosa, and Moretti to meet. They would need to stay hidden and wait for some time, something Tolly and Leigh were both used to.

They talked in hushed voices, even though Tolly checked often in every direction for anyone nearing the warehouse. They were upstairs on the second level, hidden behind a well-placed beam. If someone did come up the stairs, they could easily get out before anyone was upon them. A few times Tolly hissed that a handful of people were nearby, but so far, none were the ones they wanted.

Then the appointed time drew closer, and once again Tolly nodded after sending out his vibrations, sensing two people coming from one direction and *five* from another, before voices and a bustle of movement alerted them that these were, in fact, the people they were waiting for.

Tolly took out his phone and began recording so Leigh could message the detectives, though he had told Tolly he would wait until he was certain all the right players were in attendance.

Vaguely, Tolly recognized Jake's voice from the club that day and assumed the female to be Rosa. The only other person who spoke was Vincent Moretti, judging by Leigh's reaction.

"One thing before we start," Moretti said, and there was a scuffle, like someone being forced forward, and a far too familiar voice calling out:

"Hey!"

Leigh froze, eyes wide with dread at the sound of *Ralph's* voice.

"This little rat has been seen with Hurley a few too many times. Not sure I trust his loyalty anymore."

"He's nothing to get your panties in a twist over, Vinny," Rosa said, though she sounded half-bored and uncaring. "Just some brat. I thought he was the one who told you Hurley was alive before we could."

"He was, and now he's trying to get out. But you see, kid, once you're in, you're *in*. But if you're out.... Well. Jake, Rosa, why don't you do the honors to set the right example."

In the split second before more could be said, Leigh put his phone in his pocket *without* messaging the detectives and stepped out from behind their hiding spot.

CHAPTER 10

LEIGH HAD no idea what he was doing when he stepped out from behind the beam hiding him and Tolly from view. All he knew was that if he didn't make his presence known right that second, they were going to kill a fourteen-year-old kid.

"No wonder you have so many holes in your organization," Leigh said as he descended the stairs, causing every head to turn—and every gun to point at him. He was packing tonight, too, he wasn't stupid, but taking it out now would be. "You're relying on these two to do your dirty work, Vinny, and for what? A kid you can't muzzle? Sweeney's laughing all the way to the bank over this one, trust me. And I'd say he'll be here in about…." Leigh smugly looked at his watch. "Two minutes."

At least Leigh was a good liar, but he couldn't be sure if Moretti bought it. Everyone else looked like they might—except Ralph, who only looked terrified and was crying. They must have grabbed him from home. Leigh should have known they wouldn't let him out easy.

"Hurley," Moretti said with a sneer, lowering his weapon, though all five of the others remained aimed. He might as well have been a clone of his younger brother, just in a nicer suit. "You're sticking your nose everywhere lately, aren't you? I don't know what you did to our guys the other day, but they couldn't even remember going to see you. Came limping back all dazed and bloody."

It was different men with Moretti tonight. He probably hadn't been happy with the other three for failing to take Leigh out.

"How'd you get out of the river anyway?" Moretti asked. "Leo was pretty confident he'd offed you. A regular Houdini act? Or did you have help?"

"He's got this cute young bodyguard hanging around," Rosa spoke up, less nervous-looking than some but with a sharp eye moving about the room. "Maybe it was him."

"Please," Jake scoffed, "that pretty boy's just around to keep Hurley's bed warm."

Tolly hadn't come down the stairs. He was staying hidden—or so Leigh thought until he saw shadows moving behind the others as if *someone* had snuck around the second floor and dropped down without a sound.

Leigh couldn't give away what he'd seen. He had no idea how to fix the situation, since Sweeney was not coming and neither were the detectives, but it would have been too risky to call them with Ralph in the cross fire. If Tolly could even the odds, though….

"Don't you believe in fairy tales?" Leigh held his ground, feigning confidence he didn't feel to put Ralph at ease. "I grew gills and swam back to shore. Happens all the time."

Moretti cleared his throat, and the goons with him squared their guns on Leigh more seriously. "I'm gonna need a bit more than that, coz I don't think Sweeney knows a thing or you'd have brought more backup."

Tolly crept up on the largest goon first; Leigh could clearly see him now and took a steadying breath.

"Who says I didn't?"

The goon howled as Tolly struck him in the back, everyone spinning in surprise, but Tolly had more than a large enough shield in the man. He snapped his arm back, relieving him of his gun, and kicked him forward into the next goon, who he charged before anyone could react. Kicking the second goon in the face as he stumbled from the first man falling on him, Tolly snatched up one of the downed guns and seized Moretti by the front of his suit, spinning him around to press the muzzle of the gun to his temple—all in the span of about ten seconds.

The final goon stared dumbstruck at his fellows moaning on the ground, one with a broken arm, another with his head nearly cracked open from that kick. Jake faltered just the same, realizing Leigh's backup was indeed the pretty face he'd dismissed, but Rosa scanned the room again, working on a plan, Leigh could tell, so he pulled his gun finally and pointed it at her. Much as he had never thought he wanted a partner, he couldn't deny the logic in Sweeney's mandate for pairs.

"I don't believe all of you have met Mr. Allen. Trust me, Jake, I don't need more than just him and me to take you all out, so maybe we need to have a firmer discussion about the easy and hard way this might go down."

Ralph backed away, drawing the attention of the remaining goon. This could all unravel too quickly. Were there too many people for Tolly to sing? Could he not risk it with Leigh and Ralph there? Did Leigh even want him to?

He wasn't sure, but they couldn't take the chance of anyone finding out what Tolly was. He knew the hardness in Tolly's eyes was a front, but he also knew that if Leigh asked him, he'd pull the trigger and take Moretti out on his behalf, and Leigh didn't want that.

"Sweeney had a special mission for me," Leigh lied with that same confidence. "Wanna guess what it was?"

"He knows we've been playing him," Rosa surmised with her quick eyes and mind spinning like a top.

"There's still more of us than there are of them," Jake growled.

"Not if Sweeney knows." She turned to point her gun at Moretti— "I told you this was a stupid idea."—and shot him in the head.

Everything stilled, time frozen like a picture, until Tolly released Moretti's body and he dropped, dead weight, to the floor.

Rosa turned her gun on Jake, allowing Leigh to point his gun at the final goon. Tolly eyed the two on the ground, but neither had any intention of causing trouble, so he hurried to Ralph, who was staring wide-eyed at Moretti's body like he couldn't look away.

Tolly *made* him look away by tucking him against his shoulder, and the last goon threw his gun on the floor.

"Rosa—" Jake tried.

"Call Sweeney if he's not already on his way," she said to Leigh. "He wanted you to off Vinny. Now you have. I'll take your side if you take mine. It was all Jake. I played double agent. *I* was loyal. Deal?"

"You *bitch*."

"Right back at ya, baby." She winked at Jake. "Is it a deal?"

Leigh couldn't think. He could barely keep his hand from shaking.

"We did this to get away from Sweeney!" Jake cried.

"And how do you think that's gonna play out if he's caught us? Well, *you'll* find out. Hurley, is it a deal or not?"

Tolly cast him a plaintive look as if to ask, *Are you sure?*

Leigh could call the detectives now, couldn't he? Could he? It was such a mess with Ralph there and a body. He didn't know what to do.

So he said, "Deal," and called Sweeney instead.

He was glad Alvin wasn't with them when they arrived, but Sweeney came himself with Mark and Selene and some grunts for cleanup. They took the goons and Jake away. Jake was swearing up a storm at Rosa, but Leigh played along that he'd planned this with her help and he'd been the one to shoot Moretti, even if he was in a daze through it all while Tolly continued to hold Ralph.

"Aww, does the youngen need a pick-me-up?" Sweeney headed their direction, but Leigh grabbed his arm to stop him.

"No flowers tonight, boss. Let me take Ralph home."

Sweeney wasn't often sensible minded, but he rewarded a job well done. "We'll talk tomorrow. You did good. You too, *As You Like It*!" he called to Rosa. "As for Ralphy-boy...."

"He's done," Leigh said. "Figured helping you with Moretti would keep you off his back as he's getting older on the streets. He's no runner. He doesn't want to be. He's just a kid."

The next generation was important for people like Sweeney, starting loyalty young, having a stock of dispensable grunts to choose from as others got caught or killed, but Leigh was the hero tonight—even if it was nothing but a lie—and everyone with him was included.

"Pity," Sweeney said, "but well earned. You need a favor any time, kiddo, you say the word!"

Ralph barely mustered a shaky nod, not once having slipped from Tolly's side.

Then they were free, while feeling like the furthest thing from it.

Walking back to the apartment, Ralph had never been so quiet in all the time Leigh had known him. It wasn't all that late by the time they reached home, but his parents wouldn't be in until closer to 3:00 a.m.

"Can I stay with you tonight?" he asked numbly.

"Leave a note so your folks don't worry," Leigh said. "I'll get some extra bedding."

He was surprised by how quickly Ralph fell asleep on the sofa, though the amount of time he'd spent in the bathroom retching into the toilet might have helped. Leigh placed an extra blanket over him just in case before going to bed with Tolly.

Half of him wanted to throw up too. All these years, he'd never seen someone die right in front of him, had always managed to avoid getting his hands that kind of dirty.

Were they dirty now? Was he culpable? What else could he have done?

"What are you going to tell the detectives?" Tolly asked as they lay in bed, side by side but staring at the ceiling.

"I don't know. It might have gotten so much bloodier if I'd called them. With Ralph there…."

"You did the right thing."

"Did I?"

Tolly's hand moved beneath the covers to find his. "I am glad you were not the one to kill him. Tonight, instead, you did everything in your power to save someone."

Only Tolly would see it that way, but the sentiment made Leigh's eyes feel hot. "You sure you made the right call saving *me*?"

"Every moment I am with you," Tolly said with an honest smile.

Leigh let him snuggle close that night, though it took a long time before they fell asleep.

It WAS déjà vu the next morning when a knock at the door woke them.

Instantly, Leigh was up and panicking, wondering if it was Moretti's side or Sweeney having learned the truth and not being happy about it, but the real owner of that heavy knock was worse once Leigh looked through his peephole to see *Perez* banging on his door.

They'd found Vincent's body. That would have been on purpose, a message from Sweeney without any way to point fingers. They wouldn't find Jake's.

"Where were you between the hours of ten and midnight last night?" Perez asked when Leigh let him inside. Tolly stood back in hurriedly donned sweats, while Ralph sat on the sofa, still bundled in blankets.

"Here," Leigh said. "They can both vouch for that. We were all here, right?"

Tolly and Ralph both nodded.

"The hell you pullin', Hurley?" Perez snarled. "You said—"

"You said you'd trust me," Leigh hissed at him quietly. "Give me more time."

"Someone's *dead*."

"You mourning Vinny Moretti? I'll give you the killer, but I need time to make sure nothing else blows up in my face. Please." He pulled Perez back closer to the door, speaking as quietly as possible. "They were gonna kill Ralph. I had to think fast. Give me a little more time to sort this out."

Perez was a good man. Rough and not easy to get to know, but he meant well, and he did care about the kids in this neighborhood getting caught up with warring mobsters. "You realize that was near enough to a confession?"

"It wasn't me who pulled the trigger."

Deep scrutiny stared back at Leigh, but in the end, Perez sighed. "I got nothing real to bring you in on, but it wouldn't take much for that to change. Clock's ticking, Hurley. Don't let me down again."

It felt like a clock had been ticking since Leigh dropped into the river. He had no idea how to fix this, but at least he'd bought himself a little more time.

"Take a sick day," he said to Ralph. "Spend time with your folks. Veg on the couch."

"But I—"

"I'll keep you updated, but I don't want you giving anyone any more excuses to pull you back in. Got it?"

"Okay. It's really not the worst thing, right?"

"What?"

"That he's dead. He was a bad guy. And… he was gonna kill me, wasn't he?"

Leigh saw a lot of nightmares in Ralph's future. He wished he knew how to soothe them. "Sick day. Netflix and comfort food, got it?"

"I got it," Ralph said quietly, then thanked Tolly with a swift hug before he slipped out the door to head home.

TOLLY HAD held it together while subduing those men last night, barely a slip of his claws that no one had seen, but he would have killed them all if Leigh wished it. There was some of the monster in him all the time, but it was further proof of the good in Leigh that he would never ask for that.

There was nothing to mourn over that Vincent Moretti was dead. Who Tolly mourned for was Ralph, one so young who, like him and Leigh, wanted something better for himself but found obstacles at every turn. If they could help him move past this, that would please Tolly almost as much as saving Leigh had.

But first they had to see Sweeney.

It was quieter when they entered the club than the first time Tolly had been there. No one was hanging in the corners, just dim lighting and stillness. The first sign of life was Alvin coming out of the back, looking frantic as he pulled out his phone, only to glance up with eyes springing wide to prove Leigh was the very person he'd meant to call.

He nearly dropped his phone in his haste to tackle Leigh with a hug. "*Deal* with it," he said when Leigh tensed at the contact. "Dad told me what happened. Why didn't you call me?"

"We just wanted to sleep when it was over." Leigh sank slowly into the offered comfort. "And we had to take care of Ralph. He slept on the sofa last night."

"Is he okay?"

"Good as a kid can be after seeing his first murder."

They parted, and Tolly offered Alvin his best smile in time to be hugged just as fiercely in turn.

"Rosa said you kicked some serious ass, Tol. Secret mermaid strength?" he whispered in Tolly's ear.

"Yes. That I am Leigh's bodyguard was never a lie."

"What are we gonna do now?" Alvin asked once he pulled away.

"Ah, William, there you are," Sweeney called from the back. "Gang's all here, I see. Why don't you join us?"

The gang really was all there from what Tolly saw. Rosa, Cary, as well as the ones he knew as Selene and Mark, were gathered in the back office. Tolly signed Cary a quick hello, then passed Rosa a cold stare. She was sharp, observant, and shifted under his gaze, since she had seen his strength last night.

"Mimosas." Sweeney snapped his fingers after sliding behind his desk. "That's what we're missing. It's the a.m. and we're celebrating."

"No thanks," Leigh said.

"Ah yes, you don't drink. What about you? *Tolly*, was it?"

"Tolly Allen," Tolly said. "And I am fine, thank you."

"You did all the damage, huh?" Sweeney propped his feet on the desk. "Heard it's nearly half a dozen Moretti men in need of a medic thanks to you by now. Just where are you hiding the claws and fangs, kid?"

"What?" Tolly felt the blood drain from his face.

"It's a joke. Not too bright, is he?" Sweeney said. "Well, beauty and brawns is more than enough. If you had brains, too, it'd hardly be fair to the rest of us." He dropped his feet and patted the desktop like playing out a drumbeat. "I liked the idea of someone keeping an eye on my little boy's best buddy, so I let your appearance slide, but you're officially part of the crew now. Guess that means we got a new bruiser to replace Jake."

"I have a better idea," Leigh spoke up before Tolly could.

"Oh? I'm all a twitter."

"You get neither of us. You let Ralph walk away, and I appreciate that. Now it's my turn. I want out."

Snickers passed between the others, save Cary, who remained stoic, and Alvin, who looked unsurprised but somber.

Sweeney gave three single drumbeats on his desk in succession. "Okay."

"Okay?" Leigh questioned. "Just like that?"

"Well, *no*." He rolled his eyes dramatically, lurching out of his chair and around the desk again, like he never sat still for long. "You can be out, William, but only after the dust settles. See, Vinny was the lead man, but his brother is still around, as you know. They'll be weaker for sure, but there could still be a war brewing. And considering the way Rosalind talked up your boy, we could use the extra muscle, make sure Leo plays nice when he takes over. You help us usher in a peaceful transition, you can both go your merry ways." He flourished his hand in the direction of elsewhere.

Managing a peaceful transition with Leo Moretti would not be easy when everyone was saying Leigh killed his brother.

"Take a day," Sweeney said. "Think about it. It's a nice offer for you both. You try running off too soon, things could get… sticky. I don't like sticky. It's like licking cotton candy off your fingers. You can't go back to normal after that. You have to wash your hands or go crazy." He laughed as if quite literally unhinged. "You understand."

"Dad, you will let Leigh out if he helps though, right?" Alvin spoke quietly. "And Tolly?"

"You have my word," Sweeney said with a hand held over his heart.

THE WALK back to the apartment had never felt as stiff or cold to Tolly, maybe because of the weather, overcast and chilly, but also because there was a sense of two steps forward and three steps back.

At least the look Alvin had given them before they left said he held no resentment for Leigh wanting out of that life. It did not mean they could no longer be friends, just that their circles would diverge.

As they neared the empty shop on the corner, Leigh's steps slowed. It looked dark and barren now, save the sign in the window that said FOR LEASE.

"I do not understand enough about how money works here," Tolly said, "but you do not have enough to buy the shop, is that it?"

"I was hoping to get a loan," Leigh said. "Have a bank give me what I need with the promise I'd pay them back once I made enough. But see, banks don't trust criminals, even if they are trying to go straight."

"They will not give you a loan?"

"No. They expect collateral, a positive rep, no B&Es on record, things like that. Honestly, if someone had good enough credit and no red flags, that'd be enough. I got a lot of red flags. Come on." Leigh picked up his pace to pass the building quickly. "We didn't get enough sleep last night, and I don't feel like being out anymore."

"Sick day? Like Ralph?"

"Yeah." Leigh smiled, sad though it was. "Let's take a sick day."

They did not make it all the way to Leigh's door before being interrupted, though it was merely Miss Maggie.

"Hey, Maggie," Leigh said, taking the basket of laundry from her without being asked to finish carrying it to her door. "Feeling better?"

"Look at you being a gentleman," she said. "I am. Sounds like Ralph caught my bug, though. Poor thing's stuck inside today. At least Gert managed to avoid it. She's watching her cartoons while I finish some chores. What about you two? You look like hell, William. You didn't catch my cold too?"

"Might just have. Too much time around those kids."

"Pfft. As if you don't love it. Best kind of kids to have are the ones you can give back come the end of the day."

Leigh snorted at that, and Tolly had to chuckle too. It could not dismiss the shadows from Leigh's eyes, though, and Maggie noticed once they reached her door and she took the laundry back from him.

"You're in trouble again."

"Maggie…."

"Why do you have to go and pull this boy into the muck with you?" She nodded at Tolly. "I thought he was pulling you out?"

"It's not like that," Leigh said. "All I've been doing is trying to get out. It's the ones doing the real damage who keep pulling me back in."

"So stop letting 'em. Stop compromising or soon you're gonna run out of things to bargain with. You keep him honest, dear," she said to Tolly. "Let the bad apples pay for being rotten. Don't go getting rotten with 'em."

"Easy for her to say," Leigh said once they slipped back into the apartment. He fell against the door, forehead pressed to the wood.

Tolly took his arm and gently tugged him away, drawing him to the sofa. "Come," he said, and sat, urging Leigh to lie down and rest his head in his lap. Soothingly, he stroked his fingernails over Leigh's scalp until he relaxed and closed his eyes. "Rest. This could be good. A peaceful transition is a worthy cause to assist Sweeney with."

"If he means it. And if Leo Moretti allows it. I still don't know what to do about Perez. I promised him someone to put away, and instead he got a body bag. He won't let that slide forever. I need to figure out something that saves us, gives the detectives what they want, and keeps Sweeney from becoming an enemy. I don't know if it's possible to have all three."

Tolly, of course, had a fourth item he desired, but now was hardly the time to push for it.

Leigh did sleep for a while, and Tolly might have dozed off as well. Maybe it was because of how tired Leigh was, how sorrowful, that he began digging through his cabinets in the afternoon and declared success only after he found everything he had been looking for.

"What are you going to make?" Tolly asked.

"Chocolate chip cookies. My mama's recipe."

"Oh?" Tolly had always wanted to try those. It seemed they were magical confections with how they were spoken of in human customs.

"Technically, it's just the recipe off the back of butter-flavored Crisco, but they always turned out best when Mama made them."

"What was your mother like?" Tolly asked, since he had heard very little about Leigh's family.

"Sad," Leigh said. "But kind. I don't remember her much, to be honest. Just her smile, her voice, especially her voice singing, and warm cookies on a cold day. Don't know how a sorry excuse like my father snagged her. She died when I was young. Chronic heart trouble. Genetic thing I don't have, so don't worry. Sometimes I thought she was lucky, though, getting out early, getting away from my old man. What about you? Good things, I mean, before your parents were gone?"

Tolly watched Leigh with rapt attention as he made the cookie batter. "My parents were very much in love, and very dearly loved me. We lived the farthest from the colony. They preferred it that way, as did I. They were skilled hunters but never cruel with what they caught. They would help the injured, my father especially, which was against our ways. The injured are considered weak. They should be culled to thin the herd. But if my father found any of our kin or another creature not fit to be food, he would help them."

"Can't you just heal yourselves the way you healed my hand that time?"

"Most things, yes. But to heal ourselves, we need energy. Too deep a wound takes too much and can require another of our kind to take pity."

"And pity isn't the merfolk way."

"It is not."

"Your father was like a doctor, then?"

"I suppose he was," Tolly said with a smile. "And my mother a teacher. She would show the children she found playing near us clever ways of catching food without causing suffering, or tricks to escape nets and other human trappings. She enjoyed human culture like I do and ventured close to shore often. She taught me the start of many languages, to understand when I hear them, and to read. I learned much on my own later, but the passion for it started with her."

"You can't be the only good merfolk out there," Leigh said. "There have to be others who think like your parents did."

"Perhaps. But to change a culture's ways is not easy. Even the cruelest practices can be seen as natural and necessary when you know it all your life."

Leigh was quiet for a bit, but some of the shadows had fallen when he looked at Tolly again. "I bet your parents were as beautiful as you are."

That made Tolly blush and grin and feel very warm inside, though Leigh knew not what he spoke of.

"I bet they'd be proud of you," Leigh added, spooning drops of chocolate-speckled batter onto a pan.

"Shall we see if your mother would be proud of these cookies?" Tolly teased, stealing a finger full of batter from the bowl. It was lovely and it had not even been baked yet.

"Ten minutes in the oven," Leigh said.

Once they were ready, Tolly could not decide if he preferred brownies or Leigh's cookies best, because both were ambrosia, so different from anything he had known in the water. Certainly Leigh's mother would be proud, and he told him as much.

"I hope I can make her proud of more than just my baking someday."

"You will."

They were halfway through a second cookie each when a loud voice reached them from down the hall. It took a moment of listening close to realize it was *Ralph*.

Throwing down their cookies, they dashed for the door, rushing into the hall toward Ralph's apartment, where they could see him leaning out his doorway yelling at Rosa.

"Leave me alone!" he cried, then turned and saw them, with a surge of hope in his eyes to once again be rescued. His parents would be gone to work by now.

"You heard the kid," Leigh said. "He's not gonna rat you out."

"Pretty sure he got into this mess *because* he ratted someone out," she said.

"And once a traitor, always a traitor?" Leigh towered over her. "Leave him alone. He's out. Trust me, he doesn't want anything more to do with you."

"I'm just making sure it stays that way," she said snidely back at him, so Tolly stepped forward, offering that same cold stare. She took an immediate step back. "Be good, Ralphy-boy, and you'll never see me again." She twirled her fingers in a wave and headed for the stairs.

She would have fit in well with Tolly's kin.

"Ralph?" Leigh said after she had gone.

"I'm fine," Ralph said, though he did not look fine, arms crossed tight over his T-shirt-clad middle and eyes downcast. "She really was just ragging me about not telling anyone what really happened. I wouldn't." He gave Leigh a heartfelt glance. "But she's right. I ratted out *you*. I never should have said your name. I'm just as bad as—"

"Hey." Leigh reached for Ralph's shoulder and gave it a reassuring squeeze. "It doesn't matter. They had you scared. They still do. But I'm fine. I'm gonna be fine. All you need to worry about is taking a breath and enjoying your sick day. Order a pizza or Chinese or something for dinner—on me."

"Can I come back to your place again tonight?" he asked tentatively, already inching out his doorway.

"Sure, kid," Leigh said, and Tolly smiled in agreement. They had an entire batch of cookies to share, after all.

While Ralph looked over Leigh's take-out menus to decide on dinner, Tolly pulled Leigh aside. "She is the lowest in my mind. She betrayed her own, her lover, and is willing to sacrifice even a child for herself. And she is going to get away with murder."

"Maybe," Leigh said thoughtfully, the cleverness Tolly loved so much shimmering in his eyes like the beginnings of a plan forming. "I need to think, but tomorrow, we're gonna see Sweeney again. Rosa gave me an idea."

THERE WAS hope in their steps on the way to Sweeney's club the next morning that had been absent along the same path the day before. Even more exciting was the text message Tolly received.

I'm gonna do it. I'm gonna ask Cary out. I told him to come to the club this morning. You guys are coming, right?

We are on our way now, Tolly texted back.

I so need the moral support! But I'm ready.

Tolly showed Leigh the messages as they stopped at the final crosswalk. "How exciting. You see? There are still good things in this world."

The explosion that shook the block, erupting from the very club they had been headed toward, threw them both to the ground.

CHAPTER 11

LEIGH'S EARS rang from the explosion that had gone off so close in front of them, leaving him floundering on the sidewalk, coughing through the dust and trying to get back his bearings.

The club.

An explosion.

"Alvin!" he cried, scrambling to get up and reach what was left of the doors.

"Leigh!" Tolly hung on to him. "It is too dangerous. There is smoke and fire."

"Alvin's in there!"

"I know. And I will retrieve him." Tolly stood as if hardly fazed by being thrown to the ground, not talking as loudly as Leigh to be heard over the ringing, the headache, the *panic*. He remained calm as he headed for the carnage, Leigh left feeling helpless but unable to tell Tolly not to go when he knew he was stronger and more resilient than Leigh could ever hope to be.

The time between Tolly entering the building and coming out again could only have been minutes, but to Leigh it was still far too long. Sirens filled the air by the time Tolly emerged, carrying Alvin's unconscious body.

Leigh choked on the accumulating ashes as he sat up. The important thing was to get Alvin away from the smoke, where Tolly laid him down to make sure he was breathing.

He was. He was alive. Leigh didn't even care if anyone else had been inside. He knew Cary wasn't, or Tolly would have gone back in after him.

The fire department showed up in due course, then the cops, but by then Leigh and Tolly had helped Alvin into an ambulance headed for Cove City General. Leigh wanted to go with him, but he'd have to follow later because first he needed to find out the damage.

The fire department pulled Selene and Mark out of the back, less injured than Alvin, still both conscious since the blast had been focused at the front of the club. Sweeney hadn't been in yet; he was on his way like Leigh and Tolly. It had to have been Leo Moretti taking swift action.

Or Rosa.

Or *both*.

Leigh was in a daze, wanting to leave now and make sure Alvin was okay, but Perez and Horowitz showed up to pull him and Tolly aside.

"We don't know anything. I have to get to the hospital."

"You were almost blown up with Sweeney's kid and you're still following at his heels?" Perez barked.

"He can't help who his father is any more than I could," Leigh said. "He's my friend. He's hurt. We don't know anything. We were just headed to the club to meet him. You know who likely did this, but I got no further info to give."

"Why were you meeting Alvin Sweeney?" Horowitz asked diplomatically.

"For moral support," Tolly said.

"Moral support?" Perez repeated.

"Yes. He was going to ask the man he loves on a date and wanted us to be there. I can show you the text messages if you like." Tolly pulled out his phone, but Horowitz waved him away.

"We believe you. If you can think of anything that might help the investigation, you know how to contact us."

"Right," Perez huffed.

"Nick," Leigh tried, "I'm going to put a stop to all this. I mean it. I had no idea anything like this was going to happen. I just want to check on Alvin."

Perez's patience was clearly running thin, but he jutted his chin away from the mess of firemen and frantic bystanders to dismiss them.

For once, Leigh wasn't taking the long way. He and Tolly made it a couple streets over until they could hail a cab. Then they headed straight for CC General.

Sweeney hadn't finished his trek to the club after he heard what happened; he'd gone to the hospital first and was placing one of his larger grunts at Alvin's door to keep watch.

"Is he okay?" Leigh asked as he and Tolly rushed up.

"Leo is bold, I'll give him that," Sweeney said with his usual half-cracked smile. "He thinks he can go after what's mine—"

"*Sweeney*," Leigh cut him off, "you can't retaliate."

"Excuse me." Sweeney's eyes snapped to his like two burning coals. "Are you telling me what I *can't* do?"

The grunt shifted from the door as if he'd pull his piece right there in the hallway. Tolly pushed forward to protect Leigh, but Leigh held him back.

"I know how we can bring the whole thing down on Moretti's head," Leigh said, "but you need to do as I say. You are going to calmly call Leo, thank him for the remodel on the club, whether he did the deed or not, and ask him for a truce for everyone to get their bearings and then to meet at one of your other clubs in one week's time to talk things out."

Sweeney tilted his head with a twitch of that mad grin, right on the precipice between laughing and ordering Leigh's head on a block.

"I'll handle everything else, and everyone will know to never mess with you again. But you have to trust me."

It was a gamble. Dealing with Sweeney always was. He could probably find a way to dump a body easy in a hospital, but with Tolly there....

Sweeney's eyes darted to Tolly as if he was thinking the same thing. He only knew of Tolly's strength secondhand, but it made him pause enough to think about what Leigh had said.

"He's still asleep." He nodded back at the room. "Concussion. Too much smoke. But he should be fine in a day or two. Let me know the moment he wakes up or I won't be so accommodating," he said, as close to sounding like a normal, concerned parent as Leigh had ever heard.

"Of course."

Sweeney nodded to the grunt and left, presumably, *hopefully* to do as Leigh had asked. The plan was still forming in Leigh's mind after having to recalibrate from the explosion, but he saw no other course.

The grunt let Leigh and Tolly into the room. Alvin wasn't connected to much, just fluids as he remained passed out from the smoke, which meant they weren't worried, but Leigh still felt something catch in his throat to see him like that.

This was his fault. This was what someone loving him got him and why the promises of love and saying the words were always empty, because words couldn't protect anyone. If Leigh had been smarter, if he hadn't brought so much heat down on them....

"This was not your doing, Leigh." Tolly read his mind like always.

Leigh couldn't defend himself, so he simply sighed, looking at Alvin's smudged face. "Can you help him?"

"I would need access to water...." Tolly trailed off as he scanned the room.

There was a sink in the corner and a stack of paper cups, but filling one proved it was little more than a Dixie cup.

"It will be enough to help anything minor," Tolly said in response to Leigh's skepticism, "if he is indeed only as injured as Sweeney said. He was near the bar when I found him. Perhaps it helped to shield him."

"You're not going to dump that on your head, are you?"

"No." Tolly smiled and then drank the water but didn't swallow. He held it in his mouth as he touched Alvin's forehead and throat. After a few moments, he swallowed. "He will rouse soon enough. There will be no lasting damage."

"Thank you," Leigh said, for so much more than magical healing.

Tolly took Leigh's hand and held it, then leaned forward to press a kiss to his cheek. Leigh didn't deserve him.

It was less than an hour later that Alvin stirred.

"Leigh?"

"Hey." Leigh scooted his chair closer. "You're okay. You're going to be okay. Do you remember what happened?"

"The... the club!" His eyes sprang wide as he tried to sit up, nearly dislodging his IV.

"Relax." Leigh gently held him down. "You were the most hurt, and you're fine. It's being taken care of. Just rest."

"What about Cary? He was coming to see me. Urg," he groaned, more like his usual self. "Why do I have the worst luck, just when I was ready to ask him out?"

"We have not seen him," Tolly said from the other side of the bed, "but he was not in the club when it blew. I am sure he is well."

"Hold that thought." Leigh pulled out his phone. "I promised your dad I'd let him know when you woke up."

He sent a simple text message: *Alvin is awake and doing well.*

It was maybe thirty seconds later that the door opened, and Leigh looked over, expecting it to be Sweeney with impeccable timing, but it was *Cary*, as though Alvin had willed him to appear.

"Hey," Alvin exclaimed, sitting up again, but this time he did so slow enough that Leigh allowed it.

Cary held his cell phone, which made Leigh glance at his own with a frown.

"Did you hack my phone to intercept my messages?"

"Maybe." Cary shoved his phone away, hands staying in his pockets, dark jacket on with a hood Leigh half expected to be up, and probably had been wherever he'd been hiding outside the room.

"Why did you not join us if you were waiting outside?" Tolly asked. Leigh assumed the answer was because Cary wasn't the sociable type and didn't want to be in the same room with them for long, but the way he glanced aside said something else.

"I didn't want to see Alvin until I knew he was okay," he said softly, which lit Alvin right up, because Cary had just admitted he didn't want to see him hurt. "You're the one who wanted to talk, and while showing up just about got me killed if I'd been two minutes earlier.... What did you want to ask me?"

His eyes darted to Leigh and Tolly, which normally would have been a sign for them to scram, but Alvin was having none of it, already looking around for props.

"I had this whole thing planned with the jukebox and.... Where's my phone?"

"You may use mine," Tolly said and handed it to him, since Alvin's phone had been fried in the blast.

"Thanks."

Alvin grinned as Cary moved to the end of the bed with nervous eyes, but still he stayed while Alvin took a moment to Google something, then started playing the Righteous Brothers' version of "Unchained Melody."

"I know it should be 'You've Lost That Lovin' Feelin' but that's kinda the wrong message."

For one horrible moment, Leigh thought Alvin might sing, which no one should be subjected to, but he simply used the song as a backdrop, starting to *sign* as he spoke, hesitant at first but getting bolder with each phrase.

"I'm a mess. And not everybody likes me. But there's only one person I want to like me. I think you are *everything*." Alvin crossed his hands and spread them wide with emphasis, then moved his hands to his forehead. "Brilliant. And beautiful. And really funny when you want to be.

"I love the way you fix your glasses when they fall." He giggled, because Cary had just reached to fix them, which made him huff in embarrassment. "I love how your work has to be perfect and it always is. I love how much you love music. I love that you got stuck with me, and I'm sorry I'm not the best partner, but I'll try to be better every day even if your answer is no."

"Answer?" Cary said, tentative but anxious to hear the question.

"When I get out of here"—Alvin continued signing as he talked—"do you want to go out sometime? Get lunch or dinner or anything you want *not* as partners for work?"

Cary was a few years older than them, closer to thirty, a grown man, yet here they were, in a situation that felt so juvenile. But the reality simply made Cary laugh. "You realize it is cheating to ask me this here, now, when you almost *died*?"

"Yep," Alvin said. "I'm good at cheating."

"Just us?" Cary eyed Leigh and Tolly again. "Without the peanut gallery?"

"Of course! I just needed the support to get the nerve to finally ask you."

"I guess we could do that," Cary said, and ducked his head when Alvin practically whooped. His eyes drifted then to look at Tolly. "You taught him that?"

"He was very eager to learn," Tolly said.

"Don't suppose you'd teach me more?" Alvin asked Cary, as Leigh finally stood and moved from the bed so Cary could take his place. "Be good for jobs, too, communicating from afar. Not that we have to talk all the time. If you don't want to sign anything back to me, you can just give the universal one." He promptly flicked Cary off.

Cary laughed more openly than Leigh had ever heard.

"Why don't we leave you two alone?" Leigh had to go over to Tolly's chair and physically haul him out of it to get him to stop watching the show like one of his movies. It was time to let the budding lovebirds progress on their own.

"We will see you soon!" Tolly called as Leigh dragged him from the room, but the pair was already in deep discussion as Leigh saw Cary sign something back to Alvin that was one of the few phrases he knew.

Thank you.

The burly grunt on guard duty was still there. Glancing at his phone on their way out of the hospital, Leigh saw that he already had a message from Sweeney with the address of another one of his clubs.

Meeting set. I'm all ears for this grand plan of yours.

Good. Tell Rosa she's joining you. I'll be showing up to run point, but don't let her know that. You make everything seem like you have this well in hand, then when the day comes, you won't be going. I'll handle everything.

Bold request. Can't wait to see how it pans out.

Neither could Leigh. But in case it was one more thing that blew up in his face, he wasn't going to waste any time.

"Let's head home, and I'll tell you what I'm planning to save our skins."

A WEEK seemed like so much time, but Leigh knew it still might not be enough. He had to scope the club, figure out exactly who Leo Moretti had left on his side, who might turn traitor if Sweeney looked weak after the explosion, and he needed to get Perez and Horowitz to trust him one last time.

But all that would come later. The only thing he had to worry about for now was making sure Mark and Selene kept Rosa busy during the truce. As long as Moretti thought he had the upper hand, he'd honor a cease-fire, and Leigh shouldn't have to worry about any bombs showing up at his doorstep next.

He set everything in motion that he could, made sure Ralph was okay, got pulled into a few of the usual building chores, but when evening rolled around, all he cared about was Tolly.

"Let's go down to the pool. You won't need your trunks."

"Oh?" Tolly asked with a mischievous smile.

"The supplies we usually use won't work in the water, so…."

"A condom would likely not fit anyway when I am—"

"It's fine." Leigh didn't want to go into detail until he saw the truth for himself or he might psych himself out of this. "I just wanted to know what to bring."

"We only need each other, if that is all right," Tolly said like the Disney prince he was, though Leigh still grabbed a couple of towels— and an extra lock for the pool door.

Tolly wasted no time stripping and diving into the water to let out his tail, while Leigh stripped more slowly, nervous and excited in one great bundle of tightness in his stomach. He chose to walk to the shallow end and descend the steps slowly.

"So uhh, you can keep me lifted or…."

"No need. We will stay under the water." Tolly grasped his hands to pull him toward the deep end.

"Uh, Tolly, I need to *breathe*."

"You will have no trouble while submerged. That is one of the gifts bestowed on you with the Breath of Life."

"What?" Leigh gaped and nearly let his head dip down before he was ready. "I can breathe underwater? Why didn't you tell me that before?"

"It had not come up before." Tolly blinked innocently. "You always refused to join me."

Of course his answer would be so wholesomely simple.

They reached the end of the pool and Tolly pulled Leigh close, looking into his eyes to be sure he was ready. Leigh could feel Tolly's tailfin tickling his legs, soft like silk. He nodded, and Tolly pulled them under to sink to the bottom.

There was an instant of panic, but as Leigh opened his eyes, he felt no sting of chlorine. The water seemed clearer than it should, and when he took his first unconscious breath, water didn't fill his lungs but breathed in just the same as air. Leigh didn't understand any of it, so he chalked it up to magic and let Tolly lead.

The end of the pool was ten feet deep but seemed endless as they floated around each other. Leigh's bare legs seemed out of place in comparison to Tolly's tail.

I wish we could talk, he thought as he took in Tolly's smiling face, so similar to what he remembered from when he first saw him.

Then talk. I can hear you. Tolly's voice startled him, echoing in his mind.

Something else that never came up? Leigh thought back at him. *I must be in the water or in my true form to do this.*

And right now you're both.

... Yes.

Tolly took Leigh by the hand and guided it to his hip where human skin met red-and-gold scales. All this time and Leigh had never touched him like this. When Tolly released him, he glided his fingertips on his own. It was like the softest leather but with a sharp, almost metallic feel along each scale's edge.

Moving down Tolly's hip, Leigh continued to where his thigh would have been before moving inward to the center beneath Tolly's waist.

Tolly whimpered, audible in Leigh's mind, as his fingers traced a nearly invisible line. The scales parted there like an exhale and Leigh ran his fingers gently along the edge of the opening that was remarkably tender and slick.

For when you wish to be inside me, Tolly said, floating closer to urge Leigh's fingers to explore. It almost reminded Leigh of being with a woman, but was unique in its own way, especially with the scales moving aside. *Tonight, however, you wish for me to be inside you?*

Yes.

Then I will show you.

Tolly removed Leigh's hand, and the slit continued to part, opening wider to reveal the peek of something similar to a man's length, though it was a deep red to match Tolly's tail. As it extended longer, Leigh realized it split. All those years watching Shark Week with Alvin, he'd never paid much attention, but this was sort of like those Google images recently seared into his brain, though not really *two,* more like split halves to a whole that stayed together usually yet could also... part.

As Leigh stared at it, Tolly flexed the two halves, then folded them back together.

I have full control over it. You need not worry. Do you find it... ugly?

No, Leigh said without having to think, aware of Tolly's self-consciousness. *It's beautiful and unique just like you.*

He moved his hand to the base, amazed at how slick it felt even in the water, just like the opening.

Tolly's whimpers came through again, and he reached for Leigh to pull him into a kiss. That felt different while submerged but no less nice—the slide of their tongues and seal of their mouths. Then Tolly took Leigh in hand to touch him as he was being touched. Leigh wasn't sure how to get his bearings or find leverage in the water, so he lifted his legs to wrap around Tolly's waist as anchor.

May I open you up now? Tolly asked.

Just umm... be slow.

I will be everything you need me to be.

Leigh knew he meant that and moved his hands up to cling to Tolly's shoulders as Tolly reached to explore him more intimately. Again, it should have been more difficult in the water with that natural human wetness washed away, but Tolly's hands were slick from what he'd gathered from his sex, something resilient and smooth letting his fingers slide in, one and then two, with scant resistance.

He was careful and slow like Leigh had asked, which started to drive him mad before long, but that was when Tolly asked if he was ready for more, and Leigh couldn't deny that he was.

It was familiar at first, a gentle pressure like two fingertips, becoming wider as it pushed farther in. All of Tolly, strange and different though the shape may be, was not larger in size than his human form. It might not have felt different at all from past encounters Leigh remembered if not for how, after he was fully seated, Tolly flexed like before, stretching both halves apart.

Leigh's mouth opened with a true moan that got garbled by the water.

Is it all right? Tolly asked.

Leigh didn't know how to explain that it felt like two long scissoring fingers inside him reaching corners he didn't know could be reached, so he simply said, *So right. So good. Keep... keep doing that.*

Tolly floated back with Leigh atop him and lifted him with powerful hands, up and down as he flexed each time he pressed inside. Leigh felt tingles race up his spine and shudders wrack through him with every motion.

Why did I wait so long to let you do this?

Tolly's laughter responded. His thrusts grew more rhythmic, more practiced, mimicking what Leigh had shown him all their days together so far. Then he pulled Leigh closer with a hand at the back of his neck and sank his teeth into his pulse point, right along the tendons beneath his ear.

The not-quite but almost painful bite made Leigh moan through the water again, the act so primal, so animalistic but still not harsh. When Tolly released his teeth, he nuzzled the mark left behind with his nose, with the side of his face, all so instinctual that Leigh found himself clutching that much harder at Tolly's back to be part of it—marked, claimed by Tolly and so deeply desired.

They went on like that, Tolly's thrusts and flexing, his nips at Leigh's neck followed by comforting nuzzles and soft licks of his tongue. It made Leigh feel like he was floating, and he was, there in the water attached to Tolly, whose tail drifted beautifully beneath them. He was radiant and otherworldly, like something out of storybook, and he'd chosen Leigh.

His pace quickened soon enough, the pulses of his sex more constant, until both of them were moaning, heard between each other's minds if not through the water. One phrase stood out to Leigh clearly as he came and Tolly followed quickly after him.

I love you, Leigh.

The words were easy to ignore underwater, high on sensation and nearly overwhelmed. Leigh didn't think anything back to Tolly other than expressing elation as the water carried their release away.

It was then that Tolly turned, flipping his tail to push them back toward the shallow end. Leigh had another moment of panic where he expected to choke, but he breathed air when they surfaced as easily as he had breathed water.

Tolly brought them to the steps, where Leigh could catch his breath, and his tail changed into legs once more, while both of them sat hip-deep in the water. Leigh wanted to pretend Tolly hadn't said those words, hoped it could be left behind in the deep end and they could just enjoy the afterglow of how amazing that had been, but Tolly, sweet, romantic Tolly, gripped his chin, pulled him into a kiss, and murmured against his lips.

"I love you."

What an ass Leigh was that his reaction was to cringe. "Tolly, it's been ten days."

"I know." The smile faltered on his face. "But that is how I feel. I am yours, and I will be yours forever."

"Don't…." Leigh felt his stomach drop as he pulled away—because he didn't mean to, he didn't *mean to*. "Don't say things like that right now."

Tolly looked so stricken, hand dropping, sitting there as if alone on an island.

"Hey." Leigh reached for him to erase that awful look, and Tolly pressed his cheek to the offered hand. "I'm not trying to ruin this. I *loved* this."

"This…," Tolly repeated, because he hadn't said *you*.

"It's just… not something I say."

"I am sorry," Tolly said, scooting closer like all he wanted was to be held. "I pushed too hard. Forgive me."

"Nothing to forgive. You're more than I'd ever ask for, but right now all I'm asking is to go to bed. You wore me out." He forced a chuckle.

Tolly chuckled too, equally false. "Of course."

He looked so sad as they left the water to dry off. Leigh had ruined everything after all, but how could he explain that those were words he simply couldn't say?

Ever.

CHAPTER 12

TOLLY KNEW he should not sulk. Leigh did care for him and desire him; he could see it in his eyes even if not for the added passion he felt through their connection. But magic was old-fashioned. The pact required the power of words. Leigh had to say it. He had to tell Tolly or come the full moon, as soon as the sun set, Tolly would lose his legs and the others would come. There would be no hiding anymore.

The week passed, and Tolly dared not profess his love a second time for fear of alienating Leigh. He had to wait for the right moment, after they fixed the chaos around them.

Alvin was home and healing well, perhaps better for having Cary beside him. Tolly insisted that Leigh tell them the plan, at least Alvin, so he would not worry, and Leigh did, assuring Alvin that no matter how much the plan might seem dangerous, they had everything under control.

It was a good plan. Getting the detectives on board had been difficult, but in the end, they had agreed to participate. Tolly only wished he could help Leigh acquire the shop he looked at longingly whenever they passed it. Surely, if he helped Leigh get out of his criminal life, then he would love him. Leigh *had* to love him.

Once the week was up, there were only ten days left.

The day of the meeting, Leigh was calmer than he had been all week. He had to be to see this through, and Tolly projected as much calm as he could through their connection to keep it that way.

The other club was not very different from the one Tolly was familiar with. Open, dim, and mostly empty when they arrived, save Rosa, who had beaten them there, along with a single bouncer who opened the club for them and then left.

"Sweeney's cutting it close," Rosa said, eyeing them distrustfully.

"I'd focus on Moretti," Leigh said.

Sweeney would not be coming, but Leigh did not want her to know that.

A few tense minutes later, Leo Moretti arrived with minimal muscle to protect him as requested, two men only, though Leigh had told Tolly there would likely be more goons outside. Moretti might suspect an ambush, so they had to be ready for one too.

"You understand if I want my men to pat you down, considering we're on your turf?" Leo, the younger brother to Vincent, said. He was likely grateful to have his brother gone, Leigh had said, leaving him in power, but he would still want retribution.

This part of the human world truly was like Tolly's kin.

"Go wild, Leo," Leigh said. "We're just here to talk, but then you'll understand if we ask you and your men to set aside your weapons after?"

"Depends on what we find."

Tolly did not want these men to touch him, but he had promised to follow Leigh's lead and was prepared. The wire Leigh had asked him to wear was uncomfortable beneath his clothes. Leigh wore one as well. But as the goons came forward to check them, starting with Leigh and Tolly before one moved to Rosa, Tolly hummed ever so subtly beneath his breath.

You find nothing, he willed with a gentle nudge.

The man before him blinked as if in a daze, but he eyed Tolly hungrily when he said, "Pretty Boy's clean."

"Hurley too," the other added.

Tolly was glad when they moved away.

From Rosa they found a gun. Tolly had not used his powers to help her, but she was smart. Simply being armed was not betrayal. Leo and his men set their guns with Rosa's on a nearby pool table.

"What a good sport you are, Hurley, Miss Brookes." Leo shifted his eyes to Tolly. "Others. But Sweeney owes me the courtesy of being here too."

"He sends his apologies," Leigh said. "Alvin isn't doing well after that *accident* last week, so Sweeney was called away. I speak for his territory with full authority."

"You *what?*" Rosa spat.

"No longer part of the inner circle, Rosalind?" Leo said, but everyone was on higher alert now. The goons could easily have hidden weapons since they had not been patted down in turn.

Tolly wanted to sing again *now,* but Leigh had warned him that they must be patient to get everything they needed for the detectives.

"Let's sit." Leigh gestured toward a circle of chairs. "And we can discuss where this relationship went sour."

"I believe it was your Robin Hooding," Leo said, though neither Leigh nor Tolly flinched, for Leigh would not be held accountable for anything he was accused of tonight since the detectives had offered him immunity. "You know, I had men scour this place before the meeting. They didn't find anything."

"Why would they?" Leigh said. "I'm no coward who'd plant a *bomb*."

Leo looked curious enough to listen, but Rosa was trapped. She could not make a run for it, much as she seemed to want to.

Still, it was Leo who said, "Why don't we send the muscle into the back? We can discuss this just us three."

Tolly started. They had not planned for *that*. He could handle two on one with ease, but if he left Leigh alone and Rosa double-crossed them again....

Leigh did not allow any panic to show on his face. He looked at Tolly squarely and nodded as if dismissing nothing more than the bodyguard he pretended to be.

Tolly had to obey—they could not risk spooking Leo early—but he would listen carefully for the moment when Leigh gave the cue to sing.

Leaving the others to take their seats, Tolly led the goons into the back. There was a lounge for the waitresses, dancers, and bouncers that Tolly turned to instead of the office, but he still kept his senses attuned. He did not like the way the man who had patted him down had looked at him—and continued to look at him.

"You really the one who took out so many of our guys? With a face and body like *that*? More like a night's entertainment than a bruiser. You cover both bases for Hurley, sweetheart?"

Tolly wanted to believe the comments were merely to rile him, but this man meant his lewd words. "It is not your concern what I am to Leigh. Our orders were to give the others space. That does not mean I wish to converse with you." He glanced over his shoulder and made sure to frown in the direction they had come from, instinctually prompting the men to turn around.

Quickly, Tolly spun forward to pulse his powers into the space behind the club, checking for signs of backup as Leigh feared.

"Trying to throw us off, Princess? Don't worry, talking's the last thing I want to do with you," the man said just as Tolly felt the resonance of his powers return a picture of a man outside the back door.

He spun with his arm outstretched, hoping to catch one or both of the goons off guard, but a hand caught his wrist and twisted his arm behind his back. No matter, Tolly could easily overpower him and—

A sharp pain pricked his neck and something burned into his veins.

"Like lull you to sleep, pretty thing, so you put up less of a fight."

They had poisoned him. He could feel an instant sluggishness overtake his body.

"Will you stop chatting, for chrissake?" the other goon said. "All we need is him out of commission so we can take Hurley out."

Leigh.

Tolly pushed past the spots blinking in front of his eyes and the way everything was blurry and spinning. He could not pass out. He could not leave Leigh to whatever fate they had planned for him.

"You guys already taking down the bruiser?" another man said—the one from outside. "Why ain't ya just killing him?"

"Boss wants to see if he can be bought into playing for our side after Hurley's gone."

"*N-never*...." Tolly gasped, limbs no longer listening to him, though he managed to stay conscious as he was flipped around and pressed against a table, the needle pulling away but nausea very much present.

"Not ready for your nap yet, Sleeping Beauty?" The first goon held Tolly to the table, daring to stroke his face and down his neck as he crowded in close to his body.

No one got that close to Tolly without permission, and he wanted to tear something to pieces at the fury it built in him.

The man. The others.

All of them.

"Still raring to go, huh?" The man held Tolly tight as he struggled and willed his body to heal the poison faster. "All the better in my opinion. Maybe we can have some fun before we kill you."

"You thinking with your dick *now*?"

"What harm'll it do? All Moretti said was make sure Pretty can't come to Hurley's rescue." His hand drifted lower down Tolly's body.

"You will n-not touch me," Tolly rasped. "N-no one... is allowed to t-touch me but Leigh."

"Knew you were screwing him," the man breathed hot and unwelcome in Tolly's face.

Red flashed before Tolly's eyes as his fury grew, his claws lengthening even before he reached out to grip the man's wrist and pry his hand away, just barely able to hold him back but feeling his strength return as he burned through whatever they had poisoned him with.

"You will regret it if you do not desist," he warned.

"What's with his *hands*?"

Tolly had too few days left. Losing his form would make it harder to change back, but the man did not seem to care about his fellow's comment.

He leaned forward and hissed at Tolly, "I'm gonna have you, fight or not, and enjoy every minute of it."

Tolly slammed his head into the man's face, barely feeling the thunk of contact before he gripped his wrist tighter and twisted with the full force of his claws, like popping off the lid to a jar—enough for the hand to fall to the floor.

Before the man could scream, Tolly grabbed his neck and yanked him forward to ram their foreheads together once, twice more, then released him to leave an unconscious heap on the ground.

"The *fuck*!" one of the others sputtered, but all Tolly saw was *prey*.

He growled as his fangs extended, eyes sharpening as they darkened to their true color, scales freckling across his cheekbones and down his neck, but his legs remained strong and stable to carry him across the room where the others backpedaled to escape him.

"What—!" one tried but was cut short by Tolly slicing his throat and ramming a knee up into his stomach. He was lucky Tolly had not punctured more deeply, but still he coughed and gasped as he bled onto the floor where he fell.

The final man, the one who had come in from outside, was mute and trembling, too terrified by what he saw of Tolly to do anything but flounder.

"Only Leigh is allowed to touch me," Tolly growled with an inhuman resonance as he reached out with both hands, deep red and further spattered with blood on his claws, to grab him by the front of his shirt and haul him closer.

"Please...," the man said, soiling himself—Tolly could smell it—but it was the other voices drifting in from the main room that stopped him from sinking his teeth into the man's throat with a *bite*.

"Liar!" Rosa screamed. "I didn't kill Vinny! It was you!"

Leigh. He was out there alone going forward with the plan. Tolly had to reel in his true form. He had to calm down.

"P-please," the man said again, while Rosa kept shouting. Leigh spoke calmly but loudly back at her, and Leo said nothing, which meant he was not sure what to believe.

Tolly had to do his part. He had to act. *Now*.

Glancing back at the men on the floor, one missing a hand, Tolly felt the nausea of what they had injected him with surge up in his throat again for how easily he had fallen to his nature and what his kin were capable of.

So he opened his mouth and sang because it was something he could use his powers for that was not monstrous. It was supposed to be soft and subtle like his humming, but he was too far away from Leigh now and had to project as far as possible.

Tell the truth, he sent through the song.

The men on the floor were out, but the one at the end of Tolly's claws fell to the song with startling clarity.

"I killed my cousin, took out teenagers before, dozens of 'em, beat my girl within an inch of her life. Am I dead? Is this hell? Coz I'd rather be skinned alive than face whatever *pit* you crawled out of."

Tolly threw the man into the wall, slamming his head hard to knock him out with the others. That was hardly a truth that surprised him, because he still had claws and fangs. He could not let Leigh see him like this. With every ounce of power left in him, he willed his body to be human. He had to be human.

Before it was too late.

LEIGH HAD known the moment he heard Tolly sing to cover his ears. Rosa and Leo weren't as lucky. They turned at the mournful sound, craning to hear *better*, until their eyes turned glassy.

"I shot him," Rosa said. Then, more passionately, "*I* shot Vinny. And so what if I did?" She spun toward Leo, already on her feet. "You planted that bomb! You could have killed me!"

"I *should* have been targeting you!" Leo jumped up. "I planted that bomb to get back at Sweeney for killing my brother! I blamed him and Hurley, and it was *you*?"

"You hated your brother!"

"That doesn't mean anyone else gets to kill him! I did all the dirty work for years. I was the one manning the protection money and setting up the drug drops and gun trafficking at the docks. I planned everything around taking these streets from Sweeney. We were going to slaughter all of them piece by piece, and Vinny did nothing, just sat back and reaped the rewards."

Wow. Leigh hadn't expected that much. Rosa for killing Vincent, one of them for the bomb, hopefully *something* on Leo if he hadn't set it, but Horowitz was getting fed everything the CCPD needed to clean out the Moretti family completely, and Rosa had only incriminated herself. Sweeney would be safe, which meant Alvin would be safe, and Leigh could finally be free.

Speaking of, once Rosa and Leo stopped screaming and remembered the guns not far away, Leigh bolted. He didn't want to get caught in the cross fire or for either of them to remember he was there.

"Now would be a good time to raid the place," he hissed into his mic, rushing for the back, grateful that Tolly had come to his rescue but worried now that he hadn't reappeared.

The office door was still closed. The lounge? He reached to push open the door—

But Tolly pushed out first, looking sweaty and haggard like Leigh had never seen before.

"You okay?" He reached for Tolly's face, only to notice the ugly needle mark in his neck.

"They tried to p-poison me, but I will be all right. Are *you* okay?"

Gunshots rang out, and Leigh instinctively pulled Tolly to him, ready to rush into the lounge for cover, but an announcement of police followed and the rush of boots, so he held steady.

"Horowitz, Perez, we're in back. Moretti's men are...." Leigh peered around Tolly into the lounge where the door still swung, revealing the bodies on the floor.

"Alive, but no longer a threat," Tolly said.

Leigh wondered what Perez had heard listening to Tolly's wire compared to Horowitz listening to his, but Tolly said nothing more. He was winded yet obviously healing. By the time the police swarmed them, both their hands raised to play it safe, the mark on Tolly's neck was nearly gone and his eyes were clear.

Whatever Perez had heard, he didn't betray a word of it when he and Horowitz pushed through the uniformed officers to reach them. They had entered from the back, so they'd seen whatever carnage Tolly left behind. Tolly wouldn't meet Perez's eyes.

"Something wrong, detectives?" Leigh tried to play it cool. "You got what you wanted."

Horowitz looked green. "One of them was missing a hand," he said. "*What?*"

"I told him only you were allowed to touch me," Tolly said quietly, "but he would not listen."

If the way Tolly said that meant the goon had tried to touch him more than roughing him up, he'd gotten what he deserved, but Leigh didn't want to imagine how Tolly had removed a *hand*.

"Hear that?" Leigh turned to the detectives. "Sounds like self-defense to me."

"Sure was," Perez said, calmer than usual as if finally appeased. "Don't know who this guy is to you, Hurley, but I'm glad he's on our side."

Tolly glanced up with unsure eyes, and he and Perez shared a look of understanding.

The goon without a hand was still unconscious, as well as another being taken by ambulance, but a third, one Leigh hadn't seen, so he must have come in later, was led from the back through the club to the waiting police outside. When he passed Tolly, his eyes went wide and he scrambled to get closer to the officer holding him.

"I'm telling you, man, he's not *human*."

"Tell it to your cellmates, Russo."

There would be stories about Tolly and what had happened here, regardless of who believed what.

Rosa and Leo were broken from their siren trance, but they still spat insults at each other as they were questioned across the room, soon to be led away as well. All that remained was to talk to Sweeney.

"We might need more of a statement down at the station later," Horowitz said.

"And you better stay outta trouble," Perez added. "Still not sure why those two grew such loose tongues. Better not find anything in their systems to compromise this bust."

"You won't," Leigh said. "They'll come out clean. Maybe their consciences finally caught up to them. We free to go?"

"Yeah, get outta here. But I mean it. Stay outta trouble, you hear me?" He said the last with a touch of softness he hadn't used in years.

Leigh couldn't express how much it meant to him, meager as it was. He hoped he never let Perez down again, hoped Sweeney let him out of the life, and that somehow, he found another way to get by.

With Tolly beside him.

TOLLY STILL seemed timid, slowed by whatever they had dosed him with, but Leigh couldn't immediately tend to him. It was too dangerous to go straight to Sweeney. Someone could be following if there were Moretti loyalists—or if there were opportunistic cops about—so he texted Alvin along the path home that all was well and that they could plan for a time to meet Sweeney tomorrow.

Then he called Tabitha.

"Hey, Beckett. Before any cops knock on your door, I wanted you to know what happened."

After hearing the story, Tabitha chided him for doing something so rash and dangerous, but still she said, "I'm proud of you, William. Now we just need those pay stubs."

"One milestone at a time." He chuckled. "I'm working on it."

Phone calls and text messages done, he wanted only to talk to Tolly and understand what had happened while they were separated, so as soon as they entered the apartment, he caught him by the wrist.

"Do you need anything? What did that guy do to you? The one who can't use a full pair of gloves from now on."

Tolly ducked his head. "I need only water and I will be fine. A drink will do." He avoided the other questions by escaping into the kitchen.

"Tolly." Leigh followed him. "Please. What did he do?"

A glass of water drained down Tolly's throat before he answered. "He only *tried*. He did not succeed. But he looked at me like a thing to be used and assumed you looked at me the same. Then he tried to touch me. I do not like anyone to touch me without permission."

"I know. But even when we'd only just met, you made an exception for me."

"*You* have permission." Tolly looked at him devotedly. "Always. Anytime. I am yours. But that does not mean I am a slave or a thing. I know you do not see it that way, but I did not like for him to assume otherwise."

"So you cut off his hand?"

"I did not mean to." Tolly glanced away again. "I was angry and weakened, not thinking clearly."

"I'm not saying you should have done differently, just making sure you're okay. You're allowed to be dangerous. You saved me—*again*. You can defend yourself, defend me, and not be like the others." Leigh pulled Tolly against him, embracing him before he could pull away.

"But what if I am like the others?" Tolly said as a breathless whisper. "Would you still want me if I was?"

Leigh knew what it felt like to believe he wasn't worth anyone caring about him, so he held Tolly tighter. "I can't imagine anything you could do or be that would make me stop wanting you."

"Leigh, I...."

Leigh tensed, expecting those words again, the ones he didn't want to hear—not because he didn't feel them, but because he couldn't say them back. Not when his father had tainted them, drilling into his head again and again that love could get him killed, that it was weak and dangerous, something bad, and to this day, he could never shake the feeling that maybe that was true.

It *wasn't*. But he couldn't say those words without feeling burdened by them. Tolly deserved better than that.

He didn't say what Leigh expected, though.

"Thank you," he said.

Leigh should have been relieved, but that wasn't what he felt. "You're welcome, Tolly."

DESPITE THE trials of the day, they made love that night like their first time, with Tolly sitting on Leigh's hips, clawing at the sheets.

Clawing *literally*, he discovered in the morning, finding parts of the sheets normally hidden by pillows shredded. Tolly had barely over a week left and it was showing. He knew it had been best to not confess his love once more, but when the time was right, he had to try again.

There was no fanfare when they arrived at Sweeney's the next day, not at a club this time, but at his home, a lavish one that made Tolly unsure where to look or step, for it was quite colorful and oddly decorated. Sweeney was there, a bodyguard, and Alvin.

"So you *didn't* shoot Vinny?"

"Nope."

"Didn't shoot Leo either, just got him and Rosa locked up and looking at hard time?"

"Yep."

"You basically, nearly single-handedly, got rid of all my competition without killing a soul?"

"Basically," Leigh said as though he had planned it that way from the beginning.

"You sure I can't convince you to stay? I know you'll be around to watch out for my boy, but you're good people, William. Good at what you do. Good at things I didn't know you could do. And I am hurting for recruits."

"Sorry, boss. I won't go far, but I don't want this life anymore."

Tolly worried Sweeney might recant, but he took one look at Alvin and sighed dramatically.

"Friends?" He extended his hand.

Leigh took it—only to jump as if he'd been shocked. "Funny," he huffed, pulling back to reveal that Sweeney wore a small device on his hand that had zapped him.

Sweeney and Alvin both laughed like an echo of each other. Since nothing had been said against Sweeney over the wires, he was safe. Tolly wondered about Alvin sticking to a criminal's life, but then he remembered that Cary was part of that life too.

"Perhaps we can get together soon," Tolly said when Alvin walked them to the door, a sense of finality following them like they had to make plans or they might lose touch, though there was no threat of that when Leigh and Alvin were as brothers. "I would like to spend more time with Cary and see how your signing is progressing."

"Double date? You're on, Shark Bait. I'll drag Cary over tomorrow. We can do dinner and movies or whatever."

"Deal," Leigh said, smiling at Tolly for the suggestion, then tapping Alvin's chest. "Be good. Or as good as you ever get."

"Please, don't say it like goodbye. You're never getting rid of me."

There was a lightness that followed them like it had before, which made Tolly feel foolish for worrying he would lose Leigh or control over himself. Leigh would love him. Leigh would *tell* him. Another day or two and all would be well.

The next night, Alvin and Cary arrived together. Cary seemed awkward and unsure of himself, so Tolly endeavored to ease his mind and signed to him silently.

You are welcome here. If you need anything, even if just this so they do not know what we are saying, I am at your service.

You're a strange guy, Cary signed back, *but I like you.*

"Secrets are lies!" Alvin teased, then grinned as he clung to Cary's arm. "I can't wait to know everything you say to each other."

They decided to walk to the corner store to pick up supplies to make dinner rather than order it, which Tolly was excited about regardless of what they cooked. On their way back, however, they ran into Ralph just inside the building, pacing and looking spooked.

"*Hurley.*" Ralph rushed up to them. "I was waiting for you. I heard someone pounding on your door. I think they broke in."

"What?" Leigh immediately passed his bag to Alvin, looking ready to storm up to the apartment.

"The boss isn't planning any double crosses," Cary assured them. "Has to be Moretti stragglers. They still have loyal people."

Tolly passed his bag to Cary in kind and pushed ahead of the others.

"Wait." Leigh stopped him. "I want to check too, but going up there now might be just what they want. We should sneak out the back, go up the fire escape to see inside."

Tolly agreed, while Alvin and Cary set the overload of bags on the floor in front of the super's door.

"We'll come back for them," Alvin said. "You don't think we'll let you do this alone?"

Despite Tolly's fondness for Cary, he was surprised the man stood firm with Alvin to offer his aid as well.

"I'm coming too!" Ralph said.

"Oh no you're not." Leigh whirled on him. "You are going straight home."

"You mean upstairs to the same floor as whoever broke into your apartment?" Ralph challenged.

"Fine," Leigh said, "but you stay behind us, and once we're in the alley, you stay put. You're not coming up the fire escape with us."

"Wouldn't dream of it."

Together the five of them moved through the first floor to the back exit that led into the alley. The others being with them made things difficult, but still Tolly saw the sense in using his abilities.

"Leigh," he whispered.

Leigh let Tolly go ahead and caught the others' attention, saying something about making sure they were careful, for no one to play hero, a simple pep talk long enough to avert their eyes from Tolly so he could pulse his powers outside and see if anyone was there.

After he nodded to Leigh that the way was clear, they pushed outside. Tolly's abilities had been right, of course, there was no one in the alley, but he had not thought to look *up*.

There was a click, then everything happened in slow motion—the turn of their heads to look toward the second floor, where a figure stood on the fire escape waiting.

It was the man who had led others to Leigh's apartment once. He must have heard what happened, heard something about Tolly that triggered him to remember the events in the apartment that day when he saw hints of Tolly's true face.

He looked wildly at Tolly now, at Ralph and the others with a sneer, but it was Leigh he looked at with *wrath* as he aimed his gun.

And shot Leigh in the chest.

CHAPTER 13

THE MAN was rash but not a fool. The silencer on his gun made the noise muffled, muted through the alleyway, but still just as shocking to Tolly.

And to Leigh, who looked down in disbelief at the dark spot blossoming from his chest for a solid ten seconds before he crumbled.

"Hurley!" Ralph and Cary's voices overlapped, while Tolly and Alvin stood stunned, Tolly certain it must be a dream—a shot like that, in the chest, that could *kill* Leigh, and he was already gasping as he collapsed back onto the pavement.

Cary came to his senses first and dove down beside Leigh to press against the wound, covering his hands that could sign so beautifully in scarlet red. Then the roar in Tolly's ears sucked away like a vacuum and there was nothing but the man who had done this and who needed to pay.

Bolting for the fire escape, Tolly raced up to the apartment. Another shot rang out, directed at his pursuit, but the bullet clanged against metal and missed him. As did the next and the next as he shot up faster than most humans could match. Tolly was upon the man in moments, and he was out of bullets by the time Tolly reached him, proven by the plaintive click of his gun.

Tolly knocked the gun away and seized him harshly. Only when he saw how his outstretched hands were bloodred, with claws, did he realize he had lost control of his form again, but it did not matter. The others could not see more than indistinct figures above them for how the metal platform and stairway hid him.

"You *are* a monster...." The man stared wide-eyed at Tolly, giving him the final catalyst he needed to launch forward and sink his teeth into the man's shoulder. His cry cut off like a whimper as Tolly dug his claws into his sides as well, wanting to tear muscle from bone and make him suffer.

But no. Then he *would* be a monster, and even if Leigh believed he would want Tolly no matter what, that would not ring true if he proved he was no better than his brethren.

Tearing his teeth free, Tolly was careful not to rip out the man's jugular or puncture the artery. His claws would not be fatal either as long as he did not twist them, sliding them cleanly out again for the man to gasp in pain. *Good.* Tolly was not like his kin, but without Leigh, he would have nothing to stop him from becoming them.

"I should kill you," he said as he threw the man to the fire escape floor and crouched over him, fangs and claws dripping blood. "Why shoot Leigh and not me if I am the monster? *Why?*"

"B-because... he ruined everything by bringing you into this."

"If he dies," Tolly snarled, "after what I do to you then, you will wish I had killed you."

To feel one more rush of satisfaction, Tolly slashed the man's face, then made his second swipe a punch to knock him unconscious. He was bleeding in many places now, but not so heavily that he would not live.

"Tolly, we—" Alvin's voice reached him before Tolly realized he had been followed. The words cut off abruptly, a sharp inhale leaving Alvin before Tolly turned.

Other than the men who deserved his wrath, no human had ever seen his true form. It was incomplete like this without his tail but otherwise fully revealed—his eyes and fangs and claws, his skin red and darkly freckled with spots and scales, the change in the color of his hair to match, and the pointed shape of his ears.

"Please...." He wiped furiously at the blood on his face when he saw the terror on Alvin's. "Leigh does not know. I did not kill the man, much as he may deserve it. Please do not tell Leigh this is what I am. He will never love me if he knows."

"Guys!" Ralph called up at them, frantic. "We have to call an ambulance!"

Leigh was what mattered and that made it easier for Tolly's skin to turn back and for his other merfolk aspects to fade. Still, Alvin stared and gave an instinctive flinch when Tolly stood to move toward him.

"Guys!" Cary cried, even more urgently than Ralph had, and finally Alvin blinked, nodded at Tolly, and turned to rush back down the steps. Tolly followed.

"He's not going anywhere," Alvin said about the man on the fire escape when Ralph and Cary gaped at Tolly's bloody clothes. "We can worry about him later. We have to—"

"Get him to the pool. Into the water," Tolly said.

"*What*?" Cary said, hands covered in the blood that would not cease its heavy pulse from Leigh's chest. Leigh was awake, but only barely and unable to speak.

"You can heal him?" Alvin asked.

"Yes."

"Heal him? What are you talking about?" Cary sputtered.

Ralph seemed too traumatized by the past few weeks to add anything.

"Leigh…." Tolly coaxed his eyes up, lips stained with blood from every feeble cough choking him. Leigh had precious little time, but he looked at Tolly and there was love there, if only he would say it.

Later.

"I will save you," Tolly said and lifted him from the ground without faltering, holding him secure with one arm, while the other wrapped around him and pressed to the wound that Cary could no longer reach.

The pool was close to the alley exit, and Tolly rushed back inside to reach it, turning down hallways and around corners with impressive speed, even with Leigh in his arms. They came upon no one in the halls, but their luck ran out when they reached the pool. Deanna was there with the children, Miss Maggie lounging in a chair with a book, all so normal and benign until they saw what Tolly carried.

"Out of the pool!" Alvin called.

"Oh my God, William?" Deanna exclaimed, though she wasted no time hauling her children out as asked, and Miss Maggie threw her book aside.

Tolly wished the children did not have to see this, wished none of them did, but he could hold his kinder merfolk form for them and all would be well once he healed Leigh.

"Out!" Alvin rushed to usher Deanna and the kids free of Tolly's path.

Tolly laid Leigh down at the edge of the pool, catching his eyes again and promising without a word that all would be well.

"Cary!" he called behind him, and Cary came forward to take his place, putting pressure on the wound while Tolly stripped and then jumped into the water to pull Leigh in with him.

"This is crazy," Cary said, even as he allowed Tolly to take him. "Why would you...." But words failed him as he looked over the side at shimmering red and gold.

"You're a *real* mermaid?" Gert said, the innocence of a child finding only wonder in what she saw, even with the blood spreading out through the water from Tolly's stained hands and Leigh's wound.

"I can save him," Tolly said, stunned though the others may have been. "I promise."

He dove, taking Leigh under with him and swimming to the deepest parts of the pool. Leigh's clothing made him heavier, though it was still hardly a feat to get there quickly and make sure Leigh looked at him instead of the blood turning the water red.

T-Tolly.... Leigh's mind called where his voice had not been strong enough.

Stay awake. Stay with me, Tolly said as he pressed both hands to Leigh's chest.

Then he sang, if only to dull the pain Leigh might be feeling, but it was from his core that the healing magic flowed.

A cut on a hand barely made Tolly cringe. Healing the poison he had been injected with had been harder but still manageable. Something like this though, *fatal*, would take most of his own energy to even attempt. He had to believe he could do it without his own life being extinguished, because here in the water, communing with Leigh, his pact-mate, his *love*, he was stronger than he had ever been.

Whereas with the cut on Leigh's hand, the illumination through his veins had been minimal, this time his entire chest and every connecting vein up his neck and down into his hands glowed. If he had been without clothing, he would have glowed like a beacon. It made Tolly falter and shiver for how much toll the exchange took on him, which must have shown on his face.

Don't..., Leigh said, hands trembling as he reached for Tolly.

I will be fine. You must heal. You must survive.

I'm not... worth it.

You are worth everything.

Their eyes locked, and Tolly could feel the beat of Leigh's pulse not only through his hands on his chest but in his ears, in his mind, beating in rhythm with his own. They were one. They belonged to each other. Tolly could not allow Leigh's eyes to close.

But they did.

Leigh!

While pouring more healing energy into him, Tolly brought them down so deep in the water, Leigh's body soon lay on the floor of the pool with him floating above. The red around them was turning hazy pink. Was the blood slowing? Or did Leigh have no more to give…?

Please….

Tolly's vision dimmed, failing as he pushed harder than his own energies could sustain, but he would not give up.

Heal. Be well. Be mine, please….

Any more and Tolly would pass out. He would fail, and Leigh would be lost. If that happened, when Tolly awoke, *if* he did, he feared the carnage he would leave in his wake through the few remaining days he had left before his legs abandoned him without Leigh's love to keep them.

Leigh, he pleaded one last time, and when his strength dwindled enough that he could no longer keep his hands pressed to Leigh's chest, they gave way and started to drop—

Only for Leigh to grab his wrists and wake with a start.

Leigh!

Leigh's chest heaved with a deep breath, taking in water with the power of the Breath of Life as easily as he gulped in air. *Tolly.*

You are alive. Tolly flicked his tail forward with one last surge and wrapped Leigh in his arms. *You are still with me. Oh, my love, please never leave me again.*

Surprised but adoring laughter echoed through their connection. *I think we're destined to keep saving each other. But hopefully there won't be any more gunshots in our future.*

Tolly laughed back at him, weak, though feeling better by the moment, no longer pouring energy into Leigh, for he was well now, and simply being in the water would help him regain his strength as well.

Holding Leigh's face with both hands, he kissed him and pressed their foreheads together. *I love you,* he said, as heartfelt as he had before. *I love you, Leigh.*

I'm glad, Leigh said, despite the wave of sadness that crossed his face. *I am. I am so grateful for you, Tolly.*

Grateful. It stung like before, but Tolly was so relieved to have Leigh with him, he would not let it spoil his joy.

The water was stained, though clearing of blood as the filters set to work, and Tolly swam them through it, hauling Leigh up to the surface with a great splash and eruption of cries and questions from the onlookers. When they saw Leigh was well, there was little more they could say but to express their amazement that Tolly was not what they had thought.

Carefully, Tolly helped Leigh sit on the edge so he could pull up his shirt to check the wound that revealed a faint scar cleanly healed over. He had still lost blood and looked in need of a meal, but he would be all right.

The worry Tolly felt for so many others knowing his secret came to the forefront with Leigh's recovery, and for a moment, he thought of ducking back under the water to hide. He should not leave the pool yet anyway, not until he felt recharged.

But none of them looked at him with anything less than amazement. He was something beautiful and miraculous to them. He was a hero, for he had saved Leigh's life, and they were his dear friends who had no thoughts of betrayal to sell proof of a "freak" for riches and fame.

It was only Alvin who looked on with wariness.

"I knew you talked too weird to be normal," Ralph said with the giddiest grin.

"Who's normal in this building anyway," Deanna said, rustling his hair with teasing fondness that caused him to look at her with his usual adoration.

Miss Maggie merely shrugged. "I've seen weirder."

"I thought all mermaids were girls," Gert said, held back from getting too close to the pool by Deanna's firm hand.

"He's not a mermaid, silly," Gar said, "he's a mer*man*."

"Merfolk," Tolly corrected.

"Why 'folk'?" Gar asked.

Tolly leaned up on the edge of the pool. "Because sometimes my kin look like men. Sometimes like women. But we are neither and also both." Much as Tolly had chosen the form of a human man to match Leigh's desires.

"Oh. Cool," Gar said, and Gert nodded in wonderment.

That seemed to surprise and yet also not surprise Leigh, but he simply smiled.

"You can call me a mermaid if you like," Tolly said.

Maggie took charge from there, getting things cleaned up, getting Leigh into dry clothes retrieved from upstairs, with clothes brought down for Tolly once he was ready to get out of the water. Cary called in for "cleaners" to handle the Moretti man. Tolly hardly cared what Sweeney's people did to him, just so long as he did not have to see his own damage again.

He was glad Leigh did not ask. He was glad Alvin did not say anything, but he wished his friend was not so distant.

Leigh did not wish to leave until Tolly could join him upstairs, so while they retrieved the left-behind groceries, Miss Maggie ordered takeout, and they ate right there together, crowding in close to Tolly with the blood wiped from the floor. The water was still not fit for anyone but him, but they would have someone clean it properly tomorrow.

"We have people for that," Cary said, signing secretly to Tolly that he was *beautiful*. "Boss'll cover it."

When Tolly finally felt well enough to leave the pool, he checked to be sure Leigh was okay, kissed him soundly, then pulled Alvin aside.

"Please—"

"Don't tell Leigh. I heard you."

"Yes, but… please do not look at me like that. Please do not fear me."

"I'm not afraid," Alvin said, though he had his arms crossed like a shield to protect him. "I… I don't know what I am. You were *eating* him or something."

"I was not eating him, merely—"

"Gnawing on his neck? Shredding him to pieces?" Alvin said, then immediately pulled back. "Not that he didn't deserve it. He nearly killed Leigh, *would* have killed him if not for you. You saved him. You keep saving him. But you're also lying to him." All the headway Tolly had made in his human life seemed to crumble in Alvin's eyes, painting him as the outsider he was. "What are you?"

"I am merfolk," Tolly said simply. "That was never a lie."

"But what *are* merfolk? Really? Coz Leigh thinks it's the tail, but that's not true. It's more than that. It's old legends of mermaids and sirens drowning people for fun."

He was not wrong; that was exactly what Tolly's kin were like. "I would never do that, I swear to you, but some things I cannot tell Leigh until the pact is over."

"Pact?"

"The magic that allows me to take this form prevents certain truths from being spoken. Other things, I… I keep from him so he does not hate me as you do now."

That snapped Alvin's attention to Tolly's eyes, which he had been avoiding, and his arms dropped. "I don't hate you. You're freaky and I don't get what's going on, but…." He trailed off, frowning at himself, at Tolly maybe, but no, *himself*, because the next moment, he launched forward, enveloping Tolly and squeezing tightly. "I love you, Tol. You're the best. You *are*. But don't hide this from Leigh. Whatever you can tell him, *tell him*. I won't, I promise, but you have to. He deserves to know you really are more Creature from the Black Lagoon than Blue." He chuckled, and the tremble in his voice was a little less prominent. "Doesn't change anything else about you. I'm sorry I got so spooked."

Stunned but so grateful, Tolly embraced Alvin back with eager arms. He did not realize he was crying until he felt hot tears slipping down his cheeks. Alvin looked at him as they parted like he was truly sorry he had ever stared in fear.

"You give your vow of love so easily," Tolly said, wiping at his eyes to clear them, "despite having seen what I am. You believe Leigh could be the same?"

"He's not some shallow asshole," Alvin said, looking calmer after holding Tolly, like he had needed to touch him anew to be sure he was not sharp. "It might just be a shock, is all."

"Hey!" Leigh called to them. "What are you two talking about? Let's head up."

Perhaps Tolly was wrong. Perhaps Leigh could accept him as he was. He nodded his thanks to Alvin and went to Leigh with a fresh smile.

The others had all peppered him with questions the way Alvin once did, assuaged now, ready for sleep, and Gert hugged his legs before they retired, for he was proof of magic to her young eyes and only something to be marveled at.

Ralph, too, seemed like some of the darkness had lifted, able to move on from the death he had witnessed because Tolly had shown him something miraculous, his hope restored.

Alvin's final encouraging smile gave Tolly hope too.

"You believe we are safe here?" Tolly asked when they entered the apartment. The fire escape was already cleared.

"After Sweeney's men were here to clean up, if there are any other stragglers, they won't act tonight. Come here." Leigh pulled Tolly to him as soon as the door closed and kissed him hard. Leigh loved him. He did. He would not shun Tolly to know the truth.

"Leigh...." Tolly sighed, summoning his courage, their foreheads falling together after the kiss with the welcome weight of Leigh's hands at his hips.

"You know, for a minute there when I was passing out, I thought I saw that monster again, the one you erased from my dreams."

"Oh?" Tolly prompted, feeling his confidence sink like a rock in his stomach.

"You saved me from all the monsters. Guys with guns. A life I didn't want. Even the worst monster living in my head."

The worst....

"You mean everything to me, Tolly."

That caused him to look up at Leigh directly. "Then you love me, as I love you?"

"I can't say that." Leigh winced.

"Why?" Tolly beseeched him. It was all he needed. It was the only way.

"It'd feel hollow from me. Broken," Leigh said, withdrawing with a pained expression. "Between my dad and a life of bad choices, it's always been an ugly word. I don't mind if you say it, but I need to know it's okay if you don't hear it back. Not now. Maybe not ever."

"Not... ever?"

"I'm sorry," Leigh said and meant it, clearly resenting the part of him that could not give Tolly what he wanted, but it was Leigh's pain that further hurt Tolly, because they should not have to sidestep each other because of what had been made of them.

"It is all right," Tolly assured him, wrapping his arms around Leigh's neck. "I am sorry your father and many of those around you were as awful as my kin were to me. I am especially sorry for how much it wounded your heart. I long only to heal it."

"You have." Leigh lifted his hands to touch Tolly's wrists. "You *did*. Literally," he said with a chuckle, drawing one of Tolly's hands down to rest over his healed wound.

"Yes. But... maybe someday you could say the words?" Tolly asked, and just as quickly Leigh's good humor died.

"I don't want you counting on that. I don't want to disappoint you."

"You could never. You could never disappoint me." He pressed forward to kiss Leigh's lips once more. "It is all right. It will be all right. If you cannot say it, then let us show our love. Let me show you how much you mean to me."

While I still can.

Tolly pulled Leigh to the bedroom, intent on pouring all his love into his acts, knowing that sharing this with Leigh and reveling in his warmth, his body, his kind heart, had a time limit. Telling Leigh the truth, showing him his true form, would not be what pushed him to say the words. If anything, it would be what caused Leigh to remember him with hatred once he was gone. Tolly wanted his remaining days with Leigh to pass sweetly. He also wanted to know that Leigh would be well even if he was not around to protect him. He wanted Leigh to have his heart's desire, even if that did not include Tolly.

And, after they had taken their pleasure in each other and Tolly lay awake while Leigh slept, he thought he might know a way.

In the morning, he texted Alvin.

LEIGH HAD never been as close to death as he was when that bullet pierced his chest, not even when he had been sinking to the bottom of the river, sure to drown. Still, in both cases, Tolly had been there to save him. Leigh wished he could give Tolly the one thing he wanted and say the words, but he needed time. They hadn't even known each other a month. While Leigh might feel it, strange and wonderful as it was, he was not ready to push aside every hang-up he had ever had unless he could do so honestly.

Tolly said it was fine, that he was happy enough simply being with Leigh, but Leigh could tell as the days passed that Tolly seemed quieter, like he was pulling away. He even went out without Leigh a few times, to see Alvin about something he wouldn't tell him the details of.

It was the little things that Leigh could not explain that worried him most.

"Did you change the sheets?"

"Yes, I… like these better."

Not to mention the hesitation Tolly showed when they touched, like he feared he might hurt Leigh when he had never worried about that before.

Once, when Leigh surprised Tolly, grabbing his hand from behind, he pulled back with a start from a cut on his palm. "Shit. Those sharp nails of yours again, huh?"

Tolly looked dismayed, apologizing profusely, but he wouldn't explain why he was so alarmed.

Finally, after more than a week had passed and Leigh was out at a job interview, trying to find something to make ends meet before he ran out of stashed cash and the next rent check was due, he came home to find a stack of papers on the kitchen counter.

It took him a moment to understand what he was looking at, but it was a loan for *Tolly Allen* signed over to Leigh, everything he needed to get started with a business, as well as the beginning paperwork to purchase the building, though that would take longer, more than Tolly would have been able to accomplish in so short a time, even with Alvin's help, which was obviously how they had accomplished this.

Tolly could be made to look like a perfect candidate with flawless credit and everything a bank could want, because there were no records to say otherwise, even if the records anyone would find would be falsified. They'd gotten everything in motion to surprise him.

His eyes felt hot in gratitude, but before he could call out to Tolly, who hadn't yet appeared at his arrival, he lifted the last of the papers to find a note at the bottom of the stack in Tolly's flowing handwriting.

> *My beloved Leigh—*
> *I wish things could have been different, but with*
> *this, I hope you can finally live the life you want for*
> *yourself and remember me fondly. All I ever wanted was*
> *your happiness. Please know you gave me much in return.*
> *Forgive me.*
> *-Tolly*

"What...?"

Leigh heard the creak of the floor and stepped out of the kitchen to see Tolly setting a pile of neatly folded clothing on the sofa, wearing only his simplest outfit, jeans and a red T-shirt, as if leaving all else behind and ready to walk out the door. He startled when he saw Leigh.

"What is this?" Leigh lifted the note. "You're leaving?"

"I hoped to be gone before you returned." Tolly glanced away. "I must go before the sun gets any closer to setting."

"Why? *Tolly*." Leigh crossed to him and hated how Tolly backed away. "What did I do? What changed? I thought you were mine and I'm yours, and you weren't even going to say goodbye? How can you leave?"

"I do not want to leave."

"Then *don't*."

"You wish for me to stay?" Tolly looked at him plaintively.

"Of course I do."

"Then tell me."

"Stay." Leigh threw the note on the pile of Tolly's clothes and grasped his hands. "Whatever you need, I'll do it. I'll give you everything you want. You got me the shop, got me out of the life so I can run it like an honest man. You've made everything in my life better since the moment you entered it." Seeing the fond smile grow on Tolly's face, Leigh reached for his cheek and held it. "You're beautiful and warm like a light in the worst pits of this world when I don't think I can stand the dark anymore. You like my cooking and all my favorite movies." He laughed, and Tolly's smile twitched wider. "You love my friends. You're part of my family. I never want to be away from you. Ever."

Tolly nuzzled his cheek against Leigh's hand. "I love you, Leigh," he said with questioning in his eyes, enough that Leigh's heart hardened.

"That's what this is about, isn't it?" He drew his hands away, and with his retreat, Tolly's smile fell and he backed up before seeming to realize that he would have to go forward to get to the door.

"I have to go," he said, trying to move past Leigh.

"I thought…." Leigh clutched after him, catching his wrist. "You… you said it didn't matter. But it does. If you can't want me the same way without it—"

"I want you," Tolly said to the door. "I will always want you. That is not the problem."

"Then what is? Why is it so important? Why are you leaving?"

"Because I am out of time."

As if on cue, the room darkened with the setting of the sun, and Tolly spun, eyes bulging wide in worse fear than Leigh had ever seen.

"No... I have to go." He tugged for Leigh to release him, but that only prompted Leigh to hang on tighter.

"Why? What is going on? Tell me!"

Tolly fought him, struggling as if Leigh's touch burned his skin, but Leigh wouldn't let go without an explanation, and because he wouldn't release him, Tolly reared back and pushed him so hard, he flew across the room with an *oomph* as he struck the ground, winded.

Looking at him in shock and apology, Tolly spun about to sprint for the door at last, but before he reached it, he cried out in such agony, Leigh thought he'd missed a gunshot ring out.

Tolly stumbled, pawing at the door, but he couldn't stay upright, his legs like jelly, losing their purchase. He dove for the kitchen instead.

"Tolly!"

"No! You must not see!" He disappeared from view like he was going to be sick in the kitchen sink, though Leigh was certain he saw him falter as he crossed the threshold, stumbling forward as his legs gave way beneath him.

"Tolly!" he cried again, lurching up to give chase, not understanding why Tolly would ever run from him.

Then he turned the corner.

And his nightmare lay on the kitchen floor.

CHAPTER 14

"No...."

Leigh retreated, fear paralyzing him before he could get farther than the kitchen door, causing him to sink down on the other side of the wall, trembling and trying to shake the vision away.

"It's not real, it's not real...."

But it had looked so tangible, the monster with Tolly's fin, deep bloodred with dark red hair, pointed ears, webbed hands with claws twice the length of its fingers, large black, *empty* eyes, and a mouth full of razor-sharp teeth. It had writhed on the kitchen floor like it was seconds from crawling after Leigh to swallow him whole, and still, he could do nothing more than squeeze his eyes shut.

"Wake up," he hissed at himself. "It's not real."

"I am so sorry," came a whimper, too close, as if right in Leigh's ear. "I never wanted you to see me like this."

"Tolly?" Leigh forced his eyes open, because either he was losing his mind or the monster was real and Tolly was in the kitchen with it.

He couldn't be as close as he sounded, though. Still, Leigh inched forward to peer around the edge of the doorway to be sure.

The monster was there, only the monster, yet it wasn't any closer. It was turned away from him, fin stretched in his direction but face turned toward the wall. Its shoulders seemed to be shaking like it was... crying?

"I did not mean to lie, to keep this from you, but I never wanted you to look on me with such dread."

"Tolly...?" Leigh repeated, unable to understand, especially with Tolly's voice ringing in his ears. "How? I don't understand. What... what happened?"

"I failed. The spell is broken. I do not get to keep my legs or the form I made for you."

Made for....

All at once, the nightmare parted like a curtain, and Leigh was left looking at the truth. Tolly could not be speaking from anywhere but the figure in front of him.

"This is what you really look like," Leigh said and felt so foolish for not understanding sooner. "It was you. It was always you. Because of our connection, I…. *Tolly*," Leigh called as he crawled around the tattered remains of clothing toward the frightening form on his kitchen floor, "look at me."

Only after several moments did Tolly obey with a slow turn of his head, and while Leigh shrank back at first, he told himself to stay strong, because those eyes, black as they were, were not empty. There was love and sorrow, and Tolly was crying.

"It's okay. It's okay." Leigh was afraid, he was, but this was *Tolly*. He had all the features of the monster, but he was still Tolly; it was still his face somehow beneath the rest. Leigh didn't want to be afraid, so he reached out to hold Tolly's cheek like he had in the living room, and Tolly started to reach up and touch his hand in turn before he remembered his claws.

He opened his mouth as if to speak around his many teeth, but a mournful cry sounded instead, like something from deep in the ocean.

"You can't speak like this, can you? That's why you sounded so close. That's why I didn't remember your mouth opening when I first heard your song. I was hearing you in my head."

Tolly pressed his cheek to Leigh's hand since he did not dare touch him with his claws. *We have no need for voices underwater.* Tolly spoke without his lips moving. *The face you saw was your ideal, part of our magic to entrance potential prey. When I chose to step out of the water, that was the form I took.*

"It was an illusion," Leigh said. "But I don't understand. What failed? Why don't you get to keep your legs? What did I do wrong?"

There was such depth of emotion in the red face and black eyes. *You did nothing wrong. You simply do not love me.*

"What?" Leigh gripped Tolly's face more fervently. "What are you talking about?"

I could not tell you the details of the spell, the magic prevented it, but to keep my human form and my gentler merfolk form, I had to secure a vow of love from the one I left the water for. You did not offer such a vow and now my time is up. I had only until the next full moon, risen now outside with the sunset. I am so sorry I could not tell you. I am sorry for what I might have told you but was too afraid to.

"Vow? You mean because I couldn't say the words?" Leigh felt his heart break as he must have broken Tolly's, all because of three words left unspoken. "I don't say it, I never say it, but I... I love you, Tolly. Of course I love you. I love everything about you." Leigh pressed his forehead to Tolly's, however frightening he might have once found him, and Tolly gasped in his mind to hear it finally.

Even though you see me as I am? Ugly and terrible?

How did Leigh keep ruining everything, that Tolly could ever believe that? Now that Leigh had pushed past his fear, knowing that the creature he'd thought would devour him was simply Tolly in another form, he saw how beautiful it was in its own way.

"You're fierce, and I was afraid, but you could never be ugly to me. I still see you. This is still you. And I love you. *I love you.*" He pressed his forehead to Tolly's again for want of a kiss he wasn't sure he could risk with those fangs, but this was enough. Tolly was enough.

It is too late. Another mournful cry left Tolly's mouth. *The spell is already broken. I must return to the water to accept retribution.*

"Retribution?" Leigh snapped back.

My kin will come to slay me now that I have failed, drawn to me from the trail of broken magic no matter what body of water I inhabit.

"*What?*" Leigh realized the horror of what his insecurities had caused and couldn't accept it. "No. I won't let that happen. We just... won't put you back in the water."

I must return to the water. With my legs, it was not as dire. I could have gone days without submerging. But in my true form, I will not last long before I perish. I can already feel myself weakening. If I do not return, they will know me dead on land; if I do, they will slay me.

No, Leigh couldn't let them win and take Tolly away from him. "We'll... put you in the tub. You said all water is connected because of your magic, but the tub would be too small. They can't get you there."

It would not be large enough for me. I must be fully submerged as often as possible.

"The pool, then!" Leigh grasped at whatever options he could think of. "It's not a real body of water. Maybe they can't reach you there either."

I... I do not know. I had never attempted to connect to a pool before. But even so, it would not be a long-term solution. I cannot stay in the pool forever. Other humans would find me, see me, and they would not be as understanding.

They'd kill Tolly the second they got a look at him.

"There has to be something we can do," Leigh said, still stroking Tolly's face and holding him close. "I can't lose you just because I was too messed up to say the words."

Tolly smiled, and even with his fangs, it was somehow sweet. *To be loved by you is all I ever wanted. It is enough.*

"No, no, I can't accept losing you. I'm going to take you to the pool and we're going to figure something out. There has to be *something*."

He tried to gather Tolly in his arms before realizing he couldn't risk carrying him down to the pool like that, visible for everyone to see. He hurried to grab the sheets from his bed, and Tolly told him to look in the back of the closet.

The old sheets were there, bundled into a ball. As Leigh unfurled them, he saw slash marks as if from... claws. That's why Tolly had been pulling away from him all week; he was succumbing to his more fearsome form, and he hadn't believed Leigh could handle the truth.

Leigh almost hadn't.

But it didn't matter now. Tolly was *Tolly*, and Leigh would not let him go. He bundled him in the sheets and lifted him, struggling with how much heavier he was with his tail, but he could manage. He made it to the pool without anyone seeing him, locked the door, and carefully set Tolly in the water.

He was still beautiful, the way he swam, the glitter of red and gold, the extra spots of darker red all over his body like freckles. Leigh felt silly for having ever thought this creature could be scary. He was dangerous, he was everything Tolly said his kin could be, but he had gentleness in him that belied any ferocity.

The pool was as clear as it had ever been after Sweeney's men cleaned it last week. Leigh took off his shoes and socks like usual, rolled up his jeans, and sat on the edge to dangle his feet in the water.

You are not angry with me for lying? Tolly asked before long.

"After the way I talked about the 'monster' in my head, of course you couldn't tell me. It's okay. It doesn't matter now."

Tolly nodded. The red hair was becoming on him, but more *Little Mermaid* red than anything natural, so black made sense for his other forms, rather than ginger or looking like some punk with a dye job.

Alvin knows, Tolly said. *He saw most of this form after that man shot you. I got rather… angry.*

That's why they'd had their hushed conversation, and why Alvin was the one Tolly had turned to this past week. "He still hugged you. He loves you, Tolly. Any of them still would if they knew the truth, because they know you."

Again, a sweet, fanged smile replied. Although Tolly had to disappear beneath the water every so often, he always came back up. *It was not you who failed. We were given such terrible odds to face. When I am gone, promise me you will still open the shop and live the life you want.*

"You're not going anywhere," Leigh said. "There has to be a shelf life for this. If you don't die on land and they can't find you, there has to be a reset button so you can step out of the water again, and this time I'll say it. I'll say it every day. I thought it would sound broken because I'm broken. I didn't want you to hear it like that when you deserve better. But saying it… saying it to you feels different than I expected. I love you, Tolly. I'm sorry."

Now Leigh was the one crying, and when Tolly floated closer to him, it was insult to injury that he could not touch Leigh or hold him because his claws were too sharp. Instead, he carefully rested his palms on Leigh's thighs.

Our skin and scales are tougher than a human's. Our claws do not hurt one another unless we use force. But I hate how easily I could cut you. There is no end to the magic, Leigh. Even if they never found me, I cannot grow legs again. I can never change from this form again. I could show you a false face, an illusion, but you could not touch it. You deserve better than a monster you would have to keep hidden from the world that could never hold you again.

"You're not a monster," Leigh said, because he'd said the opposite too many times when he didn't know any better.

There had to be something they could do. Leigh was a planner. He was a good planner. But from juvie to a life of crime, magic didn't play a role. All he could think to do was place his hands over Tolly's and lean forward to kiss his forehead.

Then the tip of his nose.

Then his lips, even if Tolly had to keep his mouth closed or risk cutting him on the edge of his teeth.

Tolly pulled back with a start, and Leigh's eyes sprang wide.

"What?" he asked, but even as he did, he saw something happening in the pool, the water starting to swirl and darken, with a strange light emanating from the center.

You must leave. Now, Tolly said, pulling away and swimming out of Leigh's reach. *They have found me. Please remember me as I was.*

"No." Leigh shook his head as fresh terror filled him. "I'm not letting them take you. Who are they? How many will there be?"

Two. They are hunters.

"Only two?"

Two is all they need.

Moments passed before two dark figures appeared, swimming with the swirl of water like circling sharks, one in shades of yellow with edging in red, another nearly completely black. They circled wider, intent on trapping Tolly between them.

Leigh, please! Tolly stayed in the middle as if accepting his fate. *I recognize them. I grew up with these kin. You must get away from the pool!*

Leigh wouldn't. He couldn't. He didn't have a weapon, didn't stand a chance against even one being like Tolly, but he didn't care. As soon as they expanded their circle to encompass Tolly and would soon pounce to drag him away, Leigh pushed from the edge of the pool to drop into the water.

Leigh!

If they're taking you, then they're taking me too. But I'm not letting either of those things happen without a fight.

Opening his eyes under the water, Leigh took in the full sight of the other merfolk. In general, they were much like Tolly, only larger, one blond, mostly canary yellow with red-accented scales like the reverse of Tolly, and the other, larger still, had dark hair and was almost entirely black, trimmed in midnight blue.

Leigh, you don't understand! Tolly swam to him, trying to guard him from the others. *The spell has broken. You can no longer breathe underwater.*

Leigh thought something felt different. That certainly made things harder, but he was not deterred. He could hold his breath long enough, even if the time they had left meant they would simply meet their end together as the others circled closer with their maws open and claws outstretched.

Don't accept this, Tolly. Don't let them win. Go out fighting. You're allowed to defend yourself. It doesn't make you like them. You hear me, assholes! Leigh wasn't sure if they could, but he shouted in his mind anyway. *If you want him, you're going to have to go through me.*

Dark, foreboding laughter filled Leigh's mind in two overlapping voices as he swam to be back-to-back with Tolly and fought against the natural inclination to swim up for breath.

You wish to die? the yellow one said.

And the black one completed the thought. *Then we will gladly grant your desire.*

They shot forward in unison, Black toward Tolly and Yellow at Leigh. The strange center of light at the bottom of the pool remained with the swirling water, but Leigh paid it no mind and focused on every episode of Shark Week he'd ever seen and what parts of a creature from the deep might be vulnerable.

There were gills on this form along the rib cage, so when Yellow came at him, fangs bared, Leigh kicked as hard as he could right at that spot and the merfolk sank with a gasp.

Tolly had pivoted away and came up on Black's side to take a bite of his shoulder. Black might be larger, but Tolly was faster.

Diving down to attack Yellow before he could recover, Leigh grabbed him by the back of the neck and swam down, pushing with all his strength until Yellow's face slammed into the bottom of the pool.

I am going to rip your throat out! Yellow raged in the aftermath, but Leigh got his feet on Yellow's back and pushed off toward Tolly.

Tolly was fighting hard, slashing and biting and constantly moving to stay out of Black's grasp. While Black's back was to Leigh, he swam faster to grip him around the middle and held him in place for Tolly to strike.

Fool! Black hissed as he struggled to dislodge Leigh. *We will rend you both to pieces!*

Starting with you. Yellow came up on Leigh quicker than he'd anticipated, and Leigh was wrenched downward, pulled by stinging claws slicing his ankles, then dragged down farther and farther, deeper than the pool could possibly be, until he hit that strange light at the bottom and everything went white.

Leigh!

Leigh was still in the water, but he had no idea where when the light dimmed, and he found himself disoriented and adrift. He struggled not to breathe in as he had grown accustomed to, but his lungs were starting to burn. He needed air. He wouldn't last much longer, and he didn't know where Yellow had gone.

Then he felt arms encircle his waist, with a shock of panic spiking through his chest, until they shot upward with impressive speed and broke the surface. Leigh gulped in air as quickly as he could. It was *Tolly* who had saved him, and they were definitely no longer in the pool.

It was dark, but Leigh recognized the river by the docks. Their magic had ported them out to the nearest body of water.

Leigh, please, you must—

But Tolly did not get to finish before he was yanked back under the surface.

"Tolly!" Leigh cried, trying to stay afloat while unable to see anything. The water was too dark. The other merfolk could be anywhere.

A splash alerted Leigh to the flick of a yellow tailfin at his right. A moment later, another splash and flick of the fin was at his left. Yellow was toying with him, taunting him, while Black must have Tolly.

"Come and get me, you bastard!" Leigh yelled, running on pure adrenaline now.

Nothing happened for far too many seconds, and he worried it was already over, that Tolly was gone. Then, just as he'd been about to sink down in the hopes of seeing *something*, Yellow's arms clamped around his middle and held tight, one hand coiling loosely around his throat to tap his claws along his jugular.

Not to worry. I will wait so that Tolomeo can watch.

Perhaps you are the one who needs to be watching, Tolly's voice came next, and Leigh looked up to see him surface not far in front of them, holding Black the same way Yellow had Leigh, claws deadly and ready to sink into his throat.

Yellow hissed by Leigh's ear with his true voice, resonant and threatening.

I remember you, Tolly said. *Both of you. You are mated now, are you not? I can tell. I will kill your mate if you do not release him!*

Yellow squeezed Leigh's neck in return, before he chuckled darkly. *You are no killer, runt. That is why you fled like your weak parents.*

Too often these past few weeks that Leigh had known Tolly, he had seen him have to be brutal, but he wasn't like his kin. He was stronger because he'd had to be a survivor.

I will kill him to protect my beloved, Tolly threatened.

Beloved? Black sneered. *You still call him that? He shunned you. That is why we are here. He offered you no vow!*

"Because it was about words," Leigh said, staring at Tolly, only Tolly, not caring that he bobbed in the water with death at his back. "Words I should have said but didn't. I love you, Tolly. I'm sorry I said it too late."

I love you too, Leigh. Tolly smiled, though it was a sad smile full of terrible grief. *So please forgive me for what I must do. Release him*—he turned his attention to Yellow—*and I will stop fighting. I will surrender for you to slay me.*

"What?" Leigh cried, feeling the claws slice his skin in his struggle. "You can't! Just swim! You always said others weren't fast enough, but you are, that's why you escaped them for so long. You can outswim them, Tolly. Just go!"

If you flee, Yellow warned, *I will bleed your beloved dry and feed his corpse to the young ones.*

Leigh believed that, and Tolly's eyes proved he did too.

Release him, Tolly said again, *and I am yours.*

"No...." Leigh tried to catch Tolly's eyes again, but he wouldn't look at him.

Before Leigh could beg him to reconsider, he found himself airborne and could hardly breathe for how quickly he shot out of the water toward shore. They had only been just off the docks, but still Leigh had a long path to fall before he landed hard and rolled up onto the sand.

As dazed as he was from the force of hitting the beach, he clambered to the river's edge as soon as he caught his breath. Tolly offered him one last longing look of farewell, before the others descended and dragged him into the depths.

CHAPTER 15

LEIGH PULLED the gate up on the front of the shop, the sun just barely up, signaling the start of his day. It wasn't officially open yet, but the new sign was neatly painted with a date for the grand opening hung on a vinyl sign beneath it.

Leigh's Fix-It Shop—We can fix anything but a broken heart.

Alvin had frowned at him when he requested it, but it seemed like the perfect kind of middle finger to the universe since none of this would have been possible without Tolly.

It had been a month since Tolly was taken away to be killed. The first week had passed in a daze, not feeling real or at all fair, even as Leigh did as Tolly told him and continued to set in motion all he needed to finish buying the shop on the corner.

That night after Tolly disappeared, Leigh wandered—still barefoot and drenched—to Alvin's place. He didn't try to hide his tears or his distress when Alvin answered the door. It was one of the few times he let Alvin hug him, and he crushed his friend just as fiercely in return, needing the contact and comfort. After a hot shower and change of clothes, Leigh explained everything.

"I didn't know he was planning to leave, I swear," Alvin said, handing cocoa to Leigh like the silliest, most wonderful of comforts. "I thought he just wanted to surprise you with the shop coz he was afraid to tell you about his other face."

"It doesn't matter. He couldn't tell anyone what he needed from me because of that stupid pact and its rules. I was supposed to figure it out for myself, but I didn't. He needed the words and I couldn't say them."

"It's bullshit." Alvin shared Leigh's anger. "All that matters is what you felt, and you loved him like crazy. He knew that."

"I know. But it wasn't enough to save him. He gave up everything to save me."

"I'm so sorry." Alvin hugged him again, more freely than he ever did, and Leigh snuggled into his friend's arms, wishing it could somehow make the sting hurt a little less.

They fell asleep like that on the sofa, something they hadn't done since they were brats in juvie. It felt nice and safe and more than Leigh would ever ask for from his friend, but it didn't make the trek home to an empty apartment the next day any easier.

Tolly's shredded clothes were still on the kitchen floor. His folded clothes and other belongings still neatly piled on the sofa. The forms and the goodbye note from Tolly's last sweet, selfless act....

Leigh put it all away, back in Tolly's claimed drawers and part of the closet like maybe, somehow, someday, Tolly would come back for them.

Telling Alvin the truth had been the easy part, but with everyone else, Leigh couldn't explain the horror and didn't want to relive it again. So he told the members of their strange, extended family that Tolly had gone home. Everyone was sad to hear it, gave their condolences, wondered at why, to which Leigh simply said it was time and Tolly wasn't able to stay. He thought maybe some of them could tell he was lying, Ralph especially, but no one called him on it.

"I'm really sorry, Hurley," Ralph said. "You were great together."

He was going to be Leigh's first employee at the shop, helping him open in the morning before school and working when he got home until closing time. It would help Leigh ensure Ralph didn't get caught up in any other nefarious dealings or unsavory groups. He hoped spending that much time with the kid wouldn't be as annoying as he feared.

For now, all that remained before opening day was to keep stocking shelves, filing paperwork, advertising, all the little things that came with starting a business. Leigh would mostly repair things, but he also had a few things patrons could buy, like batteries and cords, with a growing list of things to add. He'd order anything anyone needed and play it by ear what he had to make permanent fixtures. It would keep him very busy, busy enough, he hoped, to move on.

A month. A whole month without Tolly, which was longer than he'd known him, yet life would never be the same without him. Leigh dreamed about Tolly constantly, almost every night, in all his forms. Everywhere he turned was a reminder.

In fact, he was fairly certain the full moon had been just last night.

The door chimed and his ears perked at the sound, realizing he had left it unlocked while he busied himself in the storeroom.

"Sorry, not actually open yet! Come back in a week!" he called.

"Anything but a broken heart?" an impossibly familiar voice answered. "Rather dramatic, is it not?"

A chill tingled beneath Leigh's skin to hear that voice and then to see him in the flesh when he emerged from the back.

Tolly. Standing there just inside the door like the most beautiful mirage. Dark hair and eyes. His wide, brilliant smile. Wearing clothes Leigh had never seen before.

"I'm dreaming." He closed his eyes, unable to handle the cruelty.

"No, my love," Tolly said, coaxing him to look, because soon he was right there, reaching to touch Leigh's face, "you are not."

Leigh sucked in a breath, but he couldn't deny that he felt the touch, and when a shaking hand of his own reached up to touch Tolly's, he felt that too. "Tolly," he said aloud, and Tolly smiled at him before drawing closer.

"I have missed you so much."

The press of Tolly's lips couldn't be a mirage, or his warmth, or the weight of his body pulling Leigh in. Tolly wrapped his arms around him, and Leigh clung tightly in return to be certain this was real.

"How?" he sobbed when they finally parted. "They were going to kill you."

"They planned to," Tolly said, "but their mistake was hubris. They wanted to gloat and further humiliate me, so they took me back to our kin to parade me through the colony before my death, speaking in scorn of my love and my loss. They did not realize that telling of your heroics would be their undoing. You were *right*, Leigh."

"Right?" Leigh was still in a daze, unable to look away from Tolly now that he had him.

"There are others like my parents," Tolly said with excitement. "Many, it turns out. I was the first in hundreds of years to make a pact with a human, and though it failed, even the hunters who spirited me away had to admit that you loved me in return. When they made to slay me, others came to my aid."

With a gentle touch, Tolly sat Leigh down in the chair behind the counter and told him of a fierce battle that had erupted, brewing for decades.

"Our love was what inspired the resistance to act."

"Our love inspired a rebellion?"

"Yes." Tolly gazed on him as though Leigh was the miraculous one. "And now kinder leaders have taken control, and those who wish to be more than killers outnumber the rest. Very few of the crueler ones were killed or fled. Most are willing to hear the rest of us out. The tides are changing, truly, and it is all because of us.

"When the battle ended, dozens of my kin, so many, gathered all the magic they had in order to find a way to bring me home to you. It simply needed to wait for the next full moon."

Leigh was living in a fairy tale, and his prince knelt before him like the happy ending he never thought he'd get. "You can stay?"

"Forever. We have already sealed our pact with a kiss. All that's left—"

"I love you," Leigh said in a rush, afraid he'd miss his chance again.

Tolly laughed. "And I love you. After all, it was merfolk magic that made such pacts possible in the beginning, because there were precious few of us who fell in love with the beings we were told to drown, so we had to create our own ways to be with them. The right magic can be rewritten if you have enough of it, and it was not as hard as I feared once it was discovered what a powerful tether there is between us, still binding me to you."

"I kept dreaming of you."

"I am sorry if that made you mourn me all the more, but I am here now, if you will have me."

"*Always.*" Leigh pulled Tolly into his lap to kiss him again, then had to laugh. "We're going to have to change that sign. Alvin will be thrilled."

"Actually, he already is," Tolly said.

"You mean you—"

"When the moon was at its highest last night, I stepped on land once more. But I did not want Miss Maggie to discover me in the nude again."

Leigh laughed in near delirium now, but even that was joyous. "So you knocked on Alvin's door? He was always trying to sneak a peek, you know."

"Perhaps, but Cary was the one who answered, and he covered me quickly. I asked only for clothing, a place to rest my head, and where to find you in the morning, and they gave me all I needed."

Those assholes. Those wonderful assholes.

"So." Tolly settled in Leigh's lap, straddling his thighs and coiling his arms around his neck. "Shall we change the sign to: We can fix anything—*even* a broken heart?"

We. It felt so much better now that it meant something. "Seems so," Leigh said, resting his hands on Tolly's hips.

"I cannot wait to open the shop with you, but perhaps you could delay your work this morning. There is something I wish to show you."

Leigh spared no time locking up. He was with *Tolly*. He had Tolly back. He would follow him anywhere.

Which was back to Leigh's apartment building, though not upstairs. Tolly led him to the pool. It was too early to run into anyone, which Leigh was grateful for, because he wasn't ready to share Tolly yet, especially since Alvin and Cary already knew.

I hate you. Leigh snuck a text to Alvin as they entered the pool room and locked up tight.

Love you too! Alvin sent back with a flurry of kissy emojis.

"Now, you do not get to refuse me this time," Tolly said playfully as he pulled his shirt over his head. "Will you join me in the pool, Leigh?"

Leigh pulled his shirt off too. "Never planned to step foot in that thing again, but I will for you."

They stripped, got into the water, and Tolly let out his tail while keeping his human upper half.

"You know you don't have to hide your real form from me anymore," Leigh said.

"I am not hiding. All three forms are me, but this is the one that combines the part of me I always loved and the parts *you* first fell in love with. It is the form I prefer, not shame."

"Okay." As long as it was what Tolly wanted.

Tolly drew Leigh out to the deep end and started to pull them under.

"I can breathe underwater again, right?" Leigh asked with a start.

"Yes," Tolly assured him. "You most certainly can. Come."

Leigh always felt a little awkward being naked in the pool with his legs sprawled about while Tolly looked so elegant with his tail. With effortless ease, Tolly drew him close beneath the surface and held him in his arms. He kissed him, and this kiss was different somehow, because Leigh felt something exhilarating flutter through his chest the whole time they were in contact.

Now we have a new pact, Tolly said. *An option, but only if you want it.*

Want what? Leigh asked, and Tolly smiled ever so sweetly.

Why, would you grow a fin for me, dear bird, so we may live wherever we wish?

What? The request caught Leigh by surprise. *Tolly, I can't—*

You can. If you will it.

I.... Wait. You're saying.... Right now? How?

Will it, want it, and believe.

He said it like it was so simple. Breathing underwater was simple with magic involved, Leigh supposed. Being with Tolly, a merman, was simple. Well, not a simple road, but a simple destination. Of course Leigh had to try.

It wasn't painful. It wasn't instantaneous, but it wasn't grotesque to witness either. It was... magic that one moment his legs floated beneath him, and only a handful later he was something new, something elegant like Tolly that shocked him with how comfortable it felt, not at all horrifying to have such a drastic change overtake him.

Still, though, *I'm gonna be able to change back, right?*

Tolly didn't respond initially. He stared at Leigh's tail like he had never seen anything so beautiful. Leigh supposed it was beautiful, and he dropped down lower in the pool to flick his tail outward and really look at it.

Unlike Tolly's tail, which was mostly red, Leigh's was an icy blue with trim around his scales in shimmering silver as though he was covered in frost.

Like your eyes, Tolly said. *Oh, I never imagined you would be so lovely.*

Never imagined, huh?

Tolly's eyes snapped up to meet Leigh's smirk with a startled expression. *I only meant—*

Come here. Leigh let him off the hook since he had only been teasing.

They were like fire and ice, though the pleasant shock of Tolly's touch and kiss felt more like lightning. Strangest of all was how their tails coiled so naturally around each other.

If Leigh had a tail, that also meant—wow, that was weird to think about, yet it didn't shake his psyche, only intrigued him, as if this combination of beings was what he had always been intended for.

May I have you inside me now, Tolly said, purposely reminding Leigh of many times before, though this would certainly be different than any of those.

Should have known you had ulterior motives, Leigh said.

Only to be with you. And yes, you will be able to change back whenever you wish. Perhaps one day I can take you to visit my kin.

That was a strange thought, since until now, Leigh had considered merfolk the most terrifying creatures of the deep. *As long as you trust them, you can take me anywhere.*

He pulled Tolly in for another kiss. Leigh would never tire of kissing him, touching him, feeling his tail—*their* tails—gliding around each other, smooth and tingly with the scratch of their scales.

Let me touch you, Leigh, and coax you out, Tolly said, nuzzling him cheek to cheek as he slid the fingers of one hand down the front of his chest and lower to the beginning of his tail.

Leigh could feel stirrings of arousal, and when Tolly traced the slit at the front of his scales, he gasped at how easily they parted for Tolly to press inside. It was and was not like having Tolly inside him when he was human. There was still the same warmth building low in his belly, just originating from somewhere else.

I can feel you, Tolly said, pressing his fingers along a part of Leigh that twitched in response and started to extend. Tolly drew his fingers out with an enticing, gentle tug, and Leigh's sex, changed to be like Tolly's, revealed itself, icy blue like his tail and eager to flex.

Whoa this is strange….

Bad? Too much?

No, Leigh said quickly, looking away to take in Tolly's face.

Tolly touched the newness of him with tender curiosity before wrapping his fingers tight. A moan tried to leave Leigh's throat, forming bubbles between them in the water. It was the same yet so different again. Tolly explored his new form, always watching to be sure he enjoyed what was done, and soon had him eager to find a harbor.

I am wet and ready for you, Tolly said, guiding Leigh forward, ever with his lines straight out of a porno. Leigh loved it. He loved this. He loved Tolly.

The slick slide of Tolly in this form was something Leigh was used to, but never when he also had two halves of a whole to flex and grasp with. When he entered Tolly, it felt as though he found Tolly's sex inside him and clasped on with the first sweet thrust. Only with Tolly could he imagine anything so strange feeling like everything he'd ever wanted.

They spun in the water, tailfins fluttering, swimming together in a whole new dance. Tolly's voice whimpered and gasped in Leigh's mind, and when the moment came to bite and claim, Tolly arched his neck to the side and asked for it.

Please….

Leigh didn't break the skin, that wasn't the point, but he dug in deep to mark Tolly, then licked and nuzzled the spot as Tolly had done to him. It probably meant more than a sexual ritual, something deeper and permanent, like mating, like *marriage*, yet it didn't strike Leigh as anything greater than exactly what they were to each other.

It was so easy to reach an end together, wrapped in each other, unique and whole.

I do, you know, Leigh thought when they floated there beneath the surface, blissful in the afterglow. *I didn't only say it to keep you. I love you. Maybe it is a terrible, cruel word and thing to feel for someone, but with you, it's worth it.*

Tolly held Leigh's face in both hands and kissed him soundly. *I love you too.*

It was several minutes later that they floated upward, breaching the surface while Leigh still had his tail. He liked it. He really did. He wondered what it would be like to swim far out into the ocean with Tolly at his side.

"*Dude.*" Alvin startled him as soon as they reached the air. "Were you two having freaky mermaid sex down there? Love the tail, by the way, and only slightly jealous."

"Alvin!" Leigh gasped as he crushed Tolly to him, bobbing in the water to see that Alvin had once again broken the lock to the pool room and had Cary with him. "I hate you so much right now."

"Aww." Alvin grinned from where he crouched at the pool's edge with Cary standing smugly behind him. "Come on, losers. Let's go get breakfast."

TOLLY NEVER wondered if he had made a mistake. There were no doubts, no second thoughts. This small, broken neighborhood in a large city with criminals and dreamers alike was exactly where he had always been meant to end up. As long as Leigh was with him.

Today was the day they opened the shop—together, with just each other. And with Ralph helping on and off. It would be a simple life, filled with simple but wonderful people. Tolly would never have asked for more.

After all, there were movie nights, either streamed or out at the drive-in. There were dinners. There were long swims. There was physical connection and words of devotion. There were nights with friends. There were days and nights babysitting. There were chores done to help Miss Maggie, and several for the super. Honestly, Leigh could easily add superintendent to his resume, though all his parole officer needed was to see the opening day of the shop.

"I'm proud of you, William," she said when the day came, shaking Tolly's hand too.

Miss Maggie was there that Tuesday morning as well—Tuesday because Leigh had decided they would be closed Mondays for catch-up work and side jobs for their friends.

Deanna stopped by as well on her way to work with Gar beside her to head to school, and with Gert, too, who then went along with Maggie back to the apartment building.

They all knew what Tolly was, and they accepted him as one of their own. It was a good family, one Tolly had found after losing the one he was born into.

Even the detectives made an appearance. He accepted Perez's scrutinizing gaze and Horowitz's kind smile as a sign that all would be well, and it was nice to see Leigh bask in pride for what he had become for others to witness.

"Thanks for believing in me, Nick," Leigh said before Perez walked away.

"Yeah, yeah." Perez cleared his throat with audible effort. "Don't go gettin' mushy on me now."

Even Alvin and Cary passed by on their way to work. Yes, they were still criminals working for Arthur Sweeney, who ran all the nearby streets now, but Alvin had a way of dissuading his father from the more unsavory acts like violence or murder—or asking local businesses for protection money.

Good luck, Cary signed to Tolly.

And Alvin, able to understand him well now, signed in echo, *Never stop being strange, Sharkboy. We love you.*

Tolly signed back a grateful *Thank you,* and Leigh raised an eyebrow at the exchange.

"We will have to teach you next," Tolly said.

At long last it was Ralph who came to wish them well on his way to school, though he was not alone but accompanied by a young girl his same age.

"Go get 'em, Hurley, Tolly. I'll be here for my shift at four," Ralph said.

"And who is this?" Tolly asked the girl.

"Susie," the girl said with a sweet extension of her hand. "Or Sue is fine. I live a couple blocks over and told Ralph I'd walk him to the bus stop since these streets aren't as safe."

"Ah, so you are his protector," Tolly said, shaking her hand succinctly.

"Well, I can't imagine him facing a fight himself, can you?"

Tolly of course knew that Ralph had faced many dangers, including certain death that was thwarted, a murder before his eyes, a gunshot wound inches from his face, and the reveal of a merfolk in his midst. But he nodded nonetheless.

"True. Ralph could use a good bodyguard," Tolly said. "That is how Leigh and I met."

"Really?" Sue looked between Tolly and Leigh like they were a couple to be revered. "You have a very nice shop together, Mr. Allen."

"Thank you."

"You two run along now and don't be late," Leigh said, shooing them away.

Sue waved goodbye before heading down the street.

Ralph came up quickly to hiss a harried, "Don't get excited, we're just friends." Then he gushed with a grin lighting up his face like mentions of Deanna never had, "I really don't want to screw this up. She is so awesome."

"I wish you well," Tolly whispered back, "but we are here if you need advice."

"You can fix anything, right?" Ralph said, offering a wink before hurrying off to catch up to his friend. He would be fine, in time. Leigh and Tolly would see to that.

They would see to many things, for while there had been no whispers of Moretti loyalists or angry merfolk scorned by what Tolly and Leigh had helped put in motion, there was always the chance that threats would arise to undo what they had made. One look at them dared their detractors to come and try their worst. After all, they were mated now, bonded, linked for all time, and Leigh was merfolk with Tolly—stronger, fierce and powerful. They could swap between all three forms to suit them and hold their own in any fight, land or sea.

Maybe Tolly would have been a killer if his parents had been more like other merfolk, but here, with Leigh, in a shop on the corner of a less than reputable street, he had found home.

Like coming up for air when he had most needed it.

The door chimed with their first unknown customer.

"Well." Tolly turned to Leigh. "Shall we see what they need?"

AMANDA MEUWISSEN is a primarily gay romance writer, as well as Marketing Operations Manager for the software company Outsell. She has a Bachelor of Arts in a personally designed major from St. Olaf College in Creative Writing, and is an avid consumer of fiction through film, prose, and video games. As author of the paranormal romance trilogy The Incubus Saga, young adult novel *Life as a Teenage Vampire*, the novelette *The Collector*, and superhero duology *Lovesick Gods* and *Lovesick Titans*, Amanda regularly attends local comic conventions for fun and to meet with fans, where she will often be seen in costume as one of her favorite fictional characters. She lives in Minneapolis, Minnesota, with her husband, John, and their cat, Helga, and can be found at www.amandameuwissen.com.

A MODEL
ESCORT

Amanda Meuwissen

What's the value of love?

What's the value of love?

Shy data scientist Owen Quinn is brilliant at predictive models but clueless at romance. Fortunately, a new career allows him to start over hundreds of miles from the ex he would rather forget. But the opportunity might go to waste since this isn't the kind of problem he knows how to solve. The truth is, he's terrible at making the first move and wishes a connection didn't have to revolve around sex.

Cal Mercer works for the Nick of Time Escort Service. He's picky about his clients and has never accepted a regular who is looking for companionship over sex—but can the right client change his mind? And can real feelings develop while money is changing hands? Owen and Cal might get to the root of their true feelings… if their pasts don't interfere.

www.dreamspinnerpress.com

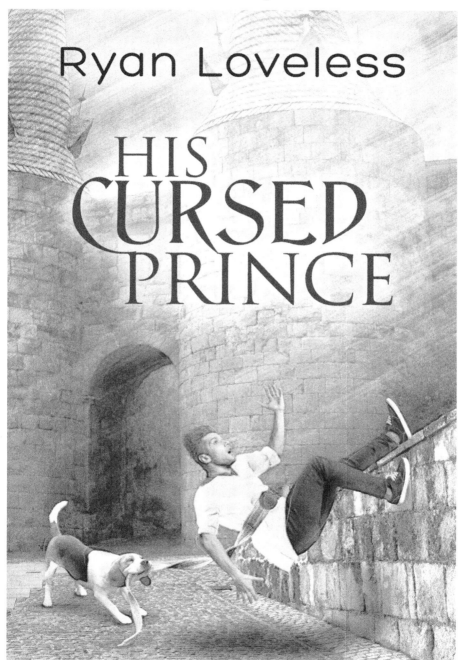

Ryan Loveless

HIS CURSED PRINCE

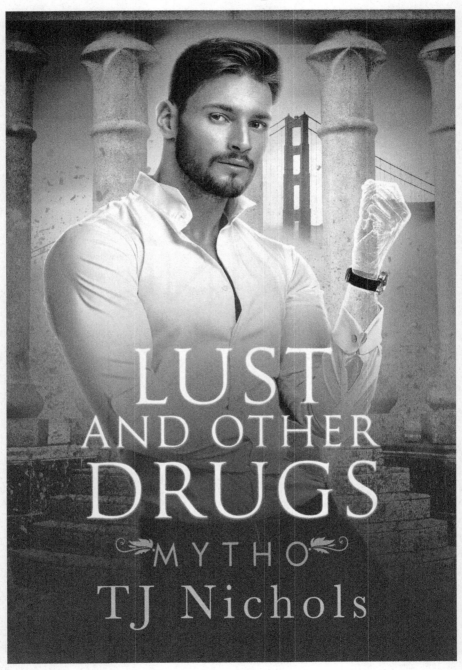

LUST
AND OTHER
DRUGS

MYTHO

TJ Nichols

Made in the USA
Coppell, TX
08 October 2021

63700429R00115